Search for Maylee

Search for Maylee

Didi Oviatt

Chapter One

Autumn drew in a lungful of California air. Although it was thick, it was somehow refreshing. She looked to her side at the sun glistening off choppy waves on the oceanfront. It sparkled in bright flashes across the horizon. She was really going to miss this stunning morning view. A thin lilac tank-top dampened with sweat in the center of her back. Her feet were growing heavy, but she pushed herself and quickened her stride. Autumn had been running along the beach every day, sometimes a few times a day, for the past three years. She found that running helped to clear her mind, and tiring her body helped her sleep at night.

Every day during this run, the thought of Maylee's disappearance raced through Autumn's mind on a loop. Every intricate detail was recalled, in order, exactly as it happened. She remembered what Maylee had eaten for breakfast, and dropping her off at school that morning. Even the conversation they had haunts her.

"Don't you want some eggs?" Maylee chirped in her perky morning voice.

"Nah, I'll just grab a coffee."

"Whatever Aunt Autumn, you're going to sneak one of those disgusting processed breakfast muffins after you drop me off, aren't you?"

Accusing eyes pierced Autumn's embarrassed face, forcing her to blush. Strange, how such a young woman could find so much fault over a simple guilty pleasure no bigger than a thin slice of cheese with sausage.

These memories continuously float in and out of Autumn's mind, circling her like a consuming shadow, just waiting for the right moment to swallow her whole. After reliving the worst day of her life, Autumn would clear her mind, steady her breath, and convince herself to focus on the present. It felt like an impossible task, to stop living in the past. Maylee was Autumn's niece, and she was seventeen years old when she was taken. Maylee was a high school senior with two weeks left until her graduation. She had her entire life ahead of her.

Now, three years later, Autumn was convinced that if she could just remember any tiny detail, something she may have skipped over, the police would be forced to pry Maylee's case back open. Autumn was more of a mother to Maylee than her junkie sister could ever dream of being – even on a sober day.

It had been nearly an hour since today's run commenced. Time seemed to escape Autumn as the worn out sneakers laced to her feet moved further down the beach. Her legs were starting to tingle and burn. They weakened, like noodles under her wearying body. The intake of air burned her chest, leaving her throat to feel like a charred tree – still intact and alive, but the edges burnt to a crisp. She could feel the color of her face darken as fresh oxygenated blood sped through her veins.

Over the course of the last few days, she had pushed herself even further than her usual run. She would be leaving her beautiful home in Northern California and moving to a cramped one-bedroom apartment, right in the center of Denver Colorado. Every detail of her life would change once again, and it was terrifying.

Autumn fell into a deep depression when Maylee went missing, and she became obsessed with the case. The only time she would leave the house was to go to the grocery store or police station. Her life's purpose became nothing more than to pester Detective Chance, or just Chance, as everyone called him. His full name and title was Detective Chance Rupert Lizhalia III. Clearly, the comfort of being referred to so casually by his first name was developed very early on in his career. The details and progress of Maylee's case were poked and prodded at by Autumn daily. It was a repetitive process until about five months after Maylee had disappeared. At that point, Chance put Maylee's folder on an overstuffed shelf to collect dust.

"We've done everything we can," he told Autumn on that bizarrely hot fall afternoon as he slowly wiped the sweat from his full, perfectly squared hairline.

"So you're going to throw her away? Just like that, you're done?" Autumn demanded, tears welling.

"Every police station in the country has Maylee's picture." Chance reminded her. "If anyone finds her or comes across anything that we can link to the case, then I assure you, Autumn, you'll be the first to know."

The short conversation had rendered Autumn mute. She stood frozen in shock as he told her to move on with her life. Chance apologized for the loss in such a way that it was clear – Maylee would never be found. Then he brushed past her in the hallway of an over-lit police station, and went about his day as if nothing had changed.

Autumn recalled it now as she ran, remembering the emptiness in Chance's expression. The excruciating heat of that day hadn't even touched the icy daggers he sent jabbing into her chest. Even his outfit was seared into her memory. He wore a dark gray suit, complementing his tan, and an orange tie.

There was no denying it, Chance was a very attractive man for his age. The stress of the job was surely the culprit of a cluster of wrinkles at the corners of his eyes, although they only added to his enticing façade. Chance was the kind of man that you could take one look at and just know, without a doubt, he could defend himself. His build was strong enough to be noticed, with broad shoulders and a flat stomach, but his eyes were key. They were light grey and deeply piercing, always with a sharp gaze – like an eagle ready to swoop.

The afternoon Maylee's case was practically declared unsolvable and doomed for a cold shelf life, all hope drained from Autumn. Her car was left in the parking lot, and dragging feet carried her home. She moved in a blurry haze. Amidst the draining three mile walk to her front porch, the heat transformed into gloom, and before Autumn knew it she was engulfed in rain. The weather was unforgettably odd.

The door swung open, and she collapsed onto the floor, unable to take in air. Anxiety surged through her body in waves, and salty tears streamed down her face. God only knows how long she lay paralyzed on the floor before she got up and ran out the door. Pushing herself through the stinging oversized drops of rain, she rounded a corner and made her way to the beach. Giant deadly ocean swells had never looked so inviting, but she refused to stop, continuing to run faster. Step after painful step in the sand, she pushed forward.

Oxygen eventually stopped reaching her lungs, and her legs gave out. Several times Autumn collapsed to her knees and stared into the water while she wheezed and struggled for breath. Each time the *slosh* of wet sand sounded beneath her fallen body, she would pick herself back up and continue to run. By the time she returned home the sky had turned black, and there were no stars to be found. Autumn was completely surrounded by darkness, a perfect match to the way she felt inside.

A haunting recollection of her own swollen, bloodshot eyes staring back at her from the hallway mirror now left an imprint in Autumn's mind. On that traumatizing day she become a ghost – an empty shell of her once prominent self. Maylee's absence was officially real, there was a sense of finality, a permanence that made Autumn sick.

That night after her first run, the world went completely black. As soon as her head hit the pillow, exhaustion and grief took over, blocking out whatever was left of her subconscious. For the first time in those five miserable months, her body gave up. She had slept an entire night through, deep and dreamless. It was the first night without nightmares and cold sweats since Maylee went missing.

Since that painful day, Autumn continued to repeat that same beachside run. Slowly over time, she's made an effort to put her life back together. So far that effort has proven unsuccessful.

This would be the day Autumn was going to take what could possibly be the biggest step of her life. Giving up on Maylee was not an option. This move was bound to uncover something. It had to. The winding road came upon a corner and revealed a small deserted parking lot. She was close to home now, with only a few more blocks to go before the first 'For Sale' sign came into view. The signs were pointing in the direction of her striking oceanside condo.

Autumn slowed her stride to a heavy footed jog until she reached the lawn in front of her newly sold home. No sooner than her sneakers sunk into the freshly cut grass, she bent at the core and clutched her knees tightly, knuckles whitening, to catch her breath. Autumn glanced up to notice the front door had been opened a crack. She squinted over the top of her right shoulder, then abruptly to the left, peering down the road as far as she could see. There were no cars out of the ordinary aside from the large U-Haul sitting a few yards away.

Paranoia was common for Autumn. A constant nagging fear weighed in her chest at all times, she was forever burdened by this. It had taken a full year to convince herself to sell all of her belongings and take this giant leap. She had to be strong, and she had to leave California, for Maylee. With caution in each step, Autumn slowly made her way up to the condo. She peeked into each window, then tilted an ever listening ear toward the crack in the door.

"Oh, for hell's sake Autumn, you're such a weirdo! You're going to pack up all your shit and take off on some 'save the world trek', and you can't even walk into your own house without panicking!"

4

The voice was shrill and mocking. It belonged to Candace, Maylee's mother. Autumn exhaled and walked inside. The sight of her sister leaning against the bar that connected the kitchen to the dining room was a lot to take in. Candace was tall and skinny. Too skinny, Autumn noted. One bony leg was crossed over the other and a thick string of smoke lifted into the air from the cigarette burning between her fingertips. She rolled her eyes at Autumn dramatically, and then flicked a long ash onto the floor.

"Candace, do you really need to do that? You know I don't let anyone smoke in my house. You think it's okay to just ash all over the place?"

"Who cares, you sold it anyway."

Candace walked over and ran what was left of her smoldering cigarette under water and dropped it into an otherwise spotless ceramic sink. The condo was empty, making it seem even bigger than usual. Autumn looked around her home, holding back the tears that were soon to inevitably flow – it was only a matter of time. The floors transformed from a dark marbled tile to white carpet in the living room. The ceilings were vaulted and the countertops were black with marbled granite.

Autumn had married at a young age and lost her husband in a car accident shortly after. She'd only known Keith for seventeen months total. A vow was made to herself when he died, she would never love another, and that was final. It'd been eighteen years since the accident, and so far she'd stuck to her promise. Autumn went back to her maiden name, Brown, in an effort to help herself move on from the trauma of his death. Keith had come from money and left Autumn a rich young woman at the time.

Initially, she bought the condo along with a dependable used car. Then she placed what was left of the settlement into a steady monthly income that was meant to last 20 years. Since then, the car had been traded in for a newer model, an end of this cash flow was rapidly approaching, and the condo sold. Autumn was trudging unfamiliar ground as her entire life was growing foreign, and that didn't even include her job.

After the loss of her young love, the years passed and the cost of living grew. Her fixed monthly income was barely enough to pay the bills and keep her fed. Enjoying nights out with her girlfriends, or buying new outfits were rare. A few years after Keith passed, Autumn picked up a job working as a waitress in a small crab shack just down the road from her condo. Surprisingly, she adored it. It didn't bring in much money, but it was enough for the little extras, and it kept her busy.

As Autumn stood across from Candace in her emptied kitchen, her mind wandered to the saddened look of shock on her boss's face when she'd quit. Autumn walked away from the steady job she loved, just over a week before. Candace cleared the tar blockage from her throat, pulling Autumn back to reality.

"How did you get in here?" Autumn asked. "And did you get me that address? I'm leaving soon. I only have a few more things to pack, so I need it. You promised."

"You always leave that window in the back unlocked," Candace said with another roll of her glassed over eyes. "And yes, I have your damn address."

Candace dug a wrinkled piece of damp paper from her pocket, along with a chunk of dirty pocket lint and a couple of pennies. The goods were slapped onto the empty countertop. Candace then shifted restlessly on her feet, her eyes darting from one side of her head to the other. The look of a wild animal had taken over her face, as if assessing the possibility of an unexpected dash for the door. Unpredictable and permanently on edge, she finally continued in her scratchy smoker's voice.

"I still don't think you should do this. Craig's not a bad guy, he just gets a bad rep because of his record. Maylee's gone because she never paid attention to anything going on around her. It's probably her own fault she was taken, I'm sure Craig had nothing to do with it."

Aside from the obvious itch to leave, Candace was without emotion, utterly careless about Maylee. She spoke as if Maylee wasn't her daughter at all, but a random girl she'd met on the street. It made Autumn's stomach wrench hearing her sister talk this way about her own child, her flesh and blood. How could she?

The thought of the opened back window in the condo was intentionally brushed aside. Autumn didn't even want to know exactly how her sister was privy to that information. The place would be deserted in a few hours, left for the new owners to deal with. The only thing that mattered now was how clearly strung-out and coldblooded Candace was. A surge of anger flowed through Autumn.

Autumn couldn't stand Candace for the evil woman she'd grown into. The fact that Candace cared more about herself and getting her next fix than she did about her own daughter was sickening. Autumn stormed over to the bar and snatched up the piece of paper. It wouldn't be out of the ordinary if Candace were to change her mind, steal back the address, and make a dash for the door. Frankly, it came as quite a shock to Autumn that her junkie sister had followed through on her promise to retrieve it in the first place. Once the address was safely in hand, Autumn finally spoke her mind.

"Maylee hated that man, and the rest of your friends. She was scared of him! She ended up here ninety percent of the time because you were a shitty mom, and your shitty friends are all terrible people. Open your eyes Candace! When are you going to understand that he was the only real lead the cops ever had? Now get the hell out of my house!"

Candace took a step back, shocked at Autumn's outburst. Her head tilted forward allowing her eyes to be shaded by the lowering of her brows. The shifty feet that struggled to hold up her stick-like legs for the first time held still. They'd gotten in several fights about Maylee over the years. They brawled more since Maylee's disappearance than ever before. Candace knew she hadn't been the best mom to Maylee, but she would never admit it out loud, and she didn't much care either way. Excuses were constantly shelled out for her behavior as she never even wanted a child in the first place. Candace justified her actions to herself in any way she could.

Autumn wasn't the only one with resentment, as Candace genuinely returned the disdain. For most of their lives Candace hated her sister for being the pretty one, the favorite. A prominent loathing of Autumn's perfection had taken up residence in Candace. There was even a slight anger toward Maylee for confiding in Autumn as much as she did. Candace would leave Maylee for weeks at a time, and then get upset when she'd find her at Autumn's house. Maylee was punished whenever her Aunt Autumn was mentioned.

Once Maylee was about twelve years old, Candace finally gave up and no longer asked or showed any concern. Candace couldn't care less whether Maylee came home or not. Candace knew that Autumn's was the only phone number Maylee knew by heart, and that's where she'd usually be. There was no point in the chase. Besides, the less Maylee was around, the more freedom there was for her. There were no whiny voices begging for food, or phone calls from teachers complaining about smelly clothes or random bruises.

Candace now stared back at her angry sister, contemplating what insult she would throw next. Whether it be about Keith dying, or about their Mom being in a nursing home, she usually thought of the things that would hurt Autumn the most before she spoke.

"You're not going to find her, Autumn. All you're going to do out there is waste what little money you have left and abandon Mom. You're leaving her here to rot while you chase a ghost."

Candace watched closely and fully satisfied as Autumn winced. The fact that their mother would be left all alone pulled fluid to the surface of her eyes. Hannah Brown, Autumn and Candace's mother had lived with Autumn for quite some time after her stroke. Once she became too heavy for Autumn to lift, Hannah was checked into the nicest nursing home within a twenty mile range. Autumn would visit her on a regular basis. Candace, on the other hand, hadn't seen their mother in years.

Autumn watched her sister strut to the door, then turn to look back as she twisted the door's handle. "Good luck on your mission, Superwoman." Candace sneered, chuckled lightly, and walked out.

Chapter Two

One single tear trickled down Autumn's face as she wondered how her sister's heart had grown so cold. The encouragement their mom had shown in finding Maylee burst into Autumn's memory. Hannah Brown was a strong woman and had raised her daughters well. There was no telling why Candace ended up the way she did.

Hannah's ability to speak clearly had been altered by the stroke, yet she was still able to consistently manage an expression of concern. She too was completely dedicated to Maylee's search, and insisted that Autumn never give up. Maylee was Hannah's only grandchild and she had all the faith in the world that Autumn could find her.

Autumn absorbed the emptiness of her home, feeling as stripped down as each wall. Her guts felt as hollowed out as the rooms she moped through. Over time she'd grown to love everything about the condo. It offered her a sense of safety and deep rooted security. She'd lived here for eighteen long years and was heartbroken to let it go. After locking the front door one last time, packing an arm full of clothing tightly between her dresser and a well wrapped mirror in the back of the U-Haul, she turned around to take a long look at the soon-to-be deserted home.

It was imperative that the move be made in one trip, so she had sold her car along with some other appliances that couldn't fit in the truck. The last two weeks had been like a free-for-all. Bargain shoppers trickled in from all over town, ready to haggle and drop the price on anything they could get their grimy fingers on. Fridge $50, stove $27, oversized propane barbeque equipped with a tank and utensils $32. With every item sold, the void in Autumn's chest widened. Everything she had left was crammed into the largest U-Haul she could afford.

"Goodbye." An airy whisper escaped her.

Autumn flew to Denver a couple months prior, and stayed for a week to find an affordable place. The one she settled on was in the nicest neighborhood she could manage, but it was dicey nonetheless. Paperwork had been signed and prepared, even the first and last month's rent had been paid along with a cleaning deposit. Despite the feeling of chaos and frigid loss, life was actually in order. Every possible kink had been ironed. She was ready for the move, physically if not emotionally.

Autumn stuck her hand in her pocket and squeezed the small pink piece of paper. Just to make certain it was still securely on her person. Everything about her future and Maylee's – if she was still alive – depended on this address. Candace sure did cut it close in getting it to her. At least Autumn didn't have to postpone her planned departure date to go flipping over rocks in search for her sister. If there's one thing that irritated Autumn to no end it was unplanned inconveniences.

The giant step it took getting into the U-Haul was awkward, Autumn had to pull her weight into the vehicle with the aid of the seat and the steering wheel. Driving something this size would surely take some getting used to. The two day trip was sure to be long and weary. Though she was nervous about maneuvering such a load on unfamiliar roads, the sickening anxiety of leaving the town she spent her entire life in was even stronger. The drive would be manageable, if she could learn to control her shaking hands. The homesickness that had settled before even pulling away was crushing, it wouldn't be so easily dismissed. Autumn took a long intense look into her side mirror as she drove off. The condo grew smaller and smaller until it was gone.

After the emotional departure from her home, the realtor's office was Autumn's first destination. It was a quick stop to drop off her key and sign the last of an exasperating stack of necessary paperwork. A stout balding man took the pages from her fingertips. He played the busy role of a secretary for the entire office of realtors. There were seven total. Autumn had only sat down with her own agent a handful of times. It was usually this same jolly man she had grown accustomed to dealing with. She didn't mind, he was always in a joyful mood and was very easy to talk to.

"And that's it, my dear." He said with a grin. "So what's your next big adventure, now that that beauty of a condo is sold?"

"I'm moving to Denver."

The answer all but stuck to the back of her throat.

"Wow, big change. Hope it all works out for you." His smile was genuine.

Autumn choked back the tears. Something about overly friendly people, they have a real gift for drawing up the waterworks. Talking about Maylee and the quest to find her wasn't exactly a subject Autumn was prepared to discuss. Especially to some strange man at her realtor's office. Despite how insane it would make her seem, Autumn was mostly worried about the puffy eyes and shaky voice that would surely accompany the explanation. So, rather than elaborate details, she stuck with a short sweet farewell.

"Thank you, Sir. I'm hoping to meet up with some family there, eventually. Good luck to you and your future as well. It's been a pleasure working with you."

"The pleasure is mine, Miss Brown."

His short chubby fingers extended toward her. She took them into hers and forced a full smile to accompany the handshake. Then she turned abruptly on her heels and practically ran for the exit. This entire day was already proving to be every bit as hard as she anticipated it to be.

Next stop, the police station. She drove up and down the street in front of the station a couple of times trying to find somewhere to park. The maneuvering of such a giant vehicle was far from an easy task. After a few ridiculously embarrassing attempts to parallel park, Autumn finally settled on leaving it at a gas station a couple of blocks down. She stepped out of the U-Haul and straightened her top.

A plain old faded black tank hung casually from her shoulders, and her most relaxed pair of jeans hugged loosely on her hips. Built for comfort, it was a great travel outfit choice. Now, glancing down the street toward the station, she wondered if it had been the best choice of dress. A short tiff in her mind commenced on whether or not to rummage through the back and at least find a dressy jacket. The practical side of her won out, and she decided to just suck it up and deal with the situation at hand. Autumn had to get past this conversation with Chance, and it really didn't make a difference on what she was wearing.

It was a short walk to the station, and she took it at quick pace. She had only seen Chance a couple of times since their awkward encounter three years earlier. Each time they bumped into each other, the pleasantries were short and awkward. There was something about this man that she couldn't quite put a finger on. Aside from the fact that his decision to put Maylee on the back burner practically ruined her life – for a second time – there was more. Something very unnerving always circled the air when she tried to talk to him. Autumn chalked it up as hate, of course. Hence, it was best to avoid him altogether.

The tall wooden door was heavy, but with some effort she was able to pull it open and step inside. The office was noisy and hectic with ringing phones and busy voices. Men and women in uniforms, suits, and skirts hustled from one side of the open room to the next. There were far too many desks crammed into such a small space. None of the faces turned to look at her. It was a sickening reminder of how ignored she'd been three years earlier. Her trips to this building were as regular as breakfast, yet not a soul gave her a sliver of recognition.

Autumn made a turn to her left, exiting the overstuffed and well-trodden entryway. The air she inhaled smelled of paper and old carpet. The hallway she moved through was stuffy and narrow. It was far too skinny and cramped to allow even a fraction of comfort. She stopped abruptly and stared at the name on the door in front of her. It read 'Detective Chance Rupert Lizhalia III' in large gold letters. She shook her head faintly and shoved the doubting thoughts out. Hesitantly, she pushed the door open and crept into his office. There was a striking young woman sitting at a small desk. The woman glanced up at Autumn and grinned from ear to ear.

"Please take a seat. Are you here for the detective?" She looked to be in her early twenties and was far too exuberant for Autumn's taste.

Lightly, Autumn eased herself down onto a thinly cushioned leather chair and replied quietly.

"Yes, please."

It was a simple response. Autumn didn't see the need for small talk with this uncomfortably attractive woman. The woman stood and walked around a small corner into Chance's slightly opened office door. Autumn couldn't help but to spectate at the age of this attractive little tart. She also wondered what happened to the white-haired woman with a pearl string on her glasses who used to occupy the desk in front of her. Anita was her name, and she was practically the opposite of the new girl.

Autumn wondered if Anita had retired or if the detective traded her in for a younger, more attractive model on purpose. There was no denying the strange swirl of growing jealousy. *Weird,* she thought, then tucked the notion away. A quick glance at the nameplate on the young woman's desk read *Vanessa.* It was beautifully displayed in swirly silver letters. A gorgeous name to match the flawless face behind it.

It didn't take long before Vanessa was back to her desk flashing that perfect toothy grin.

"He'll be just one moment, Ma'am," she confidently beamed.

Vanessa took her seat and went back to typing whatever it was she was working on. Autumn straightened her back and stretched her head toward the ceiling. What did she care if Chance had a beautiful young assistant? She reminded herself of the detest she once had for the man. After obliging Vanessa with a courteous nod, Autumn turned her head away, as to not make eye contact again.

In a matter of minutes Chance poked his head through the opened crack of his tall heavy wooden door. Clearly, he was temporarily dumbfounded. Those audacious eyes of his widened and jaw clenched, causing a tensed bulge in his neck at the sight of Autumn. She sat perched on the dark brown leather chair in front of his assistant.

"Miss Brown," he managed to cough out, "come in."

The words were stammered, he was unable to take his eyes off of her. Chance couldn't help but to notice the manner in which Autumn carried herself. She seemed much different than the frumpy, chubby, yet still attractive woman he'd grown to know and admire years earlier. Autumn was now lean, tan, and in very good shape. She wore little makeup, but didn't really need it as her skin was smooth and her bold green eyes were framed with thick, long, naturally black lashes. There was no question to her beauty, nor to his attraction to her.

Autumn swallowed her nerves and lifted her head in a managed confidence, willing him not to notice the slight shaking of her fingers. The pulsing liveliness in Chance's chest skyrocketed as he held the door open, allowing her to pass. Instantly drawn to her, he tapped a thumb on the door's handle, his growing tension a wreck. A comparison engaged through his mind, batting back and forth between the puffy eyed matted hair woman he remembered, to the clearly healthy woman she'd become. Seemed to him, she were two completely opposite people.

The old Autumn vs. the new, Chance couldn't get a grasp on the change, he was entirely engulfed by shock and disbelief. A hard lump formed in his throat causing him to choke on his spit. A balled fist was raised to his lips in aid of coughing it out.

"Excuse me." He mumbled before taking a seat across from his unexpected guest.

Caught off guard by a waft of his cologne, Autumn instantly remembered the scent. He smelled the exact same as he had years before, memory of it flooded up her nostrils, sparking a strange flutter in her stomach. *Maybe that's why he had made her so uncomfortable,* she thought. *That has to be it – it's because she loved the way he smelled, nothing more.* She chuckled in her head at the silliness of the thought, reminding herself that she hardly even knew him. That's not to mention the fact that he angered her on a regular basis not so long ago.

Autumn avoided his penetrating eyes, glancing around the room uncomfortably. After a few quick moments of confusion and an embarrassing newfound dumbness, she strained to recall the speech she had practiced. There was a reason she was here, and nothing was going to get in her way. Not the sharpness of Chance's eyes, or even his divine scent could stop her. The entire conversation had played out in her imagination, over and over the night before. Everything she wanted to say was prepared and memorized. There was no turning back now. She exhaled a hesitant breath of relief as he spoke first.

"Miss Brown, I must say you're looking well. Is there anything I can help you with?"

"I…I…I'm moving." Autumn stammered, a little confused and beside herself at his compliment.

Everything she'd planned to say evaporated out of her mind, like the rolling steam off boiling water. She now sat ashamed and growingly ridged in front of this unnerving man. A stiff torso allowed her to lean back into the chair and dig around her pocket for the crumpled up paper. If she couldn't find the words to tell him, then she'd have to show him instead. The rumpled page, still slightly moist, was set hesitantly on the desk between them.

"I'm moving to Denver to find Craig. I'm going to look for Maylee myself."

The shaking of Autumn's hands multiplied by ten while she spoke the words. There was so much more she'd intended to say, but for some uncomfortable reason her tongue wouldn't cooperate, and her chest failed to rise and fall with proper breath. These factors rendered her utterly incapable of the full speech she'd intended.

Tears welled in her eyes, stopping at the inside corners – teetering the edge of a full on meltdown. *How embarrassing.* It was easy to tuck away her anxiety and fears around her friends and family, but not so much Chance. All of her worries and doubts were somehow brought to the surface, just from the presence of him. Though so confident about the whole thing that morning, Autumn was starting to question herself at the mere sight of Chance. She couldn't decide if his facial expression read angry, worried, anxious, or what? His mind was tangled, clearly he was confused at her. The awkward demonstration of care in his face gave her a chill.

"Are you sure this is what you want to do?" He finally spoke upon reading the address scribbled across her page. "Because, I strongly advise against it."

"Yes, I'm sure. No one else seems to care about finding her anymore. He was the last person she was seen talking to. Why would he be at her school? And why would he move away right after she went missing, unless he had something to do with it? Something to hide? I'm going to find him, and I'm going to watch him."

Autumn paused, only to draw in a breath. Then she continued her venting rant. *It's now or never,* she thought, *I have to get it out.*

"I'm going to do whatever it takes to find her. I have to know if she's still alive. This is Craig's address, so I want you to write it down along with mine. I want you to have my information in case anything happens."

Autumn successfully held back those irritating tears, forcing anger and determination to take over her sadness and fear, although she was still unable to steady the shake in her voice, or of her hands for that matter. He glared at her for what seemed like a soul sucking lifetime. With her breath held she returned the look, trying her best to stare him down. *What could he possibly be thinking, why wasn't he talking to her?*

Chance watched her close, half waiting for her to spill more information, and half unsure what exactly to make of her brave attempt at salvation for Maylee. A strong feeling of respect took over. He had to hand it to her, she was bold, undeniably brave. At the same time, how could a woman with absolutely no detective experience pull off such a task? She was doomed for failure and indefinite danger. *How could he stop her from putting her life at risk?* He couldn't, there was no question to that. Ultimately, he could do nothing but stare, and drink in the returned scrutiny of her beautiful eyes.

"Well? Do you want my new address or not?" Autumn demanded, growing more and more impatient by the second.

"Yes." He quietly answered, and reached for a pen.

Autumn had expected, and even tried to prepare herself for an argument. His reaction had taken her by surprise. The stare down may have been slightly intense, but it was nothing compared to what she had imagined to happen. A sense of pride and accomplishment rested in Autumn's belly. She'd told him everything she came here to say.

Chance's strong, well-manicured fingers copied the barely readable scrawl onto a fresh sticky paper, just below Craig's address he wrote Autumn's, careful to make sure that every letter and number was correct. As soon as she was finished reciting the address that she'd memorized the very day she picked out her apartment, Chance grabbed a couple more pieces of paper. He scrawled Craig's address for a second and third time.

Autumn watched close, a little confused, but she didn't protest. Instead, she observed his hands working in silence and steadied her breath, trying to get a handle on her emotions. Chance gently reached across the desk and handed her the two new sticky papers, along with the original copy she'd retrieved from Candace.

"You might want to put a couple of these in more places than just your pocket. You know, in case you lose it." He looked down at the desk avoiding eye contact. "You can never be too careful."

"Thank you." She sighed.

Oh how Autumn wished she would have come to him sooner, she would kill for an opportunity to listen to his tips and learn a few things before taking this step. The reason she hadn't, is because she was certain he would've tried harder to talk her out of the whole thing. Already full of self-doubt, she couldn't have risked it.

"I'm sure there's nothing I can say that will change your mind, Autumn. It sounds like you already have everything in order." He was ever the professional.

"That's very correct, Chance, I'm going." She returned the proficient tone. "So, if we're done here I have to get to it. I have a long drive. It'll take me a few days to get there and I'm already running behind schedule."

Chance offered her a short nod only, no words, accompanied with softened eyes melting downward at the outer edges, wrinkles slightly ironed.

Autumn stood, looked down at her toes, and turned to exit his office. A hollow feeling swirled in the pit of her stomach. This visit didn't go at all as she expected it would. She'd imagined that he would have a load of questions for her. She anticipated his advice and was looking forward to at least a little bit of help in her journey. Disappointment gnawed at her chest, she was more than a little hurt by his reaction to her news. As she slowly and reluctantly reached for the handle, the sound of his voice made her jump.

"Wait!" He nearly shouted the request.

Chance wriggled around in his seat, and intentionally lowered his voice. "I... Um... It's about lunch time. Will you eat with me before you go?"

Was Chance asking her on a date? Even he wasn't exactly sure. Distracted by the words as they came out of his own mouth, he quickly convinced himself that it was for Maylee, rather than to satisfy the growing ache to pull Autumn into his arms. Nervously, while waiting for Autumn's response, he combed a right hand across his head. Starting just above the ear he let his tense fingers ease through his thick mane, letting it completely engulf them. The detective didn't know what he was doing. He only knew that for some reason he didn't want her to leave.

"No, I'm sorry. I had a late breakfast, and I really am running behind on time. If you have any advice for me, or any other questions, though, please call."

Autumn closed the gap between them and held out her hand in a professional manner. He took it into both of his to accept the gesture. Although Autumn's hand felt very small in his palm, she had a firm grip, an admirable quality he noted. Without any further hesitation, she again turned for the door – back straight and head held high. Despite her weak knees, Autumn forced herself to brush off his unexpected invitation, along with the fresh scent of him that seemed to follow her out.

Autumn nodded kindly to Vanessa on her way past, ignoring the chirpy goodbye and giant wave. The door shut behind her with a loud slam. Finally, she was able to exhale, leaning against the door she closed her eyes and tried to make sense of it all. *What the hell just happened in there?* The icy floor seemed to reach up and grab hold of her ankles, rendering her legs frozen in place.

An awkward silence of the tiny hallway only added to her growing anxiety. It felt like the walls were tightening, as if that were possible, the world closing in. Autumn felt as if the station wasn't a building at all, but an airtight vacuum, sealing her tightly up into a thin film of shrinking plastic. After much struggle she decided that it was just the finality of the move that made her so on edge. She would stick with any excuse to justify the weird tingling sensation Chance had just given her. Reluctant lungs sucked the air into her chest, and she found the will to move her legs.

The U-Haul seemed to be much further away than it really was, practically jogging Autumn was determined to get away from that miserable, anxiety causing police station as quickly as possible. The steering wheel and seat again offered her assistance, allowing her to swing one leg in first, then the other. As quickly as possible Autumn slammed the key into the ignition. A purr of the overbearing engine echoed in her ears. *Slow down*, she told herself.

A scattered heap of papers and books sat on the bench seat next to her. It was compiled mostly of missing person fliers, a couple of magazines, newspaper clippings, and her favorite short romance novel, all the things that she couldn't bear to store in the back amongst the rest of her random belongings. Autumn neatly straightened the stack and then repositioned her purse and the seatbelt around it, as not to disturb its neatness when met with sharp turns or abrupt stops. A framed photo of Maylee rested on the top of the pile, kind eyes burning a hole in Autumns cheek. She ran a finger softly over Maylee's hair in the picture, what she wouldn't give to see her niece again.

"I will find you." Autumn whispered to the still shot of Maylee's face.

Then she picked it up and hugged it tightly against her chest. A lone tear finally escaped her fighting eyes. She closed them tightly, refusing to let any more through the crack.

"Please God, please help me find her."

* * *

Detective Chance sat in his office for several minutes, staring at the address written on a crisp paper that was stuck to the edge of his desk. He took out his phone and pulled up her name. The numbers shouted at him from the screen, telling him to bring her back, convince her to stay with him, out of harm's way.

The realization of Autumn's free-will and determination won out. *Besides, who was he to try and convince her of anything?* After several moments of staring at the thick black letters spelling out her name, he shut the phone off and slid it into the pocket of his fitted suit jacket. Finally, he stood to leave, but not before barking orders to his daughter.

"Vanessa, get me names, phone numbers, and field positions, of every detective stationed in Denver, Colorado. Have it on my desk by the time I'm back from lunch"

"Okay, Dad." Vanessa shouted back at him.

Chapter Three

The journey was lengthy. It took three soul-sucking days, and two restless nights to make it to Denver. The drive was practically non-stop. Autumn was afraid to maneuver the U-Haul through towns, or practically any road other than a highway. Tight freeways caused her anxiety to sky rocket. Her fingers ached from the intensity of her grip on the wheel, and there was nothing left of her nails. Painful swollen nubs consumed her previously manicured fingertips. A thick coat of polish was sure to be at the top of her to do list, once she got settled. Autumn hated ugly hands. Something about chewed nails made her feel dirty and unprepared for life's tasks, like a careless teenager. The thought made her cringe.

Fear of a side swipe or fender bender stopped her from entering any fast food drive-ups along the way. This caused the consistent growling of her stomach to chew through the air. The rumble of her starving belly made her feel exactly like that annoying clock at her mother's house growing up. Not only did it mark the time, but it sent resentful homesick fumes into the air, swirling around into a giant cloud of fear and self-doubt. This was merely another reminder of how afraid and unprepared she was for the petrifying quest ahead.

The few bags of chips and bottled waters she had stocked up on in California, along with hotel muffins and single serving coffee packets had taken full responsibility for holding her over the entire trip. Autumn wanted to get there, without delay, and so she did. There was no room to dilly-dally.

Both hotels she'd stayed at left her feeling grimy. Even after her morning showers she felt under-rested and far from alert. By the time she'd arrived at the new apartment she was in no mood to unpack her things. Preparing for the move was much easier, she had no trouble convincing friends and neighbors to help load furniture and heavy items. Now that she'd arrived, there was no help in sight. Aside from a half-naked, overweight man who sat staring at her from a damaged lawn chair across the parking lot, the place looked deserted.

It was nearly dark and Autumn was silently kicking herself for not calling the landlord to help her schedule a person of assistance hours ago. It would've allowed them the time necessary to prepare for the task. It was the first of many self-disappointments to come involving her skills in moving and adventure.

Autumn realized how irritated she'd be if someone were to ask her to help in such a spur of the moment manner, so she opted out of calling, it was a request better asked in person. After locking up the U-Haul and leaving it in the parking lot, she reluctantly made her way to the building.

His was the first apartment in sight, it was on the bottom story and had a bright red door. A flimsy name plate hung from a string, just above the small peep hole, it read APARTMENT MANAGER, in bold erasable marker. It took him several minutes to open the door and greet her. Jingling of chains and clicking of locks sounded from the other side of the hollow metal door.

This wasn't the same manager that she'd spoken to when she picked out the apartment. This new guy had a much smoother and kinder face, and he appeared to be a lot younger, probably in his late twenties. *Perhaps a College drop-out?* Autumn speculated, concluding that he was most likely managing the place for the free rent that the job entails. Was she stereotyping him? Maybe… Did she care? No.

"Can I help you ma'am?" His smile rang friendly.

"Hi, yes." She hesitated, "My name is Autumn. I'm renting an apartment here. I'm sorry to bother you so late." She straightened her wrinkly top and fiddled with a gnawed off thumbnail before saying, "I'm just arriving, and I was wondering if you know of anyone that I could pay to help me unpack?"

"Oh, hey, yes, I heard about you!" His handsome smile grew causing his ears to lift, and a cute little crease to form just below the right cheekbone. "Apt 22 right?"

"Yes, that's right."

"Howdy then, ma'am, I'm Jeremy."

It was a very informal introduction yet he insisted on shaking her hand. His palm was big and his fingers were slightly calloused. A heavy free hand slapped her on the shoulder causing her entire body to jolt. He seemed like a very outgoing young man. A few husky voices rang in from behind him.

Autumn could hear a couple of men laughing and joking in the background. It sounded like they were having a blast. She couldn't quite make out their jokes or comments, but it wasn't from lack of trying. A listening ear strained to make out their words.

Autumn tried, without success, to recall the last time she was able to laugh so freely. Even with her friends, witty conversation and playful banter had been forced since the loss of Maylee. The lighthearted beam that Autumn used to carry with her everywhere, was now nothing more than a distant flicker.

It existed somewhere, but she was unable to grasp it tight enough to hang on for more than a few seconds at a time. Every time that lighthearted twinkle returned to her eyes, or a gleeful fire began to build in her chest, it was quickly distinguished with grief. Washed away before anything more than a spark could ignite. But, at least there was hope. Autumn was here for a reason and maybe someday she could get that light back.

Jeremy must have noticed her distraction by his guests because he tilted his head to the side, leaned into her personal space, and made a fully conscious effort to engage her in eye contact. That attractive crease in his cheek returned with the questioning grin he threw at her. Embarrassed butterflies escaped Autumn's chest and a lump formed in her throat.

"Care to join?" He asked, pointing over his tall shoulder with a large outstretched thumb. "I've got a few friends over. We just finished up a barbeque. I'm sure there's a burger left if you're hungry?"

"Oh no," was her very quick response.

Autumn couldn't possibly impose on a party of strangers. The pull of her tired eyelids were nagging at her to get settled for the night, and she couldn't help but to notice there wasn't a female voice to be heard. This entire situation had danger written all over it. If there was one quality Autumn truly admired about herself it was a keen sense of reserved caution. After all, you're nothing if not safe.

After declining the drink to go along with the already turned down burger that her stomach was very loudly cursing her for, Autumn again asked for help. Jeremy shouted over his shoulder toward the kitchen causing her to nearly jump out of her skin.

"Hey guys," he yelled at his guests without taking his eyes off of her. The smile he had remained intact. "I've got a quick job to do for a tenant, wanna' help?"

Autumn's eyes widened in fear, her feet shifted nervously beneath her, and she struggled to find words.

"I… Um… I can find someone else, really." She hesitated.

Jeremy leaned forward and whispered, so that no one else could hear.

"They really only look scary, and they might smell, but they're harmless, I assure you." He said with a wink.

The three men that entered the room caused Autumn's mouth to open, just a crack, and her shoulders to lower with the air that escaped her. An awkward rush of defeat crawled up her legs and stopped in her neck, threatening to drain the very life from her. The first man in sight was clearly older than Jeremy, by at least five years - was her guess.

He appeared to nearly double Jeremy in weight, and not the unhealthy kind either. There wasn't an ounce of blubber to be found, only the thick hard kind of weight that most men only dream of developing. His hair was light, short, and squared off in a boxy type cut that had a weird way of making the muscles between his neck and shoulders look even bigger. A superman symbol was tattooed on his neck, just above the collarbone. It was the first tattoo Autumn noticed but definitely not the only one in the room.

Two more men emerged from behind the giant. One looked a lot like Jeremy, with the same smile and an identical crease below the cheekbone. It wasn't really a dimple so much as a handsome dip of the skin, or a glorified wrinkle in the perfect spot.

The third man was much skinnier than the others. He was obviously no slouch in the muscular department, but his build wasn't nearly as stuffed. A full sleeve of tattoos' covered one arm and the other held a permanently detailed portrait of a winged angel, with dark hair and a perfect bikini body. Autumn pictured him to be more of a spotter in the gym, only there to elevate his heart rate and assist the others in their workout. She had a brief mental image of his tattooed arms working up a sweat as he tried to lift a dumbbell that the human machine before him had set aside with ease.

Autumn cautiously inched a step back onto the sidewalk, hoping they wouldn't notice her movement. She was at least a foot away from the door, just in case she needed to run for dear life. There was plenty of distance between her and them, and she was a fast runner. Very fast. She hadn't spent the last three years of her life scaling the beach at an abnormal pace to be rendered a slow runner. Prepared to sprint, she waited for Jeremy's introduction and gawked at the raw manpower that came in the form of his friends, and most likely brother.

"Guys, this is Autumn." Jeremy casually tossed his head in her direction, as if he'd known her for years. "She needs help moving her stuff into her new apartment."

Autumn cleared her throat to speak, but it didn't help, she was still unable. All that could be forced was a nod, and the sheer will not to pee her pants right there on the spot. A realization that these men were soon to know exactly where she lived, settled deep inside her. They would also be privileged to the in's and out's of literally every item she owned. Every. Single. One. The thought of her underwear drawer that just so happened to be sitting to the side of her dismantled dressers caused a blush.

They all stood there and stared at her for a minute. Autumn didn't really know what to say or do, so she just fiddled with the bottom seam of her shirt and let them take in the sight of her. It was a little embarrassing and uncomfortable. Jeremy looked back and forth between her and his friends. He was bewildered and fully aware of the inappropriate looks they were giving her.

Small nods and playful glances of approval were exchanged between them. The smallest of them turned to the biggest and muttered something under his breath. It was hard for her to tell for sure, but it sounded a lot like he may have said the word "milf."

This is when Autumn finally let out the breath of initial shock she'd been holding in. She dramatically forced the air out in a long drawn out groan, assisted with a dramatic eye roll. These sketchy looking men weren't a threat at all. They were nothing more than a few harmless drunken fools acting like horny teenage boys. There wasn't a hint of unkind intention on any of their faces, nor was there any sign of callous in their growing smiles. Jeremy chuckled a little at her reaction of them.

"What's wrong guys? Haven't you ever seen an attractive older woman with a tan?"

Older, he said older. What the hell did he mean by older? She wondered. Forty one really wasn't that old, although her constant anxiety made her feel at least sixty.

"I don't have much." She assured them, just before pointing a finger over her shoulder toward the parking lot. "One U-Haul of boxes and furniture, is all. I just can't lift it all myself."

"We'd love to help." The one who looked like Jeremy piped up and stepped in front of the others. "I'm Aiden, by the way. Big and little over there go by Harry and Lloyd."

"Nice to meet you." Autumn peaked around Aiden's shoulder to greet them properly, only to see suppressed giggles and spirited shaking of heads.

Had she missed something? An inside joke perhaps? Aiden burst into laughter at his own pun that she clearly hadn't caught onto.

"Haven't you ever seen Dumb and Dumber?" He asked.

"Oooohhh yeah." She said, realizing his not so funny punch line.

"I guess some people just don't appreciate good movie humor." He teased.

Autumn accepted the quick witted challenge, "I guess some people just don't know how to deliver a joke." She retorted with a mocking half-grin.

After a short but very loud rolling burst of laughter, from everyone except Aiden of course, Jeremy stepped out and draped a warm welcoming arm over her shoulders.

"You're gunna' fit in just fine." He giggled. "Now, lead the way to that truck of yours and we'll help you get settled in, without pay, and the least you can do is accept the burger Aiden is going to make you while the rest of us get started."

Aiden dropped his head to his toes and waltzed back to the kitchen causing Autumn to chuckle a little at his playful dramatization of defeat.

"Does he always do what you tell him?" She asked.

"Well, he is my little brother… Soooo."

"So no?" Autumn corrected.

"I guess you're right." He confirmed with a sigh.

It didn't take long for the bigger of the men to assume position at Autumn's side, just opposite of Jeremy. He gave her a playful nudge of the shoulder and introduced himself.

"My name is actually Lucas, and I hate to disappoint you, but I'm married." Then he wiggled a giant ring finger in front of her to show off the goods.

"Lucky gal." Autumn confirmed, mirroring his genuine smile.

The smallest man, Mr. Tattoo himself, may have been the bounciest, and funniest of them all. He wiggled himself between Lucas and Autumn, plucked Jeremy's arm from around her shoulder and tossed it aside. He pulled a disgusted face at Jeremy, as if he was diseased. Then he gently grabbed her arm and stopped them from walking. He wanted her full attention and obviously couldn't get it with Lucas walking so closely, or with Jeremy's arm in its previous position.

"My name really is Lloyd, unfortunately that wasn't a total joke, and I'm as single as they come." His voice was chirpy and confident. "Have you ever considered dating a younger man?"

Autumn couldn't help but to giggle and cheer up just a tad at his bouncy attempt at being flirtatious. She was starting to feel at home amidst their upbeat, easy-going attitudes. Despite the fact that they would clearly be hitting on her for the duration of the evening, the entire situation was still somehow comforting. She was washed over by a strange relaxed feeling around this small group of burly men, and that light hearted twinkle inside of her was trying viciously to spark. The reasoning behind her relaxation was a mystery, but welcomed nonetheless.

Autumn leaned in so that her face was a mere inch away from Lloyd's, and she slowed her breath to match his exactly. His shoulders instantly stiffened, and eyes grew wide at their closeness. She smiled big and whispered to him in the sexiest voice she could muster.

"Don't you think it's a little past your curfew? Mommy might get worried if you're out late."

Autumn thought Jeremy and Lucas we're going to fall to the ground in laughter.

"Yep." Jeremy said. "You'll fit in just fine."

No sooner than the words came out of his mouth they had arrived at the truck. Seeing the three of them stand next to the U-Haul waiting for her to lift the hatch and expose its contents, made that exciting glimpse of a light-heart disappear. The steady weight of Maylee's disappearance returned. It nestled back onto her shoulders and chest, right where she was used to it being. The short witty introduction of these men had passed, and now it was time to retreat back to her previous self. Broken and lost inside of the grief that had taken over every part of her.

Chapter Four

Light forced its way through the slow opening crack of Autumn's eyelids. She rolled onto her belly and buried her face into her pillow to escape it. There was a stale stench to the fabric of her pillowcase, probably a result of riding in a drafty traveling storage space for three days.

There hadn't been time to do a load of wash, she'd been far too tired to bother with laundry. Her dirty pillow and sheets were carelessly tossed on the mattress as soon as humanly possible. The covers were slopped together and then Autumn had collapsed, falling asleep almost instantly. Wandering hands now felt the uncovered corner of her bed. Apparently she hadn't even tucked in that irritating spot where the headboard meets mattress and side-wall. A sleepy groan rumbled in her throat as she looked over at the large neon blue letters of her alarm clock.

She hadn't actually set the alarm, there was never a need for that. Not that she intended to sleep in, although that would've been nice. Autumn knew she'd be up early on her own, as always. It never failed, once 6:00 Pacific Standard Time rolled around Autumn's eyes pulled open. This happened every day without fail. Even with her body's clock being an hour off, due to the change in time zone, she awoke the exact same as usual. The numbers read 7:05 Mountain Time. Fall would be approaching soon and then it would be back to 6:00 as normal.

Before Autumn could finish running a brush through her hair, there was an overbearing knock at the door.

"Who in the hell?" She muttered to herself.

The only people that knew where she lived was her new friend, Jeremy the apartment manager, and his rambunctious crew. If one of them were honestly knocking at the door this early to ask her on a date, then they were sure to get an earful. Autumn couldn't imagine they'd be up to the task with the hangovers they were sure to have. They were fairly drunk while moving her stuff and she couldn't help but notice two unopened thirty packs of beer sitting just inside Jeremy's door.

Nah, it couldn't be any of them, it must be a solicitor. Honestly, she wasn't sure which was worse. A hearty amount of toothpaste scrubbed harshly against Autumn's teeth, and she opted against answering the door. She didn't want to be talked into buying a vacuum and already had an appointment set up for her satellite TV installation.

Splat. A thick lump of dirtied mint foam was spat into the sink, and a low flow of water washed it down the drain. Just as Autumn reached for a hair-tie, that irritating knock sounded through the apartment again. This time it was even louder.

"Damn it."

Tip-toeing feet carried her quietly through the apartment and she glanced ever-so-silently out the peephole. She didn't want the culprit of that irritating knock to hear her on the other side of the door. To her surprise, there stood Jeremy, a coffee in each hand, and most likely the widest grin she had ever seen planted on his face. There wasn't a hint of a hangover. His eyes were white and his posture tall. The lack of paleness on his skin, or queasiness in his stance was a shock. *Who is this monster?* She wondered, feeling the extent of their age difference, for obvious reasons.

He must have sensed her watching him, because he held the coffee up and spoke toward the door, as if she'd be able to hear him better by talking directly into the tinsy looking glass. Autumn smirked to herself and shook her head at his tenacity. A reaching hand hesitated at the handle, and his voice raised in friendly annoyance.

"I know you can see me Autumn, and I know you like your coffee black because you told me that last night."

She playfully waited to turn the handle. There may have been a little amusement, and possibly even some curiosity at what would come out of his mouth next. It was an odd feeling to have adapted in one day, but she was comfortable around Jeremy. He felt like a little brother in a weird way.

Or, at least she assumed that's what a little brother would feel like, all she had to compare it to was her relationship with Candace, and that wasn't much of a comparison. There was a certain ease about Jeremy, though, something that made her relax. The consistently heavy burden on her shoulders seemed to lighten around him.

"I know. I know." He continued. "You're surprised that I'm awake and looking so dapper, right?"

Autumn chuckled and let him keep going. She wondered if the neighbors were listening, and if he treated them all the same. Probably not, who has the time for such hospitality?

"I told you I'd help you get a car today, remember? Don't think you're going to keep me waiting. It's not like I've got all day."

She hesitated at the handle. One more minute, she thought, testing his friendly patience.

"All right then. You asked for it." His voice slightly raised. "Let's talk about the contents of that bottom right drawer of your dresser. What did you call 'em? Your possibles?"

Autumn yanked the door open. "What the hell is wrong with you?" She hissed, just before pulling him inside by the front of his shirt and slamming the door behind him as if they were escaping a hurricane.

He laughed freely. "Your blush is one of a kind, Miss Brown."

Jeremy made himself comfortable by plopping down on her loveseat. Which took full responsibility of furnishing the otherwise empty living room. Beige walls were bare, and the carpet new. Her cup of coffee smelt like heaven. He was right, she needed it, and black was perfect. Autumn reached for her steaming cup like a zombie on a determined yet slow moving mission. A deep whiff of its fumes were absorbed into her nostrils before a giant gulp of it sloshed into her mouth. It tasted as blissful as it smelled.

The seat next to Jeremy cradled Autumn into its cushions as she lowered herself next to him. With a body turned to face him, she pulled her feet up under her thighs. Anything and everything that needed to be done today could wait until this delicious coffee was emptied from its cup.

"So, a car?" Jeremy asked, ever so casually.

"Yep, I need a car… Are you really in a hurry?"

"Nope." He beamed, "I've got all day. What kind are you looking for?" He shifted his weight allowing his ribcage to sink deeper into the armrest. "Something about you screams Ford. Are you a Ford fan?"

"Honestly, I could care less. You?"

"Yes, of course." He said, matter-of-fact, and with a proud smirk.

Then he took a long sip of his own drink, with steam rolling from the second hole in its lid.

"Really though, I have a friend who owns a used car lot. I'm sure he'll give you a deal, but he mostly only carries cars that are, well, let's just say aged to perfection. His lot is small, and the selection of pick-ups sucks a ball sack." Jeremy casually scowled at the wall. "The fool anyway. So, what do you think you'll want?"

"A ball sack, really?"

Autumn felt another pang of old-age, and Jeremy let out a carefree huff at her reaction to his sloppy word choice. She shook her head at his juvenile speech and continued.

"Something cheap, but dependable. I don't have much cash, but I can't be breaking down either."

An image of herself turning the key to a non-responsive ignition while stalking Craig ran through her mind, causing a shudder. The last thing she needed was to draw attention to herself. Which reminded her, she'd have to make a few changes in her appearance as well, like maybe a haircut and color. The loss of weight was huge, but that alone might not be enough to conceal her identity from Craig. God only knows what would happen if he recognized her.

She thought about asking Jeremy where to find a nice beauty parlor, but decided against distracting his young mind. A mental note was taken to ask him later. Craig was bound to see her eventually, it was inevitable, and she needed to be prepared for it.

"Are you okay?" Jeremy asked with a questioning eyebrow raised.

He'd noticed the sudden crinkle of her nose, and the stiffness in her shoulders. Autumn raised her coffee to her lips and took a long sip without averting the menacing stare of her eyes.

"I'm fine, just thinking." Finally, she exhaled and looked back at him. "Something plain." She openly admitted. "I need a plain car that won't stand out or draw attention to me. I don't want to be noticed in shitty neighborhoods, or in high class ones either. Think you could help me find a car like that?"

What the hell was she doing? Autumn couldn't believe herself. She told him too much, and now he was going to ask questions. A nervous heart pounded in her chest with anticipation, and Maylee's name was suddenly stuck in the back of her throat. Autumn wasn't ready to talk about it, yet she couldn't seem to hide it either. The simple act of discussing a car was drawing her intentions to the surface.

The look on Jeremy's face was thoughtful, he scratched at the hint of stubble growing on a hardly noticeable patch under his chin. To her surprise, and unexplainable disappointment, he refrained from asking questions.

"Hmmm," he pondered. "That'll actually be easier than you'd think. I'm sure he'll have some sort of a midsize Sedan that's just old enough to blend in everywhere."

Relief allowed her shoulders to relax some. "Good." She said, in a hurry to change the subject. "Wait here. I'll get ready fast. I don't want to keep you from your outrageously busy day." She teased. "Oh, and thanks for the coffee, it's perfect."

A splash of water refreshed Autumn's skin before she smoothed on a thin layer of foundation. Jeremy may have seen her morning face, but that didn't mean the rest of the world needed to. An unforgiving mirror hung in her uncomfortably bright new bathroom. Every single wrinkle was front and center, cursing at her in their own language. Autumn failed to see her natural beauty, to her only the flaws were visible.

Maylee's disappearance added some years to Autumn's face. The tiny crow's feet spreading from her eyes screamed 'you failed her' and the faded shade of her lips yelled, 'how could you'. Everything about Autumn's ageing was somehow intensified by the guilt of losing Maylee. After several minutes of staring at her reflection like a random stranger, Autumn finally forced out the 'if only' thoughts that were building up, along with the rapidly forming moisture behind her eyes.

Retreating to her room to find some clothing offered a distraction from that nag of a mirror. Boxes were stacked neatly next to her closet, waiting patiently to be unpacked. Each one was symmetrically taped and then labeled with perfectly printed lettering. There was a label for each season, and style. As Autumn fought the urge to place the hangers in the closet and begin the tedious task of unpacking there was a loud crash, followed by a shatter, followed by an, "Oh shit!"

In three seconds flat Autumn reached the kitchen. An opened box of silver utensils were strewn about the room, along with a mess of Tupperware containers and scattered broken glass. Jeremy was crouched down to the floor with his back facing her. Autumn couldn't tell exactly what he was picking up until she carefully stepped around him, trying her best to avoid the shining shards of glass on the russet linoleum floor.

It was Maylee's photograph. *Of course it was Maylee's photograph.* The very picture that rode through four states on the seat next to her, strapped in like a real human being. The same picture that Maylee herself had handed to Autumn on her 17th birthday. The same portrait that Autumn had had printed onto missing person fliers and plastered on every bulletin board she could find. It was Autumn's favorite picture of Maylee. Now the original was clutched in the fingers of a man who had never even met her, dropped and shattered - it was the story of Maylee's life.

Autumn's stomach jumped into her throat and then fell back down full force causing her knees to buckle. Slowly, she lowered her body to the floor and sat proper on her knees. She gently took the now glassless frame from Jeremy's hand and brushed the last shard from Maylee's face.

"Sorry." He muttered cautiously, noticing the broken-hearted sulk that was scrawled all over Autumn's face. "I was going to help you unpack and organize a few of your boxes. I guess my clumsiness got the best of me."

Autumn nodded, but refused to look up at him. His apology was clearly genuine, yet for the moment she couldn't bring herself to make eye contact. This was her stuff, and he had no right to be rummaging through it in the first place, but to drop Maylee to the floor was an unnecessary act of carelessness. After a few moments of staring into her niece's eyes, Autumn reminded herself of Jeremy's selflessness in helping her get settled. She had no choice but to let the accident go, as hard as it was, Autumn convinced herself that he wasn't at fault.

"It's okay," she breathed the words and wiped a tear from the corner of her eye before it had a chance to roam the length of her face. "You didn't mean to."

"She's beautiful by the way." He noted, pointing a finger at the picture. "Looks a lot like you, same nose and mouth. Is she your daughter?"

Emotions were tangling together causing a jumbled mass of confusion to tie a knot in Autumn's chest. It didn't matter if she was ready to talk about Maylee or not, there was no choice in the matter now. Part of her wanted to spill her guts and tell Jeremy everything. The very details of Maylee's life, and of her disappearance hesitated at the tip of Autumn's tongue. The reserved side of her emotional state defeated the sudden battle between Autumn's mind and voice.

"She's my niece." Autumn answered, and then finally looked up to meet Jeremy's eyes.

With an attempt to lighten the mood he nodded in approval at Maylee's picture, nudged Autumn's arm with his elbow and asked in a wanting voice, "So do I ever get to meet this beautiful goddess?"

Autumn only sighed. There was no quick comeback in defense of her families honor, nor was there some form of returned banter. Autumn merely whispered an airy, "I hope so."

"Come on then." Jeremy jumped to his feet behind her. "Why don't you let me clean up this mess while you get dressed, and then we'll go and get you that car."

With a tight grip of her hand and a strong arm Jeremy pulled Autumn to her feet. Another brute smack to the shoulder was offered. It must have been his way of telling her to buck up, because he followed the gesture with a quick nod of encouragement. Then he turned away from her and begin to clean his mess.

Once ready, Autumn followed Jeremy through the hall, down one flight of wide concrete stairs, and then out to the parking lot. The first thing she noticed was an empty space that held her U-Haul the night before. She had called and made the proper arrangements for it to be picked up while watching Lucas and Aiden unpack her heaviest belongings. The moving company she spoke with had told her to leave the keys in the cab, and they would be there in the morning. Surprised at their promptness, she was now completely at the mercy of Jeremy.

It was no shock that he drove a Ford pick-up. All shined up and waxed, it was black with thickly tinted windows. It was a truck that she could picture Keith driving if he was still alive. She nodded to herself in approval and then climbed in. Jeremy's light hearted conversation on the way to his friend's car lot made it easy to forget about the broken glass of Maylee's photo frame. Autumn even found herself making plans to meet his mother at a bingo house later on that week. She was happy to be making friends so quickly and hoped that Jeremy's mother was as easy to get along with as he was.

After a full fifteen minutes of weaving in and out of tedious traffic congestion, turning down a few confusing one way roads, and waiting patiently at drawn out stop lights, they finally made it. The streets of Denver would take some serious figuring out. Autumn hated learning routes and dreaded the act of 'getting used to' a new place. It would definitely be a pain in the rear, but doable nonetheless.

The used car lot Jeremy pulled into was everything he had explained it to be. There were less than twenty cars to display, and the office was nothing more than a single wide trailer with a cracked front window and peeling paint around the doorframe. It was attached at the side to a very large tin-looking garage. Jeremy insisted on talking to his friend before they even looked into the windows of any of the cars for sale. Autumn reluctantly shrugged her shoulders and agreed. *What the hell,* she thought. This place was probably the best she could afford anyhow, and she wasn't exactly excited about the test driving process.

"Don't worry." Jeremy told her as they stepped up the creaky wooden steps to the trailer. "I know the mechanic too. These cars may not look like much, but I promise anything you pick will be fixed up and runnin' proper. You shouldn't have to worry about breakin' down anytime soon."

"That's reassuring." Autumn groaned.

Jeremy flung his head in the direction of the tin shop and grinned before offering a quick waive. "Speak of the devil." He said.

Autumn was shocked to see Lloyd stepping out from behind one of the wide open sliding garage doors. Grease smeared across the tattoos on his shirtless chest. Even the picture of the woman that ran down the length of his arm now looked smudged and dirty. Okay, maybe he was in a little better shape than she initially thought. Maybe it was because he had been compared to Lucas the hulk, and even Aiden. Or, it might have been because he was now half naked and every single muscle of his abdomen was outlined in deeply defining black muck. Either way, Autumn couldn't help but to blush just a tad, and then remind herself of their obvious age difference.

Lloyd raised his voice just enough to be heard over the stretch of space between them, "Hi Autumn!" His wave was supreme. "I'll grab Benji and meet you guys inside."

"Okay." Jeremy shouted back and then let himself in.

"That's the mechanic?" Autumn asked. "Why didn't you say so in the first place?"

"I thought it'd be a pleasant surprise." Jeremy said with a chuckle and a nudge. "I think he kinda likes ya'. Don't get attached though, he's a player." He teased.

"Oh lord," She mumbled in annoyance and with a backward tilt of her neck. "Okay, I've got to ask." Jeremy turned giving her his immediate and fully kind attention. "How much beer did you guys actually drink last night?"

He laughed, "Why?"

"Because you were up buying coffee before seven o'clock, and it looks like your greasy friend has already been here for hours. How are you not all hungover and useless today?"

"Lots of practice." He winked.

"Maybe you should practice drinking less." Autumn teased.

"No, I mean lots of practice getting up early."

Jeremy corrected her in an oddly matter of fact way. He wasn't joking around in the slightest.

"It doesn't matter what you do the night before. There's no excuse for being lazy. That's one logic my friends and I all share. If you can't handle the aftermath of a party, then don't go in the first place. We all know our limit."

"Humf." Autumn was a little surprised. "Commendable," she announced. "So how early did you get up? Just curious."

"Five o'clock." Jeremy stood proud. "We meet at the gym at 5:30 every morning. Rain or shine. Hangover or no hangover."

Impressed, Autumn watched the crease form in Jeremy's cheek.

"What about you?" He asked. "You're clearly in shape."

Autumn's heart skipped a beat. "I run." She mumbled and ducked her head hoping he wouldn't pry.

Luckily, she was saved by the growing sound of Lloyd's voice accompanied by a pitchy singing laughter. *Must be Benji*, she noted, *saved by the ring of a used car salesman*. The resemblance of his rising laugh and an actual sound of a bell was the very definition of irony. A short rickety door swung open allowing the two men to saunter in.

Benji wasn't what Autumn expected another friend of Jeremy's to look like. He was notably round around the middle, and only the middle, also there wasn't a tattoo in sight. A clean, grey button up top complimented his carefully styled hair. There was a whooshing flow to the gelled mass of black on his head. It rose in the middle and then flopped neatly to one side.

Benji was a very kind, slow-moving yet attentive man. After a short introduction and pleasant conversation about nothing more than the weather and few decent mom and pop restaurants close by, they cut right to the chase. Benji's chirpy voice answered all of Autumn's questions professionally. He didn't pry into the details of her life which was a huge relief. He even promised to give her an outstanding price, since she came with Jeremy. Apparently, Benji would have never in a thousand years thought Jeremy would bring him business.

After a few winks and inappropriate compliments, Lloyd excused himself to get back to a project in the shop. Jeremy followed Autumn and Benji around at a comfortable distance as she mulled over her choices. He only jumped in with opinions when asked, and they mainly consisted of comments like "doesn't compare to a ford" and "I think a truck would be better." His opinion was quickly dismissed and Autumn decided to trust Benji's judgment on her needs and price range.

"This one seems reasonable." Autumn stated as she ran her hand softly across the hood of a small black four door.

First she tried to picture this very car in a dark alley, then she closed her eyes and imagined it in the valet line of a black tie country club. The image was a success. This car was plain, most likely the plainest one in sight, it would blend in not matter the surroundings. The windows were even slightly tinted, a convenient addition, it was perfect.

"Aww yes, the Toyota Camry. There was over three hundred and fifty thousand sold the year of this model. You said you want a car that blends, then this is most definitely the perfect choice. Wanna' take her for a spin?"

"Shit," Autumn said, "I guess."

Jeremy jumped into the passenger seat without hesitation, ready to encourage her speeding skills no doubt. Autumn's knuckles whitened around the steering wheel, and her heart nearly drummed clean out of her chest. The nerves weren't caused by the excitement of buying a new car. A distinct growing fear of exploring the back roads of Denver began to rise, causing her feet to hesitate at the pedals. They were already in a strange neighborhood that she wasn't familiar with, and it was a mere glimpse of what laid ahead. This could very easily be the car she'd soon follow Craig in.

Rather than driving straight to the freeway as she normally would've done, Autumn decided to try her own little experiment. Her foot pressed lightly on the brake before they fully crossed the dip of the exit portion on the sidewalk. Knowing full well that the question of "why" would work its way to the surface, she turned to Jeremy and made a very odd request.

"Point me in the direction of the scariest neighborhood you know. I want to see if we blend in before I buy it."

"Autumn, what the hell?" He questioned. One deep wrinkle formed between his gathered eyebrows. "I thought you wanted me to help you find a car, not be the target of drive-by? Why on earth do you want to see the worst of Denver?"

A slow exhale escaped her, and she nervously chewed at her bottom lip. This was it, Autumn knew that she couldn't avoid the conversation forever. Especially since she was accepting his help. The only choice she had was to give Jeremy something. Some kind of explanation for her dangerous request. Besides, in all actuality she was glad he was there with her. She was afraid to do it all on her own, and felt a tiny bit safer with him by her side. If she was going to do this, then she may as well clue him in… a little.

"There's a man who lives here that I want to find. He isn't a good person and based on his previous living conditions, I can only imagine what kind of shit hole he stays in now. I need to see him, and I don't want him to see me."

Jeremy's irritated eyes pierced into hers. It wasn't enough, he clearly needed more. He drummed his fingers on the dashboard and stared at her, waiting. Cautiously she continued, paying very close attention to exactly how much she let out. The haunting truth of Autumn's situation scratched at the back of her throat trying to escape, but she just couldn't tell him the extent of it all. Not yet, anyway. She'd only known him for one day after all, despite the familiarity that made the extent of their friendship seem much deeper than that.

"Look," she continued, "it has to do with my niece Maylee, the one from that picture this morning. The man I want to find might have some information about her that I have to figure out. But he can't see me, he can't know I'm here. Can we just leave it at that, for now? Please?"

Threatening tears welled in her eyes, confirming the quiver of her voice to be genuine. Of course Jeremy noticed the hesitant display of emotion. He already knew that Autumn had a secret, one that she'd reveal when she was ready, and not a minute before. It didn't matter that he wanted to push her for more information, because he didn't dare too.

Jeremy knew more than what he was letting on, and plus it was visible that Autumn might snap with violence, or even worse, cry. Soothing emotional women had never been Jeremy's strong suit, so he left it be. She'd come around eventually, and patience was always on his side.

The thinking wheels in Jeremy's head were practically visible on the curves of his face. A pulsing clench of his jaw read 'piss off' and the wrinkles on his forehead shouted 'I can't believe we're doing this'. With a mere flick of his hand, but no words, Jeremy pointed the way. It was in the exact opposite direction of the clearly visible freeway sign sitting comfortably at the stoplight to their left. Jeremy sunk himself into the seat, leaning far enough back that he could barely see out the window. Then he pulled the hood of his light jacket up over his head and crossed his arms over his chest. He was irritated, but compliant.

After a full hour test drive, Autumn learned two stiff facts. The first fact was that she had definitely chosen the right car. Not a single person so much as glanced in their direction. The second was a much more sickening fact, there were places in this city that were equally as disgusting as they were heart wrenching.

In merely one morning, and without even exiting her vehicle, Autumn had witnessed a drunken mother slapping around her toddler, a hooker sleeping on her street corner after a long night's work no doubt, and two groups of young men exchanging drugs and money in plain daylight. That's not to mention the windowless apartment buildings, and heavily 'caution' taped sidewalks.

Jeremy explained to her that these youngsters never really care who sees them because in that particular neck of the woods, if you're a nark they'll find you. It wasn't an uncommon thing to hear of drive-bys, stabbings, or even baseball bat beatings. If you were raised in certain neighborhoods, or around certain gangs, you just learn to keep your head down and move on through. Common sense is a survival tactic. 'If you don't see nothin' then you can't tell nothin' …apparently that's a well-known motto.

Autumn felt like she stepped right out of an episode of some random serial killer show from the Identification Discovery channel. Except it wasn't a television show based on someone else's story. Today was as real as life could possibly get, and it quite literally took the oxygen from her.

By the time she pulled back into the parking garage of the used car lot, every inch of her shook. From the inside out, Autumn had been poisoned with fear and by the surrealness of it all. If Maylee was alive then she could easily be living in a hell that was even worse than what Autumn had just witnessed. A new wave of understanding inched its way into Autumn's head like molasses – slow and sticky. Reality was harsh, and she knew that today was only a glimpse of what lay ahead. This journey was bound to uncover a nastiness that was impossible to prepare for.

Aside from a few quick explanations of gangs and crime rate, Jeremy remained silent for most of the drive. He made it a point to keep his eyes on the road as did Autumn. It wasn't until the car was parked and the engine shut down that he really finally spoke to her.

"Satisfied?" he asked, wholly irritated.

Autumn shook her head, unable to find the words. She now had an idea of what laid ahead, but only an idea. There was no satisfaction to settle the petrified churn of her belly, and although Jeremy had given her the cold shoulder for the last hour she was still inexplicably grateful for his company.

"I don't know," she answered honestly. "Thank you."

Chapter Five

A neatly sealed box sat on Autumn's kitchen table. The perfectly placed packing tape remained a hundred percent untouched and the label on its side read 'Finding Craig'. Every other box in the apartment had been neatly unpacked, their contents organized and put in a proper place. This was the last box remaining sealed, and it practically reached out and slapped Autumn's face every time she looked at it.

With arms folded across her chest and an antsy foot tapping the floor where old worn-out kitchen linoleum meets new living room carpet, she stood in a rounded archway of the conjoining rooms to stare at it. The contents of the box consumed every part of her wellbeing. She's refused to open it, until today, knowing that the simple act of peeling the tape would unleash everything she's avoided the past few days.

This box was like her own pandora, she might as well have labeled it that. The very fiber of this box shouts 'past meets present'. It's the letting out of ghosts, memories, emotions – mostly fear, and a petrifying anticipation of finality that can no longer be avoided. After all, the essence of this very box was the reasoning behind her entire move. Once it's open her mission to find Maylee could no longer be put off. One more day was tempting, but honestly she didn't know which was worse – facing it, or avoiding it.

Autumn had watched far too many police shows in preparation of this move. She assumed that by buying a gigantic wall sized map of the city, along with string and thumb tacks, that she'd somehow be able to figure out and replicate the process of 'tracking down a suspect' – as seen on T.V. – at least a dozen times. *Why would such a repetitive process be used if it didn't work, right?.*

It'd been exactly one week since that unnerving drive with Jeremy in the slums of the city. A recollection of a vicious mother's backhand meeting the flesh of her wobbly child's face, forced a chill to rush through Autumn's entire body. Since that heartbreaking sight, anxiety had doubled the size of its permanent home in her chest, and caused her to procrastinate and avoid her ultimate intention. Drumming fingers left an irritated pink spot on the side of Autumn's arm and she reminded herself that Maylee had been gone for three years. Three years too long!

She also reminded herself that the only thing she had accomplished in her first week here was practicing different makeup styles, and a change of hair. Her once long waterfall blonde locks were now shoulder length and black. Every day she would plaster on different faces, in a few dozen ways. She even went as far as to snap a tedious selfie each time, as to compare her pictures later on. When she's good and ready to follow through on her plans she'd pick a style.

Today, the growing disappointment in her lack of courage had drilled a hole completely through Autumn's core. A hollowed out tunnel had replaced the exact spot where her stubborn strength and a nagging perseverance used to be. It's time to fill that tunnel back up with what should've never left it in the first place.

After pacing back and forth from her bedroom to the kitchen's archway, Autumn had had enough. Speedy feet jogged to the table, this was it. With a firm plop, and a stiff back Autumn forced herself to sit. A thin wooden chair now supported her anxious weight, and an equally flimsy table clanked and vibrated in reaction to her bouncing knee.

The fingernail of her right pointer scratched and picked at the corner of the tape, not quite enough to pull it up, but just enough to disturb its neatness. Hesitant, the back and forth motion of her nail moved no further than a centimeter. Viciously, she scratched that finger until a matted little tape ball rolled underneath it and tore away from the rest of its adhesive line. Autumn exhaled.

"I'm gunna' need a drink."

Clank, clatter. The sound of moving glass echoed in her ears until she pulled a tall wine glass from behind the rest of the cups in her organized little sage painted cupboards. A long thin base was pinched tightly between Autumn's palms, and she rolled the glass back and forth between them. After contemplating between red and white for much longer than she normally would've, Autumn made her decision.

"Now I'm gunna' need company." She mumbled to herself.

Autumn stormed out without a second thought. The voice of reason that until now had pecked at the back of her brain like a hungry chicken would a pile of seeds, was ignored. Autumn was on a mission, she was going to drink, unload every single thought of guilt and intentions in regards to Maylee, and then get started. First thing tomorrow she was going to find Craig's house and make a plan. No more time could be wasted. For now she needed a victim of her own, someone to listen to her cry and rant. Jeremy was the only person she knew in this damn city, so he got to be the lucky guy. No turning back.

Autumn made a dash down the concrete steps, as quickly as her shoeless feet could carry her. As soon as her body reached his door she lifted her arm with a fist balled tight, but stopped before the flesh of it could actually touch metal. Her nervous hesitation finally took over. *What the hell was she doing?* She hadn't spoken with him since the day she bought her car. She didn't know if he was mad at her over the entire episode or not.

A heavy head shook on top of her neck. Although she couldn't bring herself to knock on the door, she couldn't leave either. She needed someone to talk to, and didn't have anywhere else to turn. Again she held up a fist ready to knock, and again stopped herself.

"Shit," she whispered with a lonely tear building in her eye.

The weight of Autumn's forehead pulled the rest of her face forward, causing her entire head to dangle loosely at the neck in defeat. Then she allowed her restless fingers to drum the crown of her head a few times before turning back to deal with things on her own.

Who did she think she was anyway? Why would Jeremy want anything to do with a friend like her? They didn't even know each other, yet he had already helped her move, found her a discounted car, and let her drive him around life threatening neighborhoods. And now here she stood at his doorstep, ready to demand more of his time, and for what? *Her own selfishness?* Nah, she couldn't knock, it was time to leave.

Two slow steps were made before the creaking sound of his opening door stopped her. Autumn froze in place, refusing to turn and look at him. She was partly afraid that he'd see the guilt plastered all over her face, and partly at a loss for words.

"Well, well, if it isn't Autumn Brown."

Autumn was relieved to hear the smile behind his words, though speculative that it may be caused by sarcasm rather than genuinity. Slowly, reluctantly, and with a bottle of wine in hand, she turned to face him. With an upturn of only one side of her smile, she held up the bottle and tilted her head to the side in question.

"You busy?" she asked cautiously.

"You stood up my mom." It was a flat faced response.

"Shit."

Autumn had completely forgotten about the promise she made to meet up with the woman who created her only friend. Now she felt lower, if that was humanly possible. Scum, Autumn felt nothing more than scum. *How could she have forgotten all about Bingo?*

Her hesitant, apologetic eyes met his, and she had no idea what to say. To Autumn's surprise, the flat expression on Jeremy's face crinkled up in a failed attempt to stop a grin. Then he shook his head, chuckled under his breath, and turned the lock on his door before closing it tightly behind him.

"I must say, Miss Brown, I was wondering how long you were going to avoid me. And lucky for you I have no plans tonight."

"I'm sorry about your mom." She mumbled, just before hooking an arm through his offered elbow.

"No worries, she actually bet me dinner that you wouldn't show," he teased. "So it turned out better for her in the long run. I treated her to Red Lobster last night."

"Nice. I guess I owe you for that now too then, huh?"

"You bet your ass you do." He grinned.

"Seems my debt is stacked."

With interlocked arms they rounded the corner, climbed the flight of stairs and retreated into Autumn's apartment.

Once inside, Jeremy leaned casually back into a chair that hardly supported his weight. The legs teetered and bowed beneath him, and the back creaked at the seams with each movement. It was ready to snap at any minute. The quiet crunching noise made Autumn cringe every time it sounded. She flinched in anticipation, just waiting for her guest to topple to the floor in a pile of broken chair fragments.

"So this is it, huh?" Jeremy asked. "The box."

It sat between them on the table, taking up what little surface space that her poor excuse of a dining table had to offer. The box was still untouched aside from the teased corner of its sealed top.

"Yep that's it. There isn't very much stuff in it, but it's the meaning of it. I came all this way, and I just can't bring myself to get started. I haven't even found Craig's place yet."

Autumn brushed a tear from beneath her eye before sniffing the loose snot back up into her nasal cavity. She had told him everything and it was surprisingly therapeutic. More so than she could have ever imagined. The weight on her shoulders lightened some as she shared the burden of it with someone else.

It must have been the way he listened that enabled her to unload so fully. He was quiet, nonjudgmental, and although he was clearly concerned he refrained from jumping in to offer obvious and unnecessary advice. Even her friends back home couldn't draw so much honesty out of her.

Every time she'd tried to open up, one of them would offer some stupid remark like "hang in there" or "I know it's gotta be tough" or even "I know how you feel" now that one really pissed her off. They didn't know how she felt, no one did, and to insinuate something so shallow, careless, and naive just flat out angered Autumn.

Now the deed was done; every detail of Maylee's life and of her disappearance was spoken. Autumn even told Jeremy about Chance and how cold he'd been, yet how concerned he seemed when she left. The details of her daily run on the beach, the disgusting facts about Candace, and the abandonment she felt for leaving their mother was explained. Once the air was cleared she felt closer to Jeremy than she had anyone since Keith died.

Jeremy poured another helping of wine into her glass whenever she needed it. The questions he asked were deep and real, not phony and assumptive. There was no visible pity in his eyes for Autumn, only for Maylee, which was exactly as it should be. Jeremy was the exact person that Autumn needed and she thanked him repeatedly just for being there. So much so, that he got irritated and threatened to leave if she kept up the nonsense.

Autumn felt twenty pounds lighter, like she may actually be able to take the next step without a heart attack along the way. She moved to the counter to open a second bottle of wine. The effects of the first bottle was settling into her fingertips, making the task of popping a cork much more complicated than it needed to be. Just as a *pop* of the cork sounded so did a *rrriiipppp*. Autumn's heart sank to her toes. Very slowly and with eyes wide she turned around to look at him. Words stuck in her throat, she was rendered speechless. He'd done it, the box was opened.

"First of all," he proclaimed, "don't raise your eyebrows at me. Second, you brought me up here for a reason, and it wasn't just to talk, right?"

"Yeah." She whispered, after clearing the surprised knot from her throat.

"Okay then, let's do this." He encouraged. "You said so yourself, right? Stop pissing around."

"I. I. I need another drink."

Autumn again turned her back to him and slowly filled her glass. Rustling paper crackled behind her, and she listened to him wrestle with the gigantic map.

"Wow, this really is big."

"Yeah." She mumbled and turned back to face him.

"I personally don't think this map is worth a damn, the way cops do things in movies is overrated. But, I do however think it'll give you the motivation you need. What better way to say 'get off your ass', than by a having an entire city plastered to your wall, right? I guess we could come up with a way to organize and use the pins for some kind of color pop, but, other than that it's useless"

"Color pop?"

"Yeah, like decor." He playfully teased, trying to chip away at her growing anxiety.

"We?"

"Yes we." Jeremy's light-hearted smile faded into a grim line. "You pulled me into this whole thing, and now I feel involved. I can't very well let you do it all by yourself now can I?"

"I guess not." Autumn agreed.

"Alright then, let's hang the damn thing and make a plan. Don't make me do this alone Autumn Brown, because I will."

It took thirty minutes and a quarter roll of duct tape to secure the ginormous map to the wall in their drunken stupor. It covered half of the kitchen, and one whole edge of it had to be bunched up and tucked behind itself in order to fit. Autumn and Jeremy stood back as far as the room would allow to admire their handywork. They both had to lean slightly against the counter to ease the unsteady motion caused by two bottles of vintage wine. It contained a very impressive alcohol content.

Autumn had been saving her wine for special occasions. They were given to her as a wedding gift, to be opened at milestone anniversaries. When Keith passed away, Autumn reset her intended use for them. After that devastating life change, they were to be opened on the biggest events of Maylee's life instead. The first one was reserved for when she finished college, next when she landed her dream job, and the last for her retirement – given Autumn lived long enough to see that day. Life then shit on the second set of plans for the wine, just as it had the first.

After tonight there'd be one bottle left in her stash and it's reserved for when Maylee was found, dead or alive. Autumn poured them each one last glass. She dumped every last drop out of the bottle, without going into detail on the back story of their luscious treat. As far as Jeremy was concerned it was just some "damn good wine." She had told him enough about her hardships as it was.

The rest of the night was a blur. They moved onto beer and together they allowed themselves to be washed away with drunken idiocy. Waking the next morning provided nothing but a headache and a new sense of urgency.

Autumn rolled to her side and reached behind herself to rub the kink from her lower back. It only took a second to realize that she was on the floor. Cuddled up to her was a very loudly snoring Jeremy. She leapt to her feet, but only to be slammed with a wave of lightheadedness and nausea. Too fast, she stood way too fast. With a firm fist, she grabbed the side of her loveseat to steady herself. Once the dark flash over her vision had passed and the ground steadied under her feet, she stood up straight and thumbed the temples of her head.

"Jeremy." She poked at him with the tip of her foot. "Wake up!"

He sat up quickly with an awkward snort, and looked in every direction with panic and urgency. ""Wha. Wha. Wait… God, you scared the shit out me." He said, just before mirroring Autumns head rubbing actions. "We drank way too much last night. I'm really gonna hear it from the guys about missing the gym this morning." He mumbled.

"Yeah," she agreed, "More importantly, why were we snuggling, and why are you wearing my shirt?"

Jeremy looked down at the pink fighting breast cancer tee that was stretched thin over his chest, and struggling to stay sewn at his armpits. He was just as shocked this morning about being able to squeeze into it as he had been the night before. Autumn clearly didn't remember insisting on him wearing it after she spilled beer all over him.

He could tell by the way she was biting her bottom lip that she had no idea how innocent his stay had been, nor about the hysterical emotional outburst she displayed over not wanting to sleep alone. He thought briefly about the rambling conversation she had with herself over where they'd pass out. One side of her conversation revolved around not wanting him in her bed, but the other side insisted on a snuggle so that she was sure he wouldn't take off. Autumn's argument with self, ended in a compromise for the living room floor.

Everything about Autumn reminded Jeremy of his late older sister, Amy. Their similarities in looks was only the tip of the iceberg. They also shared the same neurotic tendencies of rambling, and fiddling with their hair and nails when they got nervous. It was strange the way Autumn even had the same click of her tongue as Amy had when she enunciated her T's and F's.

He missed Amy and was tempted so many times the night before to tell Autumn about her, but he held back. He couldn't break the news about what happened to his sister, not yet. The guilt of keeping his secret had tripled overnight, but he was able to hold it in. Normally such an act would be simple, but because of their similarities it had proven to be much more difficult than anticipated. He actually liked Autumn, in a weird sibling kind of way.

It was no coincidence that Jeremy was the Apartment Manager at this very building. There was a reason for the previous guy's retirement. That man was very conveniently made an employment offer he couldn't refuse. The purpose of Jeremy's Apartment Manager title had absolutely nothing to do with a need for a job, and everything to do with Autumn.

Jeremy had been waiting for a break in Amy's murder for some time now, and the call he'd gotten from a fellow undercover nine days before was exactly that break. Jeremy recalled the message left on his voicemail as he stared up at the innocent and very much hungover Autumn. The low hum of Lloyd's voice, the leading detective on their team pulled into Jeremy's memory.

"Detective, we might've finally got the fuckin' clue we've been looking for. Call me as soon as you get this message, I got some interesting news from a Detective in California. I think you're going to want to talk to him."

Autumn stood over Jeremy tapping her foot nervously, engulfed by anticipation. He debated briefly at leading her to believe they fooled around, just to see the look on her face, but he quickly talked himself out of it. In all honesty, he was glad that she finally decided to clue him in about Maylee. After breaking the picture didn't work, and even the angry act while test driving her car, he was starting to wonder if she'd ever crack.

Giving her space for a week was a good move. Jeremy felt awful about leading her to believe he was someone other than a detective, but he would do whatever he needed to for Amy. Delivering justice to the men who tortured his sister, and left her dead in a gutter, was his number one priority. The similarities between her and Autumn only added to his drive.

"It's not what you think." He finally chuckled, after opting for the truth about their sleepover. "You spilled beer on me and then insisted that I stay. We only slept, I promise."

A giant breath of relief spewed from Autumn, it swept through the room like a floating ghost. "Well that *is* the biggest shirt I own," she smirked. "Sorry."

"Don't even worry about it." He soothed. Even her sulky look of apology mirrored his sister's, identically. "Besides, we have bigger things to worry about. I'm going home to shower and eat. I want you ready to go and at my door in an hour, sound fair?"

"An hour, why?" Autumn questioned. "What are you talking about?"

"We made plans, remember?"

"I don't remember forcing you to wear my clothes or even spooning you on the floor. What makes you think I remember making plans?"

"We're going to find that Craig guy's house this morning, and check out the neighborhood. Remember? You said that you need to start running again, so that's the plan. That is where you're going to run every morning. Today you prepare, and tomorrow you run."

As the very distinct plan was brought back up, she remembered. Their entire drunken night came fighting its way through her memory fog, fists swinging. They had made plans to find the place, and she did agree to set a daily jogging routine through Craig's neighborhood. Tears filled her bottom eyelids, and she wondered if she could find the courage to follow through. Jeremy scrambled to a stand and closed the short distance between them. His warm hands gripped her shoulders tightly, reassuringly.

"Don't say a word." He told her. "Don't overthink or let your fear take over you, just do what you need to. Don't dwell on your hangover either, it'll pass by the afternoon. Have some coffee and take a shower. Every time you walk into your kitchen let that hideous map remind you that you're a strong woman and that you're here for Maylee."

Autumn absorbed his advice like a sponge and wondered how she was so lucky as to stumble into such an outstanding friendship. She was completely clueless on his ulterior motives. The burden of dishonesty was now on Jeremy's shoulders, and it would remain there for as long as he could carry it. Their friendship was real by the heart's standards, but founded on a lie. Jeremy could only pray that Autumn would forgive him when his secrecy was inevitably brought to the surface.

The warmth of Jeremy's lips left a quick peck on her forehead, and then he locked serious burning eyes onto hers. No words were spoken, she only nodded and made her best attempt to swallow the growing lump in her throat.

* * *

The slow rolling tires of Autumn's car screeched to a halt at a stop sign. Two blocks to her right, and hardly visible was a narrow, broken down, two-story brick house. Half of the windows were busted or cracked, spray paint decorated one whole side, and the other displayed a large portion of black charred fire remnants. They'd circled the block twice, as well as each surrounding block for at least a five mile radius. Familiarizing herself with the surroundings wasn't exactly an easy thing to do while making a very clear effort to keep her eyes straight ahead.

Freshly blackened hair was cut over a foot from its usual length, and now it hung just above Autumn's shoulders framing her face. A large pair of sunglasses shaded her overly painted eyes. Autumn was yet to spot Craig among the busy crowds of back street Denver folk. The roads were full of other slow rolling cars much like hers, and the houses were crammed next to each other tightly. Craig's faltered brick home fit right in with the rest. They triple checked the address, just to be sure, and it was definitely his.

Autumn had counted six young kids kicking a soccer ball around a dirt yard that was no larger than her bedroom. Three houses down from the playing kids was a fenced in space, the exact same size, containing three men sitting on lawn chairs passing a bottle of whiskey back and forth, tipping it back casually. It wasn't even noon. One of those nonchalant daytime whiskey drinkers had a pistol on his lap, and another was smoking a cigar. At least it looked like a cigar. Autumn could only imagine what kind of chemically induced high was actually hidden inside its skinny brown disguise.

The one thing she hadn't seen much of, was women. It was odd, and Autumn wondered where were the mothers to the children playing ball, or the teens joining gangs, or even if there were wives to those daytime drinkers. The image of Candace pacing around Autumn's condo and peeking out the windows nervously, afraid to pick up Maylee for fear of only God knows what, struck a very loud cord. The thought settled deep within Autumn, causing a misshapen piece to Candace's puzzle to somehow fit in place.

Jeremy sat in the passenger seat, leaned back, with a hood over his head, and with ridged shoulders. It was the exact same demeanor he had the first time they drove through a similar neighborhood. Autumn wondered what he was hiding from, or if he was just as afraid to be there as herself. The latter made more sense but she couldn't help but feel like he was in fact hiding.

"Keep going for a few more blocks down, I saw a taco joint coming in." Jeremy said quietly, as if someone outside of the car could hear.

Autumn followed instructions and parked in a small slanted spot behind a grungy purple brick painted taco place. She finally exhaled a lungful of air that she'd been holding for long enough to make her head light. Everything about this place rocked her very core with terror. The one and only positive thought she had, was that ethnicity was on her side.

She had seen every single race, color, shape and size. There were literally no minorities in Craig's shady neighborhood, so her milky skin wouldn't stand out. All that she'd need to do is wear old baggy running clothes, preferably gray or black, and she could most likely go unnoticed. Especially if she ran early enough in the day that most of the people would be sleeping.

"Are you okay?" Jeremy asked cautiously. "You're looking very pale."

"I'm always pale." She breathed, staring straight ahead at the cracked fast food building before them.

"I mean… Pale-er."

"Yeah well…" Autumn didn't know what to say. She was very much *not* okay.

"Try to relax. This is the perfect place."

"I don't eat fast food unless I have to."

Autumn was still hungover, and her anxious emotions were causing the acid in her stomach to take the form of a rope and braid itself into her bowels. Fast food was the last thing she needed.

"I don't mean to eat." Jeremy said. "I mean to park your car everyday while you run. No one will notice it, and in a couple of weeks we can find somewhere new to park. Get to know the neighborhood, and be comfortable in it. Maybe you can find an abandoned house or ally to park in next. The people who see you need to think you live here."

"Remind me why they need to think I live here?"

Autumn was straining to focus. His words made sense, but were twisting together and breaking through her eardrums in fragments. There was a slight recollection about this very conversation the night before, but it was distorted. The piercing of Jeremy's glare was cutting through the skin on her face.

"Look at me, Autumn. Focus." He demanded.

Finally, she turned her head and meet his gaze. His stare was intense, forcing her attention. *Why did he care so much anyway,* she wondered? As far as Autumn knew, Jeremy was nothing more than a new friend who had only known about Maylee for a day. Yet here he was, making her concentrate, and dragging her strength to the surface tooth and nail. The intense lock of his eyes told Autumn that he wasn't going to let her give up. There was no room for that.

"Are you in there?" He asked.

"Sorry, I'm just struggling to concentrate. I'm scared out of my damn mind." She finally managed to admit out loud. It was the most she'd spoken since they reached this end of town.

"I get it." He said. "Let's get out of here so you can clear your head, sorry I'm being so pushy."

The delicate tone of Jeremy's apology didn't quite meet the growing frustration in his eyes, but Autumn's mind was too distracted to really give it much thought. The drive back to their building was quiet. You'd need a chainsaw to cut through the tension of the air. Autumn clearly needed Jeremy's coaching, but listening to it while seeing Craig's house for the first time was difficult.

The entire drive was made as if Autumn was on autopilot. The car glided perfectly between the designated road lines, but her mind was elsewhere. Everything about Maylee stuck like glue in Autumns thoughts. A haunting image of her beautiful face locked up in a dingy basement of that broken-down brick house floated around Autumn's head. She had driven past it like some scared little baby when Maylee could have easily been in there, three years aged and rancidly abused. *Was it possible? Did Autumn just witness the very place her niece has been kept?* The question caused that sickening braid of her bowels to tighten.

Autumn wanted to call the police and force them to kick down Craig's door, but she knew from experience that it wasn't possible. If anything, the notion would land her in jail, or worse, a loony bin. Nothing had ever been simple for Autumn, and this was no different. It would take time and work to get close without detection, but it had to be done.

Imagining Maylee in that disgusting place only fueled Autumn's ambition, as well as fear. Like a pulsing electricity, every beat of her heart held an unavoidable shock. She could hear the consistent pump of blood through the veins in her ears. *Swoosh Swoosh Swoosh.* Each pump circulated a different feeling within her. Pain, terror, anticipation, hate, love, loneliness, abandonment, determination, they all pushed and mixed together. *Swoosh, Swoosh, Swoosh.*

Autumn parked her car and reached for the handle, still on auto-pilot. Before she could actually open the door Jeremy wrapped his fingers around her arm, stopping her from the exit. She instantly snapped her head over to shoot him a death glare, but stopped herself from an outburst as soon as their eyes met. For the first time in their short but strangely close acquaintance, he looked vulnerable. Concern pulled at Jeremy's tightened lips, and his brows melted to a sad tilt.

"I'm sorry for not being more understanding." He mumbled. "I can get a little pushy, and I'm really just trying to help."

There was something else behind those eyes. Autumn strained, trying to see past the color of them, into his thoughts. Hoping that if she looked close enough she might be able to read where the sadness was coming from. It didn't work though, all she could detect was that there was definitely something lurking in the watery tint of them. For the first time since the very first knock on his door, Autumn looked past herself, and even Maylee. She felt bad for Jeremy, but had no clue why. She wanted to figure out the sudden flip of his demeanor. Figuring him out would be a welcomed distraction from the growing intensity of her weighted self.

"It's fine." She loosened her shoulders, and turned in her seat to face him head on. "Look, why don't we take a break and then later tonight we can order take out. I owe you dinner anyway, right?"

The skin of Jeremy's pinched face smoothed, but his eyes remained troubled. He flashed Autumn a devious smile, but it didn't touch his eyes. It did however, cause his upper cheek dimple to form just before he nodded in agreement. It wasn't much of a gesture, and it didn't seem to ease his sadness any, but Autumn decided to take it. It'd be enough for now.

Hesitant feet carried Autumn to her apartment. The homesick swirl in her guts danced, bending and twisting to its own silent tune. She closed her eyes while she reached for the handle, imagining it to open to her condo. She took in a deep whiff of the air, willing it to smell of sea salt and citrus, just as her real home always had. Instead, her nostrils filled with a bland scent of stale bread accompanied by a hint of paint. It wasn't exactly a bad smell, but it didn't bring the comfort she was hoping for.

Autumn changed out of her jeans and into a comfortable pair of running pants before retreating to the spare bedroom where she had stashed a small elliptical bike. It's one that she'd picked up from a neighbor's yard sale in California a few months before the move – knowing that she wouldn't have the luxury of her beach to run on every day. Until the treacherous relocation, this bike had never been used. She was very grateful to have it now that she was cooped up in this apartment with nothing to keep her company aside from her thoughts, and of course the repetitive meal of a Caesar Salad from a small dinner down the road.

Autumn secured her earbuds in place and then selected a soothing mix of 90's soul music that she really only listened to on rare occasions when her mood was utterly unpinpointable. No sooner than a fairly low and drawn out woman's voice hummed in her ears, Autumn went to pedaling. The queasy feeling from the drunken extravaganza of the night before resurfaced, but it only pushed Autumn to pedal faster and harder. She was determined to work the lingering alcohol out of her veins with fresh oxygen, and to wash it from her pores with sweat.

The bike had been a God send, all the past week. Autumn was able to tire her body and sleep some. The lack of her beachside running routine really put a damper on Autumn's physical state. This small elliptical bike wasn't nearly as physically satisfying, but at least it was something. Autumn closed her eyes, focused her breath, and let the therapy of her workout take over every part of her body.

After one full hour of maxing out, Autumn allowed her rubber legs to slow. A cold drink of water chilled her dry throat. She even poured a few drops on her chest to let the coolness of it run across her heated skin. The refreshing chill of the icy liquid felt heavenly as it rolled down the length of her chest before absorbing into the threads of her already dampened shirt. Autumn straightened her sweaty back and reached her fingertips to the ceiling, all the while maintaining a very slow steady pedal. Cooling down from a workout and the final stretch was arguably the best part.

Squishy new carpet then cradled her tired feet as she slipped off her burning shoes and continued to stretch on the floor. The length of Autumn's legs tightened and cramped as she reached for the floor, bending only at the middle. Thinking about Maylee while pushing her body's limits always allowed Autumn to push the stress of it aside and focus on the facts. Today was no different. Autumn knew exactly what she needed to do. It didn't matter how much she'd drank the night before, somehow the plan she set in place with Jeremy made sense. She needed to run.

Autumn knew that on foot she'd be vulnerable, but she could also make herself blend in. The streets were very active, there were people everywhere. Enough so, that she wouldn't technically be alone, and although the people she'd be jogging past were frightening and mostly criminals to one extent or another, they were also busy. Aside from the few elderly people that she'd seen scowling into the streets from the over-used recliners on their porches, everyone else that was out and about seemed to be occupied.

With fingers interlocked behind her back, Autumn leaned forward and pulled her arms toward the ceiling. The stretch was felt from her elbows, to her shoulders, and on down the outer edges of her back. While bending at the waist as far as her pained muscles would allow, Autumn closed her eyes and imagined herself jogging among the people she had seen in Craig's neighborhood less than two hours before.

The image seemed to work, if her makeup was thick, and her clothing was old and baggy enough, she could jog through without seeming out of place. The last thing she needed was to be hit on or whistled at drawing attention, so she needed to look plain. Men's basketball shorts and a tattered Tee would be fitting.

Autumn moved to one last rejuvenating body position as she thought of the last necessity of her appearance – her hair. The beautician she found did an amazing job. Autumn was shocked at the way a mere change of hairstyle had completely altered her appearance. Every time she looked in a mirror, there was a complete stranger staring back at her. The once waterfall flowing dirty-blonde hair that bounded gracefully to the small of her back was now short and black. The cut was drastic but necessary, and although the stylist tried talking her into going as short as her chin, Autumn refused.

It needed to be long enough to pull back out of her face or she'd go insane. That's not to mention the attachment she had to it. Autumn's hair had never been so short, it was the type of hair that many women envied – long thick and healthy her entire life.

The final stretches left Autumn feeling rejuvenated, mentally relaxed and ready to face her quest. Autumn was finally ready to find Maylee. Her homework was complete, and it was time to replace anxiety with courage and confidence.

Chapter Six

It'd been exactly one hour and thirty three minutes since his call. She was in the middle of dinner with Jeremy, and blew it off. She took one glance at the name ringing in, choked on the half eaten bite of cranberry chicken take-out that was rolling around in her mouth, and then quickly hit ignore. Despite her efforts to play it off, Autumn's heart had practically stopped in her chest, and then came back to life with a jolt.

Even Autumn didn't understand why she'd ignored the call. If anything, she should've jumped at the opportunity to talk to Chance, but for some reason the racing of her blood wouldn't allow her to pick it up. Instead, she lied to Jeremy and said it was just an old friend that she'd call back later.

After hitting the ignore button on her hometown detective's phone call, Autumn did everything she could to hurry Jeremy out the door. The call was random, and she was far from prepared. Seeing his name peak out at her from the screen on her phone, was unexpected, and something about it scared the living shit out of her. The remainder of Autumn's chicken dish was practically inhaled. *What if he had news about Maylee?* It was all Autumn could do not to throw Jeremy out the door, and then lock herself in her room to have a complete and utter panic attack before calling him back.

Realization of having a near heart attack at merely the sight of Chance's name, caused Autumn not to want Jeremy anywhere near when she returned the call. Jeremy wasn't exactly lacking in the observation department, and the last thing Autumn wanted was for him to pick up on her shaking fingers and nervous voice. No, Jeremy didn't need to be there. Not only that, but Autumn had to prepare herself for whatever news Chance had to deliver.

Autumn said goodbye to Jeremy, thanked him for all his help, and then practically shoved him toward the door. She apologized to him for the headache that she was lying about having, and then eagerly opened the door for his exit. He needed to leave before thinking of anything else to go over about her running plans in the morning.

"Are you sure you're okay?" he asked through a confused clench of his teeth.

"Yeah, sorry." Autumn lied, and rubbed at her temples. "I don't know why this headache hit me so fast. I'm sure it's just the stress of today after how much we drank last night. I'll feel better after a night's sleep."

Jeremy reluctantly moved through the door, and turned to lock his eyes onto hers one last time before she shut him out.

"So tomorrow then? You're going to start running at 9 o'clock?"

"Yes."

"I'm going to keep my phone in my hand all morning. If anything happens, you call me. Okay?"

His tone was as serious as the downward pull of the skin on his face. Autumn let out a lung-full of nervous air.

"Yes, I'm going to do it and I promise I'll call if I need anything."

Hearing her own words out loud wasn't as reassuring as she'd hoped it'd be. But, it wasn't a lie either. As soon as morning rolled around Autumn was going to go for a long dangerous jog right through the heart of Craig's neighborhood. She had to do it, there was no more putting it off due to her own selfish fears. Buck up, and brave up, that is what she had to do. Unless Chance had some promising news that could deter her plans, tomorrow would go exactly as plotted.

"You sure you can do it?" Jeremy asked. The concern in his voice was thick and tainted with an airy scratch.

Autumn stared at the scarlet paint on her toes for a minute before looking back up at Jeremy, "I have to." She confirmed, and straightened her back.

"Okay." He said with a small nod.

Autumn said goodbye and then hurried the door shut before he had a chance to say it back. Drawn out breaths were taken, slowly in and even slower back out. Autumn closed her eyes tightly, still standing at the door, her feet refused to carry her back to the loveseat where her phone sat waiting for her.

Finally Autumn swallowed the growing lump in her throat before it completely consumed her ability to suck in air. Making this phone call was a must.

What if Chance really did have information for Autumn? What if Maylee was finally found, alive... Or worse, dead? Finding out now, three years and a giant relocation later, wasn't going to be easy. *But would it ever?*

With each question raised, another followed. The only way she could stop this mental madness was to make the damn call - and so she did. Autumn finally made herself sit back down. Her fingers wound tightly around her cell phone, and after a few more moments of agonizing anticipation she pressed a finger on his name. The plastic face of her phone touched firmly against her cheek as she waited for him to pick up.

"Detective Chance speaking."

His voice was warm, confident, deep. It caused bumps to raise on Autumn's arms, and the weight of a rock to sink in her chest.

"Yes," she said, "This is Autumn Brown. I missed your call."

Autumn didn't understand why they had to be so completely formal. It felt like she was talking to the automated system of some multi-billion dollar company rather than an actual person. Of course Chance knew it was her, *how could he not?* And yet, he picked up with an introduction like some professional douchebag, forcing her to do the same. She listened to the sound of his breath and pictured his perfectly shaped lips as he prepared to talk. Her heart leapt into her chest and a strange heat formed at the base of her abdomen.

"Yes, Miss Brown. I'm glad you returned my call."

Autumn held her breath, waiting. She could hear the hesitation in his tone, and assumed he'd spill the beans on whatever information he was withholding about Maylee. Nothing. *He was honestly waiting for her?*

"Soooo." Autumn hesitated, drawing out her unasked questions. "Is there something I can help you with Chance?"

She felt like passing out.

"Um, yeah. I guess I was just checking up on you."

"Checking up?"

Anticipation and worry quickly flipped into something else. *Insult? Irritation? Flattery?* Nope, it was confusion. Utter confusion consumed Autumn like a plague. Some nerve this man had. *How dare he scare her like that?* To call out of the blue, and not even leave a message. The least he could've done is sent her a text, and let her know that nothing had changed with Maylee's case.

If she'd known he was calling her to chat like some irritating professional of ignorance, then she wouldn't have kicked out her guest so quickly. Autumn couldn't recall a time when she'd ever been so confused. Until he answered her question with such sweet honesty, that all of her doubt melted into some foreign sensation of gratitude.

"Sorry, if my call startled you." Chance confessed. "I guess I should've left a message." He paused in hesitation, "I just haven't been able to stop thinking about what you're doing. I'd rest better at night if I knew you were okay."

Autumn let out a sigh. *Who was this man?* She wondered, shocked that he sounded genuinely concerned about her wellbeing.

"If I didn't know any better Detective, I'd think you actually cared."

"Of course I care." His voice softened. "So, are you all settled into your new place? Are you comfortable?"

Chance was reeling with questions that he wanted to ask her. He'd been debating on the call for days. Of course, he'd been keeping tabs on her through Jeremy daily. He needed more. Chance pictured her face, and the exact expression of faltered confidence she'd shown in his office the day she left California. Every single day since then he'd recalled that look.

He knew that nothing had happened to her physically, because even though he was in a completely different time zone, he had eyes on her always. What he didn't know, was her emotional state. Normally he wouldn't care. Chance hadn't cared about the emotions of a woman in years. Ten to be exact. It had been ten years, two months and five days since his wife ran off with another man.

Chance shunned even the thought of a relationship since the very day she left him behind with nothing but a heartless note. It stated that she'd be long gone by the time he read it – with a man named Dion. *What the hell kind of a name was Dion anyway? Was he black, Italian, white, was he a midget? Who the hell knows,* Chance thought.

What was worse than caring for Autumn's wellbeing, was the fact that Chance felt guilty about lying to her. He'd been lying to her for years. He hadn't tucked Maylee's case away, as he led Autumn to believe all those years ago. Maylee had been a part of something much bigger than a single disappearance.

She was linked to several others across the western states. In fact, there had even been sightings of her. There wasn't any proof that it was actually Maylee, but several women had identified her picture. Most of the missing girls that Chance was investigating were linked to Craig himself, but until Autumn turned up in his office with a key piece to the missing puzzle, they hadn't been able to find Craig.

What's worse, was that even Craig was only a pawn. He was expected to be nothing but the go-to, the taker. Craig was one of four men expected to be the muscle of a group. The ring leaders were yet to be identified.

Chance needed Autumn, and so did Maylee. In order to cut the head off of this beast of missing girls, they needed to do more than arrest the muscle. Men like Craig were easily replaced. In order for Maylee and the fifty plus others expected to have fallen victim in this underground human trafficking ring to be found, it would take more than discretion and upholding the law. Not only did they need to be located, but the top parties needed to be proven guilty in a court of law. The secrecy was vital.

Confidentiality was key and if Autumn only knew the half of it, she'd never be putting herself in danger the way she was. Chance was well aware that he himself, as well as the entire undercover team on the case in Denver, was using Autumn as a pawn. Sometimes it took nasty tactics to catch nasty criminals, and if Autumn did end up in the wrong hands, then she couldn't possibly be forced to give away investigation details... not if she didn't know they existed.

"All of my things are unpacked, but I'd hardly say I'm settled." Autumn confessed.

Her voice on the other end of the phone pulled Chance back to reality. Guilt nearly consumed him as he listened to her discomfort. The thoughts of Maylee, and Craig, and of course of his ex-wife had him temporarily in a different place. It was time to clear his mind and focus. Chance had no idea how this conversation was going to go. But he did know one thing, for the first time in ten years he actually cared about what a woman other than his daughter and work colleagues had to say.

Autumn's voice had melted into defeat, and Chance listened to every word. He pretended like it was the first time he had heard the details of Craig's neighborhood, and that he was yet to be spotted. Chance gave her advice and encouragement. Concern seeped through the cracks of his voice, and much to his surprise he found himself being reassured by Autumn.

"I can do this, Chance. I know I can." She told him.

He contemplated calling the whole thing off, and bringing in another undercover to make a presence in Craig's neighborhood every day. On one hand it was an excellent thought. It would keep Autumn at a safe distance. On the other hand, he knew that she wouldn't stay put. Letting Autumn follow through with her plans was risky, but it was the only way to insure that she wouldn't get in the way of the investigation by forcing herself in the middle of it in other ways. Now that she knew where Craig supposedly lived, there'd be no keeping this determined woman away from it.

Chance reminded himself of the way she came to his office every single day when Maylee went missing. She interrupted important meetings, caused distractions. She even came face to face with a couple of undercovers from Candace's neighborhood. If she'd given away their identity it could've caused them the entire case, or worse, their lives.

No, Autumn was better off left in the dark. At least this way, she'd be watched. They could protect her from a distance. Chance promised himself that he'd tell her the truth personally. He wouldn't let her hear of his lies from some random Denver dickhead. He'd even fly out and tell her in person when the time came, he owed her that much.

"Are you sure you can do this?" He asked again. "You're putting yourself in a very dangerous place Autumn, I don't think it's a good idea." he omitted more truths, despite himself.

"Yes. And please stop trying to talk me out of it." She begged. "I don't need your permission. Technically all I'm going to do is jog and explore my new city. I haven't broken any laws."

"I'm just worried about you."

Finally an honest statement, and it washed him over with a wave of humility and defeat.

Autumn could feel the concern in his words. It purred in her ear and then absorbed into her body through the branching of each vein. The longer their conversation lasted the more she yearned to be home. The vision of her condo danced in her head like a ballerina to the sound of his voice. With eyes tenderly shut, she imagined having this very conversation from the comfort of her real home, the one she left behind. The smooth hum of Chance's words left a familiar taste in her mouth, and it was delicious.

Sixty minutes after that initial irritating 'hello', Autumn and Chance were both completely beside themselves. Comfort and ease had consumed them, allowing the conversation to transform into more than just a routine checkup.

Autumn soon confided in him with details of her family, and even Keith. Things that she'd never opened up about before, were now spread all over the surface of her existence like butter. She held nothing back, and it was comforting. Chance was easy to talk to. A part of her wished they would've had this very conversation years earlier. There was absolutely no small talk. Every word spoken was real and had meaning.

To Chance's surprise, even he was able to pry his heart back open a crack. He talked about his wife, and his daughter Vanessa, which caused Autumn to mentally slap herself about the previous judgmental assumptions she had when she'd met Vanessa. Autumn soon became very familiar with the miniscule truths of Chance's personal life. But, it ended there. His personal life. Everything about the importance of the present was held back. Chance kept his secrets about Maylee and the other girls missing at Craig's hand.

They said their goodbyes. Chance exhaled a long guilty breath and then went back to the stack of paperwork piled up on his desk. The familiarity of Autumn's voice pounded in the back of his mind like a hammer on a nail. It became a background noise that wouldn't go away anytime soon.

Autumn sucked in a healthy fresh breath of relief and then retired to her bed. For the first time since Maylee went missing, she felt like she was exactly where she needed to be. Defending her plot to watch Craig's house gave her the very confidence that she needed. As soon as Autumn's eyes closed she drifted off to sleep.

After three years Autumn was finally ready to step up and do the job herself. The hours, days, and even weeks ahead no longer brought about fear, but purpose. Determination and courage was finally on her side. Who would've thought that the very man who had pushed Autumn away from Maylee's disappearance, was now the most supportive in her fresh approach on the search for her.

When morning rolled around, Autumn woke refreshed and fearless. She took on the task of her run an hour early, and proudly reported to Jeremy when she returned home.

Three Weeks Later

Autumn pulled her silky dark hair into a twisted bun on the crown of her head. Both shoes were double-knotted, and she checked the car door, again, to insure it was locked. Her nervous fingers patted her pockets and felt for the keys. The fact that she'd been running this exact same route for three weeks now, didn't make her any less nervous. Each and every day the frightened pain in her chest thumped and it forced anxiety from her toes to her fingertips.

The playlist marked 'my new favorite' on her phone was selected, just before she placed a tiny fitted speaker in one ear. She need the other ear to listen for anything out of the ordinary on the streets. This had been Autumn's exact routine every single day for three weeks. The only difference between every other run and now, was that the sun was starting to sink into the background of the city. It was nearly dark out, and up until this day she had never ran the streets so late at night.

Three weeks was long enough to chase her own tail in circles without actually sinking her teeth into anything with flavor. She still hadn't seen Craig, and time was ticking away. Shaking things up and taking new risks was necessary, the truth of it crawled beneath her skin and itched on the inside. Today's second run was a last-minute decision.

Autumn had had enough pacing around her apartment. Suffocation from the feeling of failure was chipping away at her newfound bravery, and it nearly let the paranoia and anxiety back out of her sealed up mental closet. The permanence of this suffocating feeling had created a whole new beast, and pushed her to make a change.

This was the very day for a change. Autumn was as comfortable as could be with her morning run, so it was time to put herself on a new playing field. A night run was a risk that until this day she'd avoided for obvious reasons, but it was time.

Skinny fingertips reached to the sky in a preparation stretch. After counting to ten Autumn bent at the waist and hugged her legs tightly to her chest. She continued with a few more very quick stretches in the empty parking lot before pushing her body to move in the irritatingly dry Denver heat. She started off in a slight jog down the street, leaving her plain car hidden in the parking lot of the taco joint approximately six blocks away from Craig's house.

The heat was almost unbearable and she was forming beads of sweat in her hairline before her feet could cover the length of a block. Autumn picked up her pace so that she could cover all the intended ground, and be back to her car before the darkness settled in completely. After all the things she'd already witnessed on her daily run, the last thing she wanted to do was push her luck too far on her very first night run.

Nearly each block she'd been jogging through now had unpleasant memories. She'd seen men beating their wives, girlfriends, and hookers. It was unfathomable how much could actually happen in three weeks' time. Understanding the depths of time and how unforgiving it can be, only reminded Autumn of the possibilities of Maylee's existence, if she were even still alive.

On this very street Autumn had seen children who were filthy and appeared to be starved, and whores getting in and out of vehicles on a regular basis. It was a miracle that no one had approached her yet, and she was well aware that her luck in the matter could very easily run out. With her head bowed slightly down, and her eyes glued to the sidewalk, Autumn had been able to avoid any real contact with anyone thus far. Aside from a few whistles and hollers, people have left her be.

Drugs seemed to be a regular part of these people's lives, and even in the mornings there had been a few times that the sound of gunshots rang through the air. It slammed her eardrums like a gong each time and sent chills across every inch of her skin. Naturally, Autumn expected tonight to be even worse. She was as prepared as she could possibly be, *as in not at all*, because who in their right mind could honestly prepare - physically or mentally, for that matter.

The first police cruiser of the night passed her after three blocks into the run. Autumn felt completely wretched for the children who had to grow up in this environment. She just couldn't quite fathom how a mother could sleep at night knowing that her own flesh and blood could overdose or be gunned down at any moment.

Autumn picked up her speed as she passed the block just before Craig's house. There were usually two caged pitbulls on this particular block. Some days they growled as she passed, and some days they were bloodied and quiet. Healing from the night before no doubt. Autumn assumed they were fighting dogs, and tonight the cages were missing. Not just empty, but missing all together. The homes were eerily quiet, which was rare. Speedy feet hurried Autumn past the haunting of the street's stillness.

With eyes wide open and alert, she kept her focus. She could only pray that the dogs hadn't been taken somewhere along her route to fight. There were quite a few other places with similar dogs that were held in similar cages, so avoiding those roads were next to impossible. There was no way to prepare for an encounter like that, and no way to avoid it either. Autumn steadied her breath and her stride. It was imperative that she stay alert and keep her wits.

As Autumn neared the address Candace had given her just over a month before, she slowed to a sluggish jog, as she had every other time she's passed it. Close attention was paid to the doors and windows of his home. In the yard next to his there were five men sitting around a table on the small lawn playing cards. It was the same men that she'd seen in the exact same place every few days. *Do they really play all day?* She wondered.

Every time they'd been there Autumn had taken as close a look as she could at them, without being noticed. Their faces were etched into her mind in excellent detail, all except for one. This particular man had only been there a hand full of other times, and he always kept his back to her. He never seemed to want to look her way. Even on the occasion that the men would heckle her or whistle as she ran past he'd never even glance in her direction.

Autumn always made it a point to run on the other side of the road when she approached this block. She never wanted to be within arm's reach, just in case one of these men decided to grab her as she ran by. Such an event wouldn't be surprising, it was best for her to stay cautious.

These mischievous card players weren't the only reason Autumn ran on the other side of the street. She also didn't want to end up running into Craig face to face. Only God knows what would happen to Autumn if Craig recognized her. Before Maylee went missing Autumn had only seen Craig in person once, but their encounter was memorable.

She'd fought with him on Maylee's behalf. The memory of Craig's grubby fingers all over Maylee when Autumn showed up to her rescue caused a shudder. He'd had her pinned against the door trying to force one hand up her shorts, while the other hand was firmly griped around her neck. Autumn flipped. It took every ounce of body weight she possessed to push him away. When Maylee slipped out of his clutches, he chuckled at the both of them and then casually lit a cigarette. He sauntered into the house with a careless flick of the wrist as Autumn yelled at him. He didn't give two shits about what she had to say.

If Craig didn't recognize Autumn from that incident, then he could easily do so from all of the news briefs and family photos that were plastered all over their local news when Maylee disappeared.

Every detail about tonight's jog seemed a little different than the mornings. The men playing cards weren't quite as loud as usual, and the street even appeared to be emptier. To Autumn this was particularly odd. She expected the neighborhood to be quite a bit livelier, assuming that scary places came to life at night. She couldn't have been more wrong. She'd mentally prepared herself for chaos, but not for this. Not for the creepy silence that seemed to be swallowing her whole. Being alone on these darkening streets wasn't something Autumn was ready for.

There wasn't a single child playing outside, and all of the regularly occupied porches were suddenly vacant. Another difference in tonight was that the man who usually had his back turned to the road while playing cards had moved from his regular spot. He was now sitting a little sideways with his head up. This was the first time she was going to get a glimpse of his face. This was also the first time that Autumn felt comfortable enough to carry a gun with her while jogging.

Jeremy, Aiden, and Lloyd had been teaching her to shoot and practicing with her practically every day. Lloyd was particularly insistent on the matter. Like some protective self-proclaimed boyfriend that she didn't want. Autumn was reluctant at first, insisting that guns were not for her. But, tonight she was grateful to be packing heat, and to have the skills to use it if needed.

Jeremy had taken her shopping two days before and helped her pick out a semi-automatic nine millimeter handgun with a holster that was very easily hidden around her waistline. As long as her shirt was loose, no one would be the wiser as to what she was hiding beneath it.

For the last two mornings Autumn had securely attached the holster around her middle, and then wandered around the apartment until she talked herself out of carrying it. Up until tonight the gun had been left behind, tucked away in its safe place under her bed. Perhaps having it in general is what gave Autumn the boost of confidence needed to test drive a night jog. No matter the reason, here she was - running on foot through a dicey neighborhood with a nervous thump in her chest, and a handgun strapped around her middle.

Just as Autumn approached the intersection at the start of his block, she made the split second decision to cross the street. This may be the only chance she had to get a closer look at the mystery man who up until tonight has kept his back to her. Getting a look at his face now while he's turned to her, may be an opportunity that never presents itself again. It was imperative that she not pass it up, so she took yet another risk. *This better pay off,* she thought.

Autumn set her focus straight ahead, and continued her pace. The steady sound of her running shoes padded the outer edge of the sidewalk and drummed through the otherwise quiet air around her. She reached into her pocket and turned off the music that was blaring into one ear. As Autumn closed the distance to the men at the card table, she allowed her eyes to glance up just long enough to perform a quick study on the man she'd yet to lay eyes on. The air caught in her lungs as the familiarity of him settled. Autumn had seen his face before, but couldn't seem to place where.

A surge of panic ran through her as he glanced up from his hand and they made very unmistakable eye contact. The familiar man's flat emotionless expression didn't change when they locked eyes. He didn't seem to pick up on the panic or recognition in her face. It wasn't until Autumn was a mere foot away, ready to stream past them at full speed ahead, that his features lifted in a smile. It was a drunken grin that matched the glassy burn of his eyes.

The smell of whiskey wafted the air. This man must have been hammered, as he no longer tried so hard to conceal his face from any and everyone who usually crowded the block. Perhaps it was a mix of the street's emptiness and the booze that prompted his sudden lack of discretion. As soon as the grin consumed his face Autumn realized who he was. That face was familiar because she'd recently seen it on the television.

Front and center on the evening news, she'd witnessed this very man standing in uniform shaking the hand of a government official. As an outstanding local police officer, he'd accepted a recognition of honor. *Why the hell was he here?* Not only was he mingling proudly with likely criminals, but right next to Craig's house nonetheless. Autumn could hardly breath as she passed, her eyes shot directly back down to the sidewalk just inches in front of her feet.

A fairly overweight man with clearly bad hygiene was sitting next to Mr. Honorable himself. He stood to his feet and faced Autumn as she sped by them. They were within inches of each other. He placed his hands on his hips, and he thrusted his crotch in her direction. Back and forth he humped the air, as he whistled in excitement. All of the men laughed at his gesture.

Autumn moved her feet at an excruciating pace until she passed them, and Craig's house. Speedy legs rounded the corner at a stop sign at the end of the block. It was just two houses down from the rambunctious crowd, but at least she was now hidden by some shrubs and out of sight of the men. She bent over, clutching her knees.

Autumn looked around and held back the threatening tears of fear and confusion. She grabbed the back of her head with both hands and pinched her face up tight. She wanted nothing more than to scream at the top of her lungs and go home to her condo in California, but she couldn't. Autumn needed to think, and fast. She'd had enough running around in circles getting nowhere. After shaking the nerves from her fingers, she managed a slow release of air through tight lips.

Autumn decided to use the anxious feeling in her favor. She was stuck in Denver on that very street at that very moment for a reason. Already being scared to the point of no return, she decided that she might as well make the most of it. Craig's house seemed to be just as quiet at night as it had been every morning leading up to this point. Since the only men that seemed to be out in this oddly quiet street happened to be busy playing cards, she concluded it might be her only chance to look into the windows of Craig's house undetected.

There was only one small home between her and Craig's house, and there were shrubs all the way around it. Autumn ducked down behind the greens and crept into the yard of Craig's neighbor. There was a light on and noises coming from inside. *I have to make this fast*, she thought. She moved as quietly and quickly as possible through the yard and past the shrubs to the other side. There was a tiny space between the unforgiving bushes and the cracked bricks of Craig's house. Autumn wedged herself there.

Her alert ears listened carefully, but she heard nothing close. There were weeds to her waist and little space to move around. The rowdy men still playing cards and drinking beer was a faint sound in the distance. She strained her ears as hard as she could, but was unable to make out what they were saying. With a stomach sucked in tightly, and breath held, Autumn inched her way around the side of Craig's house and to the junk filled yard behind it.

The first filthy window she snuck by was hard to see through. Nothing was visible except an abundance of garbage that covered an old battered couch and coffee table. Finally, she made it to the back door and ever so slowly she reached for its handle. Her eyes were wide and searched in every direction. She prayed that the house was empty. The metal was warm in her hand, a scorching reminder that she was in fact trespassing in a very dangerous place. Several deep breaths filled Autumns lungs as she mentally pep-talked herself into twisting her wrist to open the door.

The hinges creaked allowing the door to open, and for some inexplicable reason she pictured Chance. A clear image of his piercing eyes and the angry words of caution he'd be spitting in her direction right now, barged into her thoughts. Had he known what she was about to do, he'd likely have a heart attack.

They'd grown close over the last three weeks. That first call with a professional hello and very personal goodbye had been the beginning of something more – much more. Since then, every single day without fail he'd called. Which reminded Autumn that she hadn't silenced her phone. The last thing she needed was Chance or even Jeremy ringing in to check up on her, only to alert Mr. Cop-Of-The-Year. She most definitely didn't need a tattling ringtone.

Autumn reached into her pocket and quickly pressed the silence button. Then she gagged down her fears and stepped inside Craig's dark and deserted house. With each quite tip-toe she thought of Chance and his endless words of caution. A tear rolled down her cheek and she whispered to herself.

"God please help me make it out of this house alive."

Autumn pulled her pistol out of its holster, jacked a bullet into the chamber, and clicked off the safety. The movements came natural. All that practice Jeremy and his crew of overbearing misfits insisted on was paying off. The house smelt like old cat pee and body odor. It stuck to the inside of her nostrils and dried up there like super glue.

It was a scent that she'd become acquainted with years before. The very smell had been on Maylee's clothes several times when she was a baby, and although Autumn was aware of Candace's hygiene problem, there was just something about it that had rang different. This wasn't merely a smell of uncleanliness, there was something more to it.

The memories of this familiar scent broke Autumn's heart. At the time, Autumn asked her mother about the smell, and she only shook her head in disgust, refusing to give an explanation. It wasn't until Maylee was years older that Hannah Brown finally broke down and told Autumn that the smell could've only come from the smoke of hard-core drugs settling into everything it touches like a plague.

This scent was overwhelming in Craig's house, or at least she still assumed this was his house. She had yet to find reason to believe otherwise. The smell made Autumn sick to her stomach as she gently continued to move her hesitant feet.

The door she entered through placed her directly in the kitchen. It was dark but her eyes were starting to adjust and she could at least see shapes and shadows. She knew that if she were to flip on a light then the men outside would see it, so that was clearly not an option. The room was empty aside from a few spray paint cans on the dusty counter tops and some stacked up and broken dirty dishes.

Autumn squinted and strained to get a closer look at one of the plates. It was apart from the rest, setting on the edge of the counter, and it appeared to be somewhat clean. A half-eaten sandwich was placed perfectly in its center. There was no mold or discolor to be seen with such little light, so she assumed it to be fresh. Reluctantly, Autumn reached over.

A rock of a lump formed in her throat, and she struggled to swallow it down. With a clammy nervous hand she felt the bread to see if it was hard or squishy. Sure enough, just as she suspected, her finger sunk into the soft piece of bread. The lump came right back up and she gagged on it, struggling to keep herself from losing her dinner.

Autumn hadn't seen any movement coming from inside the house when she ran in the mornings, so whoever was permeating the air with this putrid stench, and eating sandwiches, must have been doing it later in the day. Her ribs fought hard to keep her racing heart in place. She debated on turning around and making an escape now while she still could, but she changed her hesitant mind.

If there was anyone there now then there would've been lights on, and there wasn't. This opportunity to get inside would likely never present itself again so she continued, racing heart and all. She snuck through a narrow doorway into the next room.

It led into a living space with one ripped couch, a busted coffee table, and a cracked fireplace. Dried up mud chunks were strewn across the cracked floorboards, and illegible writing was spray painted all over the walls. It was hard to make out details without a light, but a swastika stood out promptly amongst the rest of the vandalism. *Typical*, she thought. This was the room she'd seen from the window, therefore the only one she knew what to expect in. Everything beyond this point was a gut churning mystery.

A main door that led out the front of the house was barely hanging on its hinges. There were several locks securing it in place, and a rickety wooden staircase sat directly before the door. Beneath the tallest part of the stairwell there was a second set of stairs going down. Autumn decided to check the upstairs first and save the creepiest part of this small town house for last. She slowly walked up the creaking steps. Each one she took was louder than the next, so she placed her feet on the very edges against the wall to try and hit the most silent parts possible.

The second story was fairly open and seemingly empty. There were only two rooms and neither of them had a door. Autumn squinted her eyes as she still struggled to see. The shade of night was consuming Denver and darkening the inside of the house along with the out. There were few windows that weren't boarded up and the light they offered was slim.

Autumn still had to make it back to her car when she left here and the thought caused a chill to dash up her spine. Again, she forced her breath to steady and continued to move through the house. The first doorless room she entered was a disgusting bathroom. The smell was horrendous. It had a toilet and a shower, no sink. For the first time since Autumn broke into this house she was actually grateful for the lack of lighting. She could only imagine how much more disgusting this room would be if she could see it in full.

She quickly turned her attention to the next doorway. It led her into a far from ordinary bedroom. There was a mattress on the floor with something dark streaked all over it. There were also chains hanging from the ceiling with cuffs on the edges. Canes and whips leaned casually against the wall, along with a seemingly expensive camera on a tripod.

Autumn couldn't tell in the dark what the streaks were on the bed but she could only imagine it was blood. She shivered at the thought. Her mind wandered to Maylee and a haunting image of her being chained up above a disgusting mattress in a repulsive old crack house. Autumn involuntarily conjured up the picture of her niece being whipped and beaten. The disgusting false image caused a cold sensation to take over her bloodstream, and her head to grow light.

She could taste the bile as it rose in her stomach and stopped at the base of her throat. Being here now seemed to cause every negative 'what if' thought she'd ever had about Maylee's disappearance to resurface. It was all so real, front and center in a house that was supposed to belong to the lead suspect in Maylee's case. With jittery fingers Autumn pulled out her phone and snapped a few pictures.

In the corner of this obvious torture room there was a small tattered table with what looked like a shoe box sitting on top of it. Tip-toeing, Autumn slowly crept to the box and looked inside. There were a stack of photographs with a large rubber band holding them together. It was too dark to make out what they were pictures of, but it didn't take much to imagine their contents.

Autumn tucked the stack against the skin of her chest, underneath her gun's holster that was secured around her waist. She fastened them in tightly so they wouldn't fall out. Giving them a thorough examination would have to wait until later, when she was safe in her own apartment.

The floor continued to creak as Autumn cautiously made her way back down the steps and to the basement door. A steady finger was held on the cold metal of her gun, as close as she could get it to the trigger without actually touching it. Jeremy taught her well, there'd be no accidental discharge of her weapon, not tonight. So far Autumn had lucked out. The crack house seemed empty of people, but the basement called to her next.

Securely in front of her, Autumn held her gun, as she closed the distance between herself and the daunting basement door. She prayed that the culprit of the half eaten sandwich wouldn't show up while she was down there, or worse, already be down there himself. The basement stairway was significantly darker than the rest of the house. She could hardly make out the last step.

When she reached the bottom she could see a small light shining from underneath a doorway at the end of an apparent hall. Autumn held her breath and very slowly walked toward it. The door was metal and locked from the outside, she gently placed an ear against it. There was a faint noise coming from inside, and Autumn strained to make out what it was. It sounded much like a wheezy breath, then a cough, followed by the soft moan of a girl in pain. Autumn's heart sunk in her chest. *Oh my God, could it be her?*

The cracked concrete floor threatened to swallow Autumn whole. Her nervous fingers reached for the lock, but she paused before flipping its latch. *Who was behind this locked door*, she wondered, *what if the pained cougher wasn't alone?* Autumn waited for a few more moments with her ear pressed firmly against the cold metal. Then, a quiet woman's voice sounded from inside. It was raspy, pained, and dry... *But not Maylee.* A tear rolled down Autumn's cheek, and her closing throat finally sucked in a lungful of the rancid smelling air.

"Please. Please." The voice begged. "I know you're there. Just please stop doing this to me, I have a family, please let me go."

Autumn's heart hesitated, nearly failing to do its job. She gasped and quickly flipped the lock. The door swung open with the push of one hand, while she gripped her pistol tightly in the other. In the small and otherwise empty room was a young brunette. At first glance she appeared to be in her early twenties, or younger. Swollen skin forced one eye shut and her ribs and hips were protruding, she was battered and starved.

The girl was tied by her wrists and ankles, she hugged her knees in the corner. There was a shining flashlight in the opposite corner next to a tin bucket, rusted at the handle. The girl stared at Autumn speechless and sobbed. She was wearing a sports bra and underwear, browned by sweat and filth. Every inch of her body was dirty and bruised.

Autumn ran to her side and started struggling with the ropes that bound her. It took a few minutes to get them untied. While she tugged and ripped on the restraints, Autumn did her best to assure the girl that they'd get out and that everything would be okay. The words were unconvincing, they spewed from her mouth in hesitant fragments.

Autumn told the girl that she would have to hide outside in the bushes while she ran to her car. The girl could do nothing but sob. As soon as the ropes were untied, Autumn helped her to her feet. They struggled up the stairs and hurried silently past the dingy living room and into the kitchen. The girl's battered arms clung to Autumn, depending on her completely to steady her feet and hold her weight. Frightened tears of relief poured down the girl's face, leaving streaks of dirt and grime.

Autumn whispered in the girl's ear, as they approached the back door. "Stay quiet, there are men outside the house."

Just as Autumn twisted the handle, a group of blaring voices blasted into the front door. One of the voices belonged to the man who had whistled at her, she recognized it immediately. Tonight wasn't the first time he'd whistled and shouted profanities in her direction. It was a distinctly husky voice, one that stood out. The girl tightened her grip around Autumn's shoulders, and they slipped out as quickly as possible.

The men were laughing and cussing on their way into the house, too drunk and distracted to hear the creaking of the backdoor. Autumn pushed it shut behind them, with a nearly silent click, then she grabbed the hunched over girl around the waist and hurried her into the bushes along the side of the house. They moved quickly with the profane sounds of the rowdy card players ringing behind them. They found themselves squished tightly in the same place Autumn had crossed the neighbor's yard, hardly fitting in the space.

"Stay here." Autumn whispered. "I'll run as fast as I can."

Their eyes locked, and the girl offered her a nod. Too afraid to speak, or even to cry in protest of being left alone, she slowly sat down and resumed the same position she was in when Autumn found her. The sight was too much to take in. Autumn couldn't bear the thought of her being found by the time she got back to her car. She kneeled to the girls level and quickly repeated her reassuring promises.

"I'm going to get you out of here. If it kills me, I'll do it."

The girl was now curled up into the fetal position in the weeds directly under Craig's living room window. A fresh stream of tears overflowed and her shoulders shook.

"I have to get my car and come back before they notice you're gone. Wait here, and stay still. If they come out I want you to run through this yard and down that street." Autumn pointed in the direction she was talking about.

This was the best plan she could come up with. She knew that if the girl was able to run away and escape before she got back to her car then at least she could look for her in the direction she was headed. Autumn stared into the girls petrified eyes until her attention was captured.

"Do you hear me? Do you understand what you have to do?"

The girl nodded, she understood the plan though she knew that running was hardly an option. Even just standing was difficult. The girl knew that being caught in an attempt to escape would mean nothing less than death, but she looked into Autumn's eyes and agreed either way.

Autumn crept back through the neighbor's yard safely. When she reached the sidewalk on the other side, she unloaded the bullet that was ready to shoot in the chamber of her gun and holstered it. Then she took off at full speed toward her car, running faster than she ever had.

The neighborhood was relatively empty and extremely dark, no people, no headlights. The majority of streetlights were busted out, leaving nothing but an increasing blackness. Autumn could only assume that they'd been shattered by rebellious teens, or even gangsters who didn't want to be seen at night. The thought of it froze a dagger in her chest and she willed her legs to move faster.

Autumn was almost to the last block that she knew of containing dogs. *Please don't let them be loose in the night*, she prayed in thought. As she neared their usual spot, barks, growls, and shrill yapps rippled through the darkness. Several parked cars came into focus and dozens of men's voices shouted and cussed from behind a broken down shed. There was no one on the road, it remained as empty as the rest. Autumn tilted her head back and ran straight past the chaos. A gunshot nearly stopped her in her tracks.

It caused her to jump and gasp, but she kept going. An image of the broken girl in the fetal position that she'd stashed in the bushes outside of Craig's house kept her moving. Autumn's head turned as she ran, checking for followers, no one was there. The shot wasn't aimed at her, *thank God.*

Maybe it was intended for a dog, or even a person watching the fights. Autumn didn't know and didn't care, she was grateful for their distraction. The dog fights, and the gun shot apparently had the entire neighborhood distracted, and it took the attention off of her. Her thoughts circled back to how quickly she needed to get to her car. With a steadying breath she maintained her stride. One more block and she was there.

As soon as Autumn's car was in focus, she reached into her pocket for the keys. She could see lights on inside the fast food place, and a few young workers ready to prepare tacos for their evening customers. The car came to life with a twist of the key, and she debated on calling Chance or Jeremy as she drove. As quickly as the thought entered her head, it was pushed back out.

Involving Chance would mean involving the police, and that couldn't be risked, not yet. Until Autumn could talk to this girl, alone, about Maylee, no one else needed to know about her. Especially with the drunken cop who was running around with the very men who had her locked away.

The shaking of Autumn's hands made it hard to grip the wheel, and her nervous legs struggled to manage the foot pedals. Autumn tried her best to maintain speed, and drive back to Craig's house carefully. The last thing she needed was to get pulled over, or draw attention to herself in any way. Within minutes her car crept past the putrid house. The tires slowed and Autumn strained to look past the weeds and garbage at the side of the house. There she was, the girl hadn't moved. It was hard to make out her silhouette in the dark, but it was definitely there. Still in the same fetal position directly under the side window.

Autumn breathed a sigh of relief, and pulled her car around the corner to park by the shrubs of the yard she needed to trespass through for a third and fourth time. Autumn locked the door, drew her gun, and again crossed into the stranger's yard. The lights inside the house were now off, Autumn hoped the occupants were also at the dog fights, and wouldn't be coming home soon. That's all she could do at that point, hope.

This secluded little back yard made things much easier for Autumn. She could only imagine if she would have had to escape on the other side of the house where those men had come from. Only God knows what would've happened, had this yard not been there. Autumn reached the girl and threw her arms around her cold trebling body to help her to her feet. Then she listened toward the window to the grotesque men inside. They were arguing on who would get to have their way with "the bitch in the basement" first. They were joking around about the sick things they'd done to her. One of them even wanted to chain her back up upstairs.

"Screw you guys, it's my turn." The husky memorable voice stood out above the rest.

The girl jumped and cringed at the sound of him, tears rolled down her face in a steady stream. Autumn covered her mouth and whispered for her to be quiet. Before they had a chance to maneuver completely through the hedge, the same voice sounded off again. This time he was shouting and the basement door slammed behind him.

"That little bitch is gone!" he yelled. "Get off your asses and help me find her!" There was a rustle inside as the men started to panic.

Autumn grabbed the girl around her waist and shoved her through the shrubs. She forced her to run over the grass to her waiting car. As quickly as possible she placed the weak and battered girl inside and slammed the door shut. As Autumn rounded the car back to her driver's side she heard the men yelling at each other from behind the house.

"What the Fuck!" One shouted.

"Didn't you lock the fucking door?" Another yelled.

"If we don't find her, Craig's gunna' kill us."

Autumn shut herself into the car breathless, and stomped on the gas, speeding away. The girl sobbed and mumbled as they drove off.

"They're gunna' find me. I know they're gunna' find me, they always do. They're gunna' kill me. They're gunna' kill you too."

In a complete and utter panic, Autumn shoved a picture of Maylee in the girl's face. She couldn't wait, she had to know. Her pounding heart fed by anxiety and fear. This was happening, it was really happening. If Chance knew the risks she'd just taken he'd flip, and so would Jeremy and his friends for that matter, especially Lloyd. But it worked, she'd rescued a woman, and was finally a step closer to finding Maylee.

"Have you seen her? This is my niece, I've been looking for her."

There was no comprehensive reply from the girl, only useless mumbling nonsense.

"Please, answer me." Autumn begged.

The one eye the girl was able to open fully was wide, staring straight ahead at the road, she refused to take a good look at Maylee's picture. She glanced down at it for a second, but the face didn't instantly ring a bell. The crack house was soon gone, not even a flicker in a rear view. Autumn assumed that the men were searching for this girl on foot, because there were no headlights behind her. She signed a breath of relief and bee-lined it straight for the freeway.

There was a mugshot of Craig in the glove compartment. Autumn had printed off two copies of it, after pulling it from public records. One copy stayed in her car, and one hung proudly on the overbearing map in her kitchen. What was meant for motivation, now would be used to snap this girl out of her trance.

Autumn pulled onto the freeway, and then reached across the nearly naked, filthy and bruised girl who sat trembling on her passenger seat. She pulled the photo from the compartment, and then shoved it in the girl's face.

"Have you seen this man? Is he the one who took you?"

The girl's contorted face dropped and her breath came in shallow. The shaking of her fingers intensified as she reached up and took the photo from Autumn's hand. She stared into his face and sobbed, clearly familiar with him. The girl hung her head forward, chin to chest, and let the overwhelming tension take over. The photo dropped to her lap.

"Thank you." She whispered.

"So you know him?" Autumn continued, unable to accept the girl's show lived gratitude as an answer. "Have you seen this man?"

"Yes."

Again, Autumn grabbed the picture of Maylee, and shoved it in the girl's hands. "And her? Please tell me you've seen her!"

The girl stumbled over her words. "I. I. I don't think so, I'm sorry."

She sniffled, and wiped the tears from her dirty cheeks.

"Where are you going to take me?" She asked. "Please don't take me to the police."

The girl's request screamed experience. Dirty legs curled up to the girl's chest as she hugged them tightly. The look in her face changed from one of fear to one of acceptance. The skin on her forehead smoothed, and aside from the bruises and swollen eye, Autumn could finally get a decent look at her. Her brows were thick and defined, and her lips were plump with sharp peaks. Aside from the hair color, this girl actually looked a lot like Maylee. They shared a few distinct similarities. This made Autumn sink into her chair, confused and still completely beside herself.

"Why?"

Autumn asked calmly, already knowing the answer as an image of the card playing cop flashed in her mind like a caution light.

"It's happened before. They've taken me twice."

It wasn't a direct answer to Autumn's question, but it was enough. Autumn reached behind the passenger seat, careful to keep the other hand steady on the wheel. She grabbed a small gym bag that she was yet to use, despite repeated invitations from Lloyd. She placed it gently in the girl's lap.

"There's a shirt and some sweats in here." She told her softly. "We'll go to my apartment. You can hide out there while we make a plan."

The girl nodded, wincing in pain as she pulled the shirt over her head. Then she picked the picture of Maylee back up to take a closer look. She shook her head slowly and whispered.

"I don't remember her, I'm sorry."

Autumn nodded an acceptance, wiped a lone tear before it had a chance to roam the length of her face, and asked, "What's your name?"

"Josie," the girl breathed quietly, and with another wince, "My name is Josie."

Chapter Seven

Josie ducked down while they pulled into a vacant parking space as close to the building as possible. Autumn's face crinkled up tight as she strained to get a closer look at Jeremy's apartment from the safety of the car. They'd have to go unnoticed while sneaking Josie past his door and up the stairs. They couldn't allow themselves to be seen by anyone, the cost was too high, the risk too steep. Even Jeremy couldn't be involved, not yet anyway. When the coast seemed clear, it was time to make a move.

Autumn opened the passenger door, and slowly helped Josie to her feet. The most recent beatings had rendered Josie fairly immobile. She was in terrible shape and unable to stand up straight on her own. Josie continued to hunch at the middle as they made their way up the steps and safely into Autumn's apartment. Autumn secured the locks as soon as the door shut behind them.

Sneaking Josie inside was much easier than Autumn anticipated. She helped her to the bathroom, and slowly lowered her to sit on the edge of the tub. Then left her to find some clean clothes and a towel. When she returned with the fetched items, Autumn informed the severely beaten Josie to take her time in the shower while she made a couple of phone calls and prepare some food.

The thought of Autumn on the phone caused a burst of anxiety to consume Josie. She snapped her head up, pulling her eyes from the freckle on her right foot that she was used to staring at. She looked deep into Autumn's eyes, searching for some sort of answer in them. She found nothing but loss and compassion.

"Who are you calling?" She asked through a dry throat.

Autumn gently placed her hands on Josie's shoulders.

"I won't say a word about you." She promised.

Josie nodded in an unspoken agreement, although the spark of fear on her swollen face remained distinctly intact. The contour of Josie's jaw was small but sharply squared, and her matted hair was thick. It sprouted from a beautifully shaped half circle at the top of her short forehead.

Dozens of needle marks tracked up the length of Josie's arms. Some were encircled with fresh purple bruises, some healing with old faded yellow ones. One vein in particular was littered with a pencil eraser sized scar with the remnants of a hole in the middle. Josie was permanently marked by her daunting past. The scars would forever be a reminder of the torture and pain she's had to endure by the hand of multiple men. They'd drugged, raped and beat her repeatedly. Turned her into an addict no doubt.

Autumn looked deeply into Josie's swollen eyes, only to see Maylee staring back out at her. A bleeding heart drummed inside Autumn's chest, and she nearly crumpled to the floor at Josie's feet. The memory of Josie's earlier statement chimed in her thoughts, '*It's happened before, they've taken me twice.*'

A suddenly overwhelming thought barged through the suffocating feelings of empathy, and Autumn clung to it. Hope… If Josie had been kept alive more than once, then there was hope that Maylee could still be out there – a beating heart in her chest, and air flowing through her lungs.

"I'm so sorry for what they've done to you," Autumn whispered through a crackling throat.

Josie had hardly been able to form a word without bursting into tears. She held her breath and hesitantly allowed Autumn to scan over her wounds. Her voice was stuck in her throat, it allowed nothing to pass. *Please don't ask more questions*, she willed. An awkward calm was finally beginning to settle in her stomach. This was a feeling that Josie wasn't used to, it was comforting.

A hint of relief washed over her, accompanied by a small pinch of hope. Not hope for life, or even safety, that was gone. It was merely hope for a night of peace and the ability to relax. Josie knew deep down that she'd never be able to feel completely safe again, that luxury was a victim to her past. Forever lost in a void of filth and blackness. They'd find her, it was inevitable. Only this time they wouldn't let her walk away alive.

Josie knew for certain that she'd pay dearly for escaping the group, escaping *him*. Her life would be the cost to pay for such defiance, and it likely wouldn't be quick and painless. Josie knew that she belonged to someone, a man that would never let her walk away so easily. A tortuous death would be her punishment this time, there was no escaping it. She let out a slow breath of acceptance. At least for tonight the raping would stop.

Even if it was only for a night, or an hour, Josie was grateful for the break. She could shower, feel clean, and rest. Her body may even have the time to heal before they found her, the hope was reassuring. For now, she was away from the evil that had taken over her. For now, she could rest. Josie was nothing but grateful for that. Instinctively, she threw her arms around Autumn and sobbed.

Autumn finally allowed the tense flex of her shoulders to relax while she held the broken down Josie in her arms. Her hand caressed softly over Josie's hair and she closed her eyes tightly, holding back a rush of sobs of her own. Autumn imagined it was Maylee safely engulfed in her arms. Maylee's tears being absorbed into the fibers of her shirt. Maylee's bruises, swollen skin and surely broken ribs. Busted, but alive. *God, how she wished this girl were Maylee.*

If Autumn could save Josie, then there was hope, and she grabbed ahold of that hope with every part of her. Josie winced in pain beneath her grasp, forcing Autumn to realize that she'd squeezed her too tightly. Instantly, she released Josie from the suffocating embrace, but kept her hands around Josie's shoulders.

"I'm sorry." Autumn sighed. "Take your time, okay? I'll be just outside the door if you need me."

Autumn finally let her arms slip away from Josie, and she forced herself out of the room. She stood by the door and listened for the click of the lock and the running water before walking into the kitchen. The cupboards and fridge were lacking ingredients. There wasn't enough to make a fresh and healthy meal for Josie, the kind that she deserved. It was irritating, but Autumn knew she couldn't risk leaving Josie alone, or even calling anything in. So, she settled for something quick and easy, opting to whip up a couple of chicken burgers. Autumn lit the burner, and slapped two frozen patties in a large pan before digging in her pockets for her phone.

There were seven missed calls from Detective Chance. Autumn's heart sank to her guts. They'd been talking every day, but he was yet to call so many times in a row. There had to be a reason. Autumn hesitated briefly at listening to his messages, but instantly decided against it. Adrenaline was already pooled in her bloodstream, consuming the very fiber of her being.

As far as Autumn was concerned, Chance had no idea about her split decision for an evening run. So whatever was so urgent, was better off heard by his own mouth rather than relayed by a heartless machine. It rang only once before he picked up. His voice was husky as if he was out of breath, clearly he was strained.

"Autumn," he breathed heavily. "Where are you?"

Autumn noted the concern in his voice, so she spoke slowly and with caution. "Home, why?"

"No you're not." He accused, suddenly sounding cross.

Suspicion swirled inside her. *Why was he being so weird?* And *why didn't he think she was home?* He was in a different state entirely, he had no place to make any kind of accusation, especially as it pertained to her whereabouts. Just as Autumn was about to ask Chance if he felt alright, he blurted a four word statement that caused her knees to buckle beneath her already tired body.

"I'm here, in Denver."

Autumn grabbed the kitchen counter with a tight fist, it helped to hold her body upright. Her mind flashed from Josie's swollen face to Chance's piercing eyes. *He wasn't here, he couldn't be.* She'd spoken to him the night before and he didn't say a word about coming to see her. He had promised to eventually, but not now. There was no plan set in place. Autumn was a planner, she would have struggled with a surprise visit on a regular day, let alone with a kidnapped woman in her bathroom. *How could she hide Josie with him here?* She couldn't. Anticipation and guilt consumed her, rendering her speechless.

"Autumn." Chance repeated, pulling her back. "Where are you? I've knocked on your door three times in the last hour. I'm at Detec…" he paused, voice catching in his throat. "I'm here, downstairs."

"Where?" she breathed, hardly understandable.

"Downstairs, waiting at your friend's apartment."

"Why?" Her voice was merely a whisper.

"Excuse me?" he asked.

Autumn only waited. She didn't need to explain herself. The surprise of his visit seemed tainted, she could feel it in her bones. The urgency in his voice only told her that something was wrong. The questions rose as she waited in silence for him to respond with some sort of explanation. *Why was he there? What was he about to say when he caught himself. Was this about Maylee? Why would he be with Jeremy?* The questions stacked, one after another, higher and higher. Her mind was a volcano ready to explode at any minute, but she held tight-lipped for the sake of Josie.

Chance sighed a long breath of surrender. "There's something I have to talk to you about. It's not an emergency so don't panic, but it's important."

Autumn's mind raced. She had to think fast.

"I just got home, I've been running."

"At night?" he jumped. "Never mind, I'm coming up."

"Don't!" Autumn shouted. The yell was unintentional, and the sound of it made even herself jump. "I mean..." *think fast Autumn,* "I was just stepping in the shower. You said it wasn't an emergency, can you give me thirty minutes?"

"Really?" He asked. He was wholly irritated, but compliant nonetheless.

"Yes, I'll hurry." Autumn disconnected her end of the phone, leaving no room for an objection.

By the time Autumn packed up the dinner that she'd just barely started to cook, and slapped together a peanut butter and jelly, she heard the water to the shower turn off. *Thank God,* she thought. Josie was quick in the shower. She glanced at the clock on the stove. There was still twenty five minutes left of the thirty she'd requested. Unless Chance decided to come knocking on her door early, then she had just enough time. Autumn threw the poor excuse of a meal onto a paper plate and stood outside the bathroom door. She tapped lightly on the hollowed wood, and leaned toward the crack of the doorframe.

"Josie?" She exhaled slowly, searching for the words. "Something came up. I need you to hurry out of the bathroom, okay?"

Naturally, Josie assumed the worst. Her feet froze to the linoleum and she dropped her hair drying towel. It fell around her ankles in a wet lilac scented heap. A comfortable set of flannel button up pajamas were folded neatly on the counter for her. She dressed quickly and silently, listening carefully for *his* voice. Only a second hushed request from Autumn rang in.

"It's okay honey, just come out."

Autumn coaxed her guest from outside the bathroom door as if she was an abused animal hiding under a bed or a porch. Maylee had a puppy once. It was a skittish stray Labrador, that she'd talked Autumn into letting her bring to the condo. Autumn remembered the way it shook and peed itself in the corner. It lasted for one week, scarfing down every last drop of puppy food until it got sick and died.

The vet had explained to them that the puppy had a virus called Parvo. Not only was the puppy's fate inevitable, but he also infected the ground around Autumn's home with its sickness. She would never be able to keep a pet again.

Autumn wasn't sure why she thought of that dog at that very moment. The irony made her sick to her stomach. A sweet and innocent creature turned beaten and infectious. Endangering everyone who it came in contact with.

Josie twisted the handle, allowing the door to crack at the hinges. Not completely open, just enough to peek out and lock eyes with Autumn. No words were necessary, everything Josie needed to know was painted all over the urgent sympathy in of her savior's face. Josie knew that look well, she'd seen it on her mother several times as a child when her father had drank too much and was out for blood. Everything about the downward pull of Autumn's tight lips, and the strain of her burning apologetic eyes told Josie that she needed to make herself invisible, and fast.

"Where can I hide?" She whispered.

Autumn released a lung full of air, completely relieved at Josie's unspoken understanding. There was no time for a drawn out explanation. She was down to twenty minutes before Chance was to come physically barging into her life, and she still had to jump in and out of the shower to wet her hair before it happened.

"In my room." Autumn said, as she assisted Josie in draping an arm around her shoulder to help them move a little faster. "I'm so sorry. I wasn't expecting company."

Josie didn't respond. She only watched as Autumn tossed a few blankets and pillows onto the floor in a small space between the bed and the wall. It was perfect. She wouldn't be seen from the doorway if anyone were to look in at a glance. As long as they didn't come searching she'd be safe. If they did come looking, there would be no hiding anyway and Josie had already accepted that fate.

The comfort of the pillows and the cleanliness of the blankets called to her. She hadn't seen such luxuries in weeks. Not since she was last with *him*, being injected by a needle in *his* bed. The memory caused Josie to shudder. She pushed out the recollection of her burning veins and the blackness that followed.

Autumn's bedding cradled Josie as she lowered herself to the floor. The pillows smelled of fresh linen, and the comforter was clearly down. It felt like she was hiding in a cloud. A familiar cloud like something from a dream. Autumn handed her the sandwich, along with some Advil and a tall glass of Iced Tea. Then she scurried away to rummage herself some new clothes from her closet.

Josie realized at that very moment how much she admired Autumn, and envied her innocence. The sharp pain in Josie's ribs was excruciating. She gulped down the Advil with one replenishing swallow. Then she pulled her legs up into the fetal position to nibble her meal in the cramped little hiding space that only somewhat concealed her.

Autumn hurried to the bathroom. She pulled off her shirt and took a quick awkward look in the full length mirror at her side. She stood tall thin and muscular with a gun strapped to her middle.

"Who are you?" she whispered at the reflection staring back at her.

Her bony fingers unhooked the strap to her gun holster. As she peeled it away from her sweaty body a thick stack of pictures fell to the floor with a *thud*. The sound made her jump and gasp. With all the events of the night and the adrenaline building and bubbling inside of her, Autumn had completely forgotten about the pictures she'd stolen from Craig's place.

She held a hand over her heart and stared unbelievingly at the disgusting stack of polaroid. They were face down, still secured together with the large rubber band. Pointlessly, she looked around the knowingly empty room before slowly bending at the knees to pick them up. It felt like holding a scorching hot pan in her fingertips. Before flipping the stack face up she glanced at the time. It couldn't wait, she had to know if Maylee was in the photos.

There was still fifteen minutes, and this would only take two at the most. Autumn closed her eyes and took in a breath while she removed the rubber band and flipped the stack face-side-up.

"You can do this Autumn."

The first picture on the stack was of Josie. Her eyes were closed and she was naked, sprawled out on the stained mattress with no blankets or sheets. She was obviously drugged, she looked dead. Autumn flipped through the next few pictures as quickly as possible. Still, they were of Josie, placed in several different humiliating positions and tied up in places that forced her skin to purple. A silent tear ran down Autumns cheek as she made herself keep looking. The nausea in her stomach grew into something stronger. It felt like she was suddenly stricken with food poisoning or the flu.

"My poor girl, what have they done to you?" she whispered into the quiet of the bathroom.

After a few more pictures were scanned over, a new girl appeared. This girl was also drugged and placed into the same positions that Josie had been, but she was in an entirely different bedroom. Autumn's eyes widened at the shock of a new face, and flipped the pictures even faster. *There is more,* she thought, *Maylee has got to be here.* Faster and faster, see shuffled through them in a panic, searching the faces of several naked girls.

One girl after another, the faces practically blurred together. Autumn's vision was increasingly disturbed by the growing tears. No Maylee... In less than a minute she'd reached the end of the pile. There had to have been at least a dozen young girls photographed in this stack of pictures, probably more, and at least five different locations. Autumn crossed the room in two giant steps, gripping the photos with a tight fist. The first wave of vomit came up violently. It lurched from the bottom of her stomach, and escaped into the porcelain bowl of her toilet.

Who could do such terrible things? Autumn forced the rubber band back around the stack just before another wave of throw up forced itself to the surface. *They were all so young and innocent. How could there be so many monsters out there to allow and participate in such torment?* Autumn tucked the stack away safely in the bottom drawer next to the sink and quickly jumped in the shower.

His knock on the door soon pounded through the apartment. Autumn barely had enough time to throw on some clothes and rush a pick through her tangled wet hair.

Josie froze in place. She laid still in pain and anticipation, listening to Autumn's footsteps. The feeling that followed the knock was all too familiar. The fact that she knew nothing about Autumn's unexpected guest left her feeling hollow. Not afraid, just empty. She was too mentally drained to be scared, and too physically exhausted to tense. Josie was used to unfamiliar guests. Like a worn out seat on a train, she was used to strangers. On the inside she was numb and empty.

Nervously, Autumn hurried to the door. Before opening it, she took a quick heart-throbbing look out the peephole. There he was, the man she'd spent her evenings swooning over while listening to the steady hum of his voice over the phone every night. A man that she once detested, and now ached for. There were so many things she wished could be different about this moment. She would have prepared herself, dressed nice and fixed her hair. Probably in an updo and swept out of her face. She would've picked something with a low neckline to wear, lathered her skin with her silkiest lotions, and even taken the time to shave.

Rather than the romantic reunion Autumn had anticipated, she was being forced to see him in dreaded conditions of her own, and clearly of his too. It was going to take everything she had to shoo him out of her apartment. She had every intention of telling him all about Josie, but not until she had the time to speak with her first. Josie needed to warm up to Autumn, and rest. That wouldn't be a possibility if she was thrown to the wolves before given a chance to catch her breath. Autumn had to keep Josie a secret, at least for tonight.

Chance stood outside the door waiting impatiently. It'd been a long trip, he'd caught the first flight possible after hearing news of another sighting of Maylee. Right here in Denver nonetheless. It was time to be completely honest with Autumn, and he had to do it in person. Anxiously, he held his breath as her metal door creaked open. All he could do was come clean about his lies and pray for her forgiveness.

Their eyes locked and for one brief moment they were the only two people in the world. Josie, Craig, Jeremy, and even Maylee faded into mere background. The sharp grey shards of color in his eyes pierced through her, and she drank in their naked vulnerability. There was a sense of surrender in the upward pull of his brows. It was a look she was yet to see plastered on his handsome face, a look that melted her insides.

As she welcomed him in, the familiar scent of him threatened to consume her. It smelled like spruce bark and ocean, and it followed him into her apartment, her heart, her future. They had opened up to each other in a way that there was no turning back from. Even if it had only been by phone. No matter what he had to say, there was sure to be a way around it. Autumn was confident of that.

Their greeting was somewhat awkward at first. Chance didn't know whether to fall to her knees in apology, or to scoop her into his arms for the embrace he'd been pondering about for weeks. He opted for neither and took a seat.

"I'm sorry to barge in like this. I wish I could have come on different terms." He openly admitted with a hint of surrender bleeding through.

"It's fine," Autumn lied.

She tried her best not to look back toward her bedroom as it contained an overwhelming secret of her own. Lingering post-vomit body chills shot up her spine, and her stomach continued to spin. She took a seat next to him, close enough for their legs to brush. The heat of his body left an impression on every part of her that was close enough to feel it. The fluttering in her chest turned rapid as he gently placed his hand on her exposed knee. *Tight lengthy yoga shorts were definitely a good choice,* she thought.

Chance leaned in toward her, ready to spill the beans on his entire operation. But, as soon as he opened his mouth to speak he realized the lightened shade of her skin, the warmth of her leg under his wanting palm, and the cloudy haze that was covering the whites of her eyes.

"Oh my God, Autumn. Are you okay?"

She had to clear the lump from her throat before words could push through. The only thing she could see in his devilish eyes was concern, and all that she wanted to do was bury herself in his arms. She toyed with the possibility of crawling onto his lap and allowing the smell and comfort of him to engulf her while she cried like a baby.

"I don't know," she confessed, containing her childish urges.

Autumn wrapped an arm around her stomach. It wasn't exactly a lie. Looking at those photos triggered something in her guts, and the two rounds of vomit she'd experienced might not have been enough. There was no question about it, she was most definitely sick.

"Why didn't you say something?" He asked.

Instinctively Chance reached a hand up to feel the burning heat of her forehead.

"And you ran?" He demanded. "Why were you out running? You're obviously sick, you should rest!"

Autumn laced her fingers in his and pulled his hand away from her head. "I'll be fine." She instead. "It's good to see you."

Finally, a moment of solace beyond the initial glance of intimacy when she'd opened the door to let him in. For the first time since Keith, Autumn felt comforted by the presence of a man. She could tell by the way he held her gaze, and tightened his fingers around her grip, the feeling was mutual.

With a surrendering slump of his shoulders Chance let out a therapeutic sigh of relief. He leaned his forehead into hers and squeezed his eyes shut tightly. He couldn't bear to say the words out loud. There was no way to express how badly he'd wanted to see her – to feel her skin against his. Since their very first call, the sound of her voice had remained in his mind. It'd become a part of him.

To be in the same room as the woman he's spent the last three weeks of his life obsessing over was everything he'd imagined it to be and more. Even if she was sick, and even if he did have to break her heart with the biggest secret he'd ever kept. He was still glad to be there, to have her within arm's length. Chance knew he had to do it now. There was a reason he came, and it wasn't to keep up the deception. She'd opened herself up to him, and it didn't matter how badly he wanted to take her right there on the spot, his conscience wouldn't allow one more second of the secrecy.

"I have to tell you something important." He whispered inches from her face, foreheads still lightly pressed together.

Autumn breathed in the warm peppermint air that escaped his mouth, and then pulled away to look into his face. Not a word was offered, only a nod and a squeeze of his hand. She was ready, whatever he had to say, she could take it. Autumn held the air in her lungs, thoughts racing from the way he looked in his suit, to the battered girl hiding in her bedroom.

Autumn didn't know what would be worse, the confession that he came all the way to Denver to get off of his chest, or having to kick him out of her apartment afterward in order to conceal Josie. She already wanted him to stay – to feel the warmth of his body in her bed as he lay next to her.

"I haven't been completely honest." He said, cutting right to the chase.

"What do you mean?" She asked lightly, with her heart sinking lower with every word.

"About the case, about Maylee."

Chance stared into his lap, unable to face her fully. He was expecting her to panic and shout at him demanding answers, but she didn't. She remained still. Her grip loosened and she pulled away from the hold on his hand, but she didn't push him away. A quiet sniffle sounded, and she reached up to clear her face. The room was still, so he continued. There was no turning back now.

"It's confidential, all of it. But it's been eating me alive keeping it from you."

Chance finally looked up to meet Autumn's cloudy eyes. Her skin seemed yet another shade lighter. He wanted her healthy, and in a reasonable frame of mind, rather than sick and clearly exhausted. He drew in a long breath of nervous air and then let it all go. The burden on his chest was slowly lifted and then tossed aside. He watched the pain in Autumn's face transform from one emotion to the next. Her brows would pull and then smooth. Her lips would tighten into a thin line and then relax when she swallowed. Consistently, she gnawed on the bottom right corner of her lip and fiddled with her fingernails.

Autumn listened carefully to every single word. Hurt and betrayal swirled and twisted, intertwining itself with relief and hope. She heard the words.

"'Maylee's been seen, or at least we think she has. It was here in Denver, last night."

And the rest was history. Everything else blurred together, spouting from his sharply defined lips in waves of mush. Autumn hated him for lying to her all this time, yet she loved him for caring now. She loved the way his voice was laced with concern every time he said Maylee's name, and she adored the way his eyes fogged with emotion every time he met her gaze. When he was completely finished, and the entire three years of Maylee's not so cold case was exposed, Autumn struggled to find her strength.

"Yesterday?" she finally croaked.

Every other part of his confession was placed on the back burner. She tucked it away in a place to be reckoned with, after she'd had the time to truly process.

"You said someone seen her? Here?"

"I said they might have." He corrected, emphasizing the might. "We have quite a few undercovers, and one of them thinks he might have seen her. He said it was from a distance so it was hard to tell, but the girl he did see looked exactly like Maylee's picture."

Autumn placed a hand on her chest, unable to speak.

"Autumn," Chance said in a low smooth voice. "The girl he saw was with Craig."

Autumn squeezed her eyes shut instantly in an effort to stop the flow of tears. She leaned into Chance and let a full round of sobs roll through her.

"We couldn't have found Craig without you, Autumn."

He spoke into her hair as she cried, knowing she was still listening – tears or not.

"There are two other men just like Craig who we've been watching, but it wasn't until you decided to move here that we've been able to watch him too. That house is only one of four that Craig stays in. They bounce around a lot, all of them. Who we can't seem to find is the head of the beast, or even how they move the girls from place to place. Until we figure that out, we have to lay low and wait."

Autumn pulled herself together and pushed away from Chance with both hands on the dampened portion of his suit. She brushed the tears from her face and searched her soul deeply for a way to cope.

"I think you should leave."

It was the first full sentence from her mouth. The pained look of confusion in Chance's face shoved a dagger through her heart.

"I'm sick, Chance, and I need time to process everything." She quickly explained.

"Anything," he said. "Anything you want me to do, I'll do it. However much time you need I'll give it to you."

Autumn shook her head and stared at the floor. There was too much to do, too many things had happened in one day. The situation needed to be handled before it escalated even further. Autumn didn't want to wait for anything, but she knew that before any decisions were made and before she could take the time for herself, to decide what to make of Chance and their strange relationship, she had to deal with Josie.

Josie was her priority that night no matter how badly she wanted to storm the gates and demand answers from the man who'd seen Maylee. Jeremy was also on her list of forces to be reckoned with, but right at that very moment it all boiled down to space, and quiet, and Josie's trust.

"Just for tonight. I need to think… about everything," Autumn's stare burned a hole in Chance's face. "About us."

"Okay," he whispered.

"I'll call you tomorrow when I'm ready to talk."

Autumn stood, reached for his hand, and then walked him to the door. There was no kiss goodbye, she merely stared at the floor with the door open. He loosened the grip and left without a word. No sooner than the door was shut, Autumn leaned against the wall and allowed herself to slide down the length of it to the floor. With her face buried into her hands she let the tears flow.

Every part of her heart had been shattered into tiny bite sized pieces and devoured by the man she was finally ready to hand it over to. A man that she'd went from pestering, to loathing, to wanting, to trusting. There were only three things Autumn knew for certain. Three distinct facts – she hated him, she still wanted every part of him, and that she already forgive him.

* * *

Josie woke to the smell of bacon and eggs. The scent was amazing. She couldn't remember the last time she was able to indulge in a nice breakfast, even before she'd been abducted. Anything more than a bagel or protein bar on her way out the door was a rarity. She drew in a deep lungful, letting the scent illuminate her nostrils. That's when a sharp painful twinge at her ribcage brought her back to reality. Every recent act of violence she'd been forced to endure was front and center. The malnourishment was felt in her muscles, and the beatings in her face and bones. Josie winced in pain as she sat up in Autumn's bed.

Slowly, Josie pulled herself to stand and cautiously wander toward the heavenly scent of a real breakfast. Autumn was sitting at the kitchen table with a concerned furrow of her brow, staring at a framed photo. Josie's stomach flipped at the sight of the room. Behind Autumn was a gigantic map of the city, and tapped in the upper left-hand corner of it was a mug shot of Craig. Plastered all over Craig's face was the usual lowered in anger eyes, mixed with a proud and wholly satisfied smirk. Josie shuddered, the feeling of pins and needles crawled up the length of her.

As soon as Autumn looked up at Josie, her pinched expression smoothed into a gentle and caring gaze. A half-hearted smile filled Autumn's face, and she stood to greet her not so solemn guest.

"Why don't you go have a seat where it's comfortable, honey? This is ready to eat, I'll get us a plate."

Josie nodded in appreciation and turned to make herself comfortable on the loveseat. She found the remote to the already powered on television, and started flipping. Josie had all but forgotten how nice it was to do such mundane things like aimlessly flipping through channels on a television. The normality was awkward, and for no reason at all it made her feel guilty, as if she was doing something wrong.

Momentarily, Josie settled for an old episode of *The Family Guy*. A cartoon she used to love, but as she sat rescued in an unfamiliar place the sound of Peter Griffin's voice pierced her right through the middle. It made her think of the life she lived before the rapes and the drugs.

There'd likely never be another day when a simple cartoon could brighten her spirits. After staring blankly for a few second and reminiscing about what could have been, as opposed to what actually was, she changed the channel to the news. Reality was what she'd grown used to. At least with the news she wouldn't feel so much like she was pretending at normality.

Autumn delivered a perfectly portioned plate along with a tall glass of orange juice. It was the type of meal Josie had dreamed of having for months. A dish that had been cruelly denied. A replenishing gulp of the juice went down smoothly, and the bacon was perfectly crisp. Josie thought about the conversation she'd overheard the night before between Autumn and Chance.

"Can I see her again?" she asked.

"I'm sorry?" Autumn questioned.

"Your niece. Maylee was her name?"

The food rolling around in Autumn's mouth hesitated to go down with a hearable gulp.

"Yes. Absolutely."

After setting down her plate, Autumn fetched the photograph she'd been staring at while waiting for Josie to wake up. It was early and Autumn didn't have a clue on how to proceed with the day. Having Josie request to see Maylee's picture right off the bat was helpful. She'd ignored three calls from Jeremy already and was sure that he'd be knocking on her door at any minute. Even though she'd warned Josie the night before about Jeremy, she was still hoping to make some sort of progress before his inevitable appearance. Showing Josie Maylee's picture in the calm of the morning, would be a great start.

Autumn returned from the kitchen with the same photograph Jeremy had knocked to the floor weeks before. Except it was now framed with fresh new cherry wood. She eagerly handed the picture over to Josie, and remained standing next to her.

"This is my favorite picture of Maylee. It was taken on the beach by my condo. My mother snapped this picture the day before her stroke. It was one of the happiest days of my life."

"I don't think any of my family has ever loved me as much as you love her." Josie said, staring at the picture. Her voice was quiet and shaky. "I'll do everything I can to help."

Josie was overflowing with pent up truths, just waiting to be let loose. She was ready to tell Autumn as much as she could. Josie knew they would come for her, so she had to help now while she was still alive to do it. No matter how hard it was to say the words out loud, she continued.

"As much as I want to see my family, I know I have to do this first. I feel safe here with you, and they'll find me if I go home. I don't want to go to the police either."

Josie shook her head in disgust at the memories pooling in her mind. She looked up at Autumn, took another large gulp of juice, and then continued.

"Your niece... her face looks familiar but I don't think I've actually seen her in person. In a picture maybe, but I can't be sure. They have a lot of girls, but I've only met a few. They said this was my last day at Craig's before I'd go to the healing house and be sold."

"The healing house?" Autumn asked.

"Yeah. I've been there before. You don't fetch as high of price with fresh bruises." Josie continued to speak with a blank stare, as cold as ice. "They said something about having enough out of this city. Something about a requirement and a deadline. I'm not sure what they meant, and I haven't seen Craig since he left with Mary a few weeks ago. She's a girl that was in the house with me the longest."

Autumn reluctantly accepted Josie's explanation of Maylee's familiarity. She set the photograph of Maylee back on the kitchen counter, and then returned to her breakfast. The remainder of their food was eaten in silence. Autumn stared at the last bite on her plate. The distinct churn of her stomach from the night before returned with vengeance, threatening to force up her freshly eaten meal.

The thought of the disgusting stack of pictures hiding in her bathroom swirled around her. She debated on telling Josie about them, but held back. There was more than one elephant in the room and the suffocation of them was scratching at Autumn's spine.

A brunet woman with gorgeous facial features was being aired on the news. She was flawless, her makeup thick. She spoke very professionally. There was one point in Josie's life when she'd considered journalism as a career. Her mind was quickly changed after taking a few classes – she'd absolutely hated the sound of her own voice recorded. She watched the lady speak for several minutes without hearing a single word. Everything the broadcaster reported blurred together.

Josie was a blank slate, careless about local politics and small business growth. That is until a missing person alert broke through, interrupting the regular news. The protective wall around Josie's blank thought process came tumbling down, and her attention transformed into complete. Josie gasped as she recognized the girl's face peering back at her from Autumn's television screen.

"Oh my God." She whispered with hesitation.

Autumn's attention snapped up to see the increasingly pale shade of Josie's face continue to lighten. She noted the widening of Josie's healthy eye, and the hyperventilating gasps for air. Instinctively, she reached for the remote and turned up the volume to the television.

A young beautiful girl was freshly missing, and her name was Jessica Barnes. She was seventeen years old, and she was taken from the high school just a few blocks up the road from the college campus where Josie had also been abducted. A new broadcaster explaining Jessica was shown on the left hand side of the television. Next to him flashed two pictures. One of Jessica and one of Josie. Front and center, the bolded words 'Missing today' was stamped on Jessica's chest.

"I know her." Josie choked. "She lives down the street from me. They took her because I got away." Josie spoke the words in a pitchy petrified voice as her body shook. "I know they did."

The two stared at the television screen and listened to the tall handsome newscaster explain the specifics. First he described how Jessica Barnes had last been seen in the parking lot of her school. The similarities between Jessica and Maylee's disappearances were uncanny. Next, the newscaster explained how Josie had gone missing from the same place nearly two years earlier and was yet to be found. Autumn glanced over at Josie and watched the tears slowly roll down her face.

"We have a lot of work to do, and not much time." Autumn mumbled, just as much to herself as to Josie.

Autumn left Josie to ponder the statement as she retreated back into the kitchen to clean up their meal. The breaking story only lasted a few minutes before returning to the pretty brunette and her pointless speech on a survey regarding local sandwich shops. Josie was left to deal with an overwhelming mix of emotions. She felt empty, lost, and most of all guilty. Another girl had been taken in her place, all because she choose to leave with Autumn.

They'd been talking about a quota and a deadline. *Of course they needed a replacement for her, how did she not see this?* Josie thought about how she should've stayed behind to save another. *She could've told Autumn to leave her there.* Josie's heart was nothing but a thick lump rising into her throat. *Why Jessica?*

Josie stared blankly at the screen until Autumn came back in the room. Together they formulated a short term plan – just for the morning, and then they'd take things from there. It was really all they could do. Autumn had made up her mind on the morning run, and now she had to follow through.

After being seen the night before, if she didn't run that morning then it might be noticed. So far her daily jog had allowed her to become a part of the neighborhood. She blended into the background. Her presence was normal, and more importantly, if there would be any changes due to Josie's escape then they had to know.

Josie promised to lock up and stay hidden in Autumn's room until she got back. And even agreed to meet up with Chance and Jeremy upon Autumn's return. She was reluctant, but they decided that this couldn't be done on their own. Besides, if Jeremy had been under cover this entire time, then he had to be on the right side. There were too many things that could've gone wrong with Autumn's run had he been in cahoots with the wrong crew. Autumn had been running for three weeks, so surely he would've put a stop to her nosey ways if he would've been batting for the wrong team.

Autumn was sure to have some words with him. She was heartbroken that he hadn't come out and told her who he really was in the first place. Car shopping, all their evenings at the shooting range, their drunken map night, and even waking in a cuddle with him wearing her shirt seared a hole completely through Autumn. She considered him to be a genuine friend, probably the best friend she'd ever had for that matter. She'd even finally met his mother for bingo, and he hadn't said a word.

There'd be some serious answering to be done on Jeremy's part, eventually. But, for the time being, Autumn was just glad that she hadn't told him about her spur of the moment decision to run the night before. They must not have been watching her because Chance clearly had no idea she'd gone. She never would've been able to keep Josie hidden if they'd been following her.

Josie was willing to take the risk of meeting with Jeremy and Chance. For Jessica if nothing else. If Jeremy and Chance were on the wrong side then the outcome would be inevitable. Whether she met them on her own free will or not, she didn't stand a chance. Josie was positive that her odds in making it out of this whole mess alive were slim either way, though she'd never admit it out loud to Autumn.

The plan was set. Autumn would run, and then they'd meet up with Chance and Jeremy together. Autumn and Josie decided to face the day head on, no matter the cost.

Autumn practically ran past Jeremy's door, praying that he wouldn't catch her on the way out. With fingers trembling and a shortened breath she was able to speed away from the apartment. Autumn didn't much care that she'd be watched during the run. Apparently, she had been all along, and a part of her felt safer now because of it. As long as she was able to avoid the actual conversation with Jeremy until after the run, and no one found out about Josie, then she could handle the morning.

The drive to Craig's neighborhood went quickly. Autumn parked at the taco place as always, stepped out of her car, and looked down at her phone. There was nothing. No missed calls, no text messages. Autumn wasn't sure what she expected, but she took the lack of popularity as a good sign. If something had happened with Josie there would've been an attempt to contact her surely. It didn't matter that her phone was by her side the entire drive, she still didn't want to miss anything. She slipped it back into her pocket, and completed her stretches before taking off.

There was a slight overcast and welcoming breeze. Which was very irregular compared to the previous days. Oddly, she was grateful for the change and a break from the heat. The crisp air reminded her of the beach and helped her to focus. Starting off, her pace was steady. She made a conscious effort to tuck her fears deep down inside. Slow breathing came naturally as she ignored the chaos on the streets. It was a regular day in this part of town with children screaming and couples fighting.

In no time at all she was rounding the chilling and familiar corner by Craig's small brick house. A memory of the spray painted walls, smelly bathroom, and blood stained mattress flashed across her mind as she made her way toward it. A chill ran down her spine, she prayed silently. *Please don't let them notice me. Please don't let them realize I ran by just before Josie escaped their grasp.*

There was a car in the driveway that she hadn't seen before. It was an old Lincoln town car. It was all black with dark tinted windows. There were three men on the porch smoking and talking quietly to each other. Autumn recognized one of the men from the group the night before. The other two had their backs turned to her and she couldn't see their faces.

Autumn kept her pace steady, and she stayed on the opposite side of the street as usual. It was the exact same time of day, and she wore the exact same running clothes as she had every other morning leading up until now. There were a group of children playing soccer in a small fenced in yard. They were there every day, and Autumn clung to the fence line. The children were used to her running passed them, as was she. This helped feed into the normality and routine of it all. She watched across the street out of the corner of her eye as she ran.

One of the men in front of Craig's house was wearing a black ball cap, and the other had red hair with a noticeably large bald spot on the back. They paid no attention to her as she made her way down the sidewalk. She glanced at the license plate on her way past, and then whispered it under her breath, repeating it over and over as she continued down the street.

Autumn rounded the stop sign and onto the sidewalk that was hidden by the all too familiar shrubs. There she stopped, and hunched over slightly grabbing her sides to catch her breath. She didn't linger too long. Everything about Autumn's run was to notice any differences at Craig's house since Josie had gotten away. The out of place, clearly expensive car was a big deal, and the fact that she'd gone unnoticed was also huge. It only took a second for Autumn to catch her breath and steady the wobble of her knees, then she pushed herself full speed ahead.

She cut the run short, and willed her feet to move as quickly as possible. Rather than working her way around a five block radius after passing Craig's house as usual, Autumn headed back, repeating the license plate number silently under her breath. Over and over she chanted the short mix of numbers and letters, again and again until the sequence of them seared permanently in memory. There'd be no forgetting this vital piece of information. Autumn was determined to instill it into her brain, just the same as she had her very own address the first time she came to this city.

As Autumn reached the parking lot at the taco joint she smiled slightly to herself. She'd done it. She'd made it through another morning run, after rescuing one girl, and she remained unharmed. This time she made it out with even more information. Finally she was getting somewhere, and she felt closer to Maylee now than she had in years. An awkward accomplished smile began to form as she started the engine. Autumn thought about Chance, how he told her Maylee might have been seen.

"Please God, let it be true."

Just as the car roared to life there was a loud startling pound on the window, only inches from her face. Autumn jumped nearly out of her seat. She looked over to see a sickeningly familiar face staring right into hers, with a toothy grin.

Autumn realized instantly who he was, and was momentarily dumbfounded. *Do I lock the doors and take off? Do I talk to this man and keep my cool? Do I play stupid like I have never seen him before?*

The card playing crooked police officer of the year stood outside her window staring. Autumn decided to go with her gut and talk to him. *What choice did she really have?* Autumn knew that if she were to speed off, it would only cause more trouble. Then they were sure to know she was a guilty party in Josie's escape. It took everything Autumn had to calm her racing heart. Reluctantly she rolled down her window.

"Can I help you with something?" She choked.

"Yes ma'am," his voice was smooth, and his smile remained cool and confident. "Aren't you the woman I saw out running last night?"

"It could have been, I guess, I run every morning and night." Autumn lied. The night before had been her first time out at night. She could only pray that he didn't already know better.

"I knew it." He smiled.

There was something about the calm and collected look in his face. Nothing rang callus, or even suspicious. He actually seemed friendly, which made Autumn cringe all the way to her toes. Suddenly, Autumn had a bone chilling understanding on Josie's fear of going to the police.

If there were even more men like this one, who were perfectly capable of maintaining an innocent looking grin amidst such touchy circumstance, then Josie had every right to want to avoid every man on the planet. *Who could blame her?* Autumn didn't know what to say, she hesitated at an excuse to quickly leave, but he spoke again before she had the chance.

"Look, I'm sorry about my friend whistling at you like he did. That was completely inappropriate."

Autumn's brows pulled in the middle. That wasn't at all what she expected him to say. There was no mention of Josie, or even a hint of suspicion in his expression.

"Yeah," Autumn agreed, staring him straight in the eyes.

Who was this man, to be trying at a conversation with her? Maybe she was being paranoid, she thought. *Maybe he really didn't expect her to have anything to do with Josie getting away.* He seemed to be trying at a genuine conversation with her. *Or was he?* Autumn felt beside herself. She was even starting to relax a little, which was completely out of character. Mr. Honorable Mention didn't seem to intend any harm at all. Autumn knew that she had to play off the entire conversation as casually as he was, or else it would risk everything.

"Oh, I'm sorry," the man grinned, "Where are my manners? My name is Alex."

Autumn's heart sunk as he reached a hand out to her. He was still crouched down, leaning toward the driver's side window. Her car was running, and the conversation was awkward, but she knew that she had to play along. It didn't matter if his entire facade was an act or not. She had to seem innocent, it was everything. Autumn reached her hand out the window, ever so casually.

"Erin," she lied.

"Well, have you had anything to eat? Do you care to join me?" He pointed over at the fast food with a welcoming grin on his face.

It was an odd request. One that Autumn never expected. *Why on God's green earth would he be asking her to eat?* His voice was smooth, no underlining of concern. Had Autumn met this man anywhere else or under any other circumstances, she probably would've been obliged to join him for a meal. This Alex creep was handsome with a genuine looking smile and a kind glint in his soft-blue eyes.

The thought brought a sickening realization that literally anyone out there could be a creep, and no one would be the wiser. For the first time in Autumn's life she understood the expression, 'trouble could be lurking around any corner'.

"No thanks, I already ate."

She started to roll her window back up when he grabbed the top, holding it still.

"Well okay, if you insist on turning me down today, then will you at least let me take you out another time?" His grin widened.

"Sorry Alex," Autumn struggled to steady her voice. "I don't make it a habit to date men I meet in the parking lot of fast food joints." *Smooth*, she thought, proud of herself for the seemingly innocent yet quick and honest response.

"Look Erin, I don't usually do this."

The man's cheeks actually flushed some. Autumn was shocked. There was no way anyone could blush on command like that, if there were actually some sort of hidden agenda. She stared at him with utter disbelief, frightened, lost, and partially intrigued.

He continued, "you're a beautiful woman, and I'm truly embarrassed about my friend last night. Just say yes, I owe you one."

Autumn watched his adam's apple sink to the base of his neck then bounce back into place as he swallowed the obvious lump in his throat. She looked at him cautiously out of the corner of her eye. The vision of Josie bound, bruised, and frail reminded her of who this man really was and what he was capable of doing. After a deep exhale of air Autumn opened her mouth a crack to speak.

"I'll have to think about it." She finally said.

Every alarm in her body sounded. *What was she doing?* Autumn knew that allowing herself to be around this man could take her another step closer to Maylee. Despite the clear danger, letting a dirty cop take her out was an option that couldn't be ignored. Autumn was a stranger to herself, and the bravery was completely foreign. She wanted to stomp on the gas and speed away from this place, this man. Yet she didn't. Clear eye contact was made as she waited for him to make the next move.

"Erin, you won't regret it." Alex grinned as the fake name she'd given him spewed from his lips. "I actually have very good taste. Well, better than fast food anyway," he chuckled and tossed a thumb over his shoulder.

Autumn forced a smile accompanied with a short giggle. Her stomach lurched.

"Why don't you give me your number?" He asked.

Autumn's response was quick and sure, just as it would be any other time with any other man asking her out.

"That's also against my rules." She smiled. "But… give me yours, and like I said, I'll *think* about dinner."

"Sure yeah, do you have a pen?" He asked.

Autumn rummaged through the console being careful not to expose the pictures of Maylee or of Craig. She pulled out a blue pen and a torn piece of paper from an old envelope. She handed the utensils to him through the opened crack of her window.

He leaned against her car using the roof to write on. He was way too close for comfort. Autumn looked away from the half rolled down driver's window with his stomach smashed up against the glass of it. Her mind was racing. The elbow of his right arm was dangling down in front of the windshield while he wrote with the left. He had a small tattoo of a four leaf clover on his forearm. Autumn pulled out her phone and quickly snapped a picture. She set it back down on her lap just in time for him to lean back and hand the paper to her thru the window.

"Alex." She said the name as she looked at the paper.

"Yes ma'am," his voice was sweet.

"Okay then," She said back with another fake smile. "Now, if you'll excuse me I have to go."

After stepping back away from her window, the un-uniformed officer flashed her a full handsome grin and a small wave. Autumn waved back, rolled up her window, and as calmly as possible she threw her car into reverse. She could feel his eyes on her as she slowly pulled out of the parking lot and drove away.

"What the hell just happened?" She asked herself out loud.

Its official, she thought, *I'm in way over my head.* Danger surged through her, it was thrilling and terrifying all at once. Autumn wondered if this was the way Jeremy felt being undercover the whole time. The want and need to hate him faded some, as it merged into a fraction of understanding. She didn't have a clue of what to make of that strange yet exhilarating encounter.

How could this Alex guy's eyes be so friendly and his voice sound so kind if he was suspicious of her? Autumn was almost certain that he couldn't suspect her of a thing in regards to Josie's get away. Autumn had never been so nervous. Her veins buzzed and vision nearly blurred, yet for the first time ever her hands were steady. Confidence dug its way to her surface.

"This is it Maylee," Autumn whispered into thin air as she pulled onto the freeway. "I promised to find you, and I will. I swear to God I will."

Chapter Eight

Chance's rental car was sitting in the parking lot, parked right next to the only vacant space. Autumn pulled next to it and slid her own car into park.

"Please let Josie still be locked in my apartment." She looked up and whispered as she stepped out.

For the second time that morning Autumn was able to hurry past Jeremy's door undetected. A listening ear was alert as she passed, wondering if Chance was inside or if he would be waiting at her own place. Only silence was offered. Autumn entered her locked apartment slowly. There was still no sign of Chance, or of Jeremy. She let out a breath of relief, locked the door behind her, then quickly made her way to the bedroom to check on Josie.

Josie was fast asleep on the bed with a Nicholas Sparks novel slipping from her relaxed hand. The scars and bruises on her wrists were front and center. New and old, they mixed and mingled. Bearing the mark of a truly tortured woman through and through.

Autumn sighed before she walked over and placed a hand on Josie's shoulder. Instantly awakened, Josie jumped and scrambled backwards on the bed. Instinctively, she kicked her legs and shook her head in a panic. The fear in her eyes was completely unmistakable. No sound came out of her, no scream or squeal, only a gasp.

Almost as quickly as the fear had consumed her upon waking, she calmed at the site of Autumn's face. Josie's chest lifted and dropped as she struggled to calm her breath. Fear had become a common part of her life, and violent attacks upon waking was regular. The compassion in Autumn's eyes was the very unspoken comfort that she needed.

"Sorry to wake you honey, I know you need sleep, but we have a lot of work to do."

Autumn shrunk with guilt for waking her frightened guest. Josie needed some very serious therapy. She could desperately use some time to heal physically mentally and emotionally. Autumn very well knew that, but time was no luxury – not this day. Josie nodded her head slowly and winced at the effort to straighten her back.

As they made their way into the kitchen, the sound of voices from below them came into range. Autumn looked at Josie with a finger to her lips to keep her quiet. A small cement patio with a barbecue and a few fold up chairs sat directly beneath Autumn's kitchen window. They belonged to Jeremy and led to the sliding kitchen door of his apartment.

Autumn leaned a straining ear as close as possible to the window and listened carefully. Both Jeremy and Chance's voices were recognizable. They were accompanied by Lloyd and Aiden. Autumn motioned with her hand for Josie to join her. They eves dropped together, silently with eyes wide and hands held.

"What the fuck do you mean, she ran this morning?" Aiden demanded. "We let her get away on a very first night run without even knowing about it. No tail, no protection, no nothing! And now she still went back out this morning?"

"Yeah, she's getting brave." Lloyd mumbled.

"It's a good thing she's been shooting." Jeremy added.

"Is Lucas tailing her?" Aiden asked.

Autumn pictured Lucas, his giant frame and the way he waived his ring finger at her the day she moved in. There was no way he could have been the man Chance had spilled the beans about following her. He was way too large, he surely would have stood out, *right? Were all Jeremy's friends cops?* She wondered as the distinct feeling of betrayal thumped in her guts. With a pinched face, she tightened her grip on Josie's hands and tried to sift through the rest of their conversation.

"Yeah," Jeremy said, "Lucas stayed on the morning post. He called about fifteen minutes ago to report her getting out quicker than normal. She made it to the freeway safely, but she talked to Alex. He cornered her in her car."

"Alex?!" Aiden cussed. "That mother fucker. God, I wish we could pin something solid against him already." Aiden's voice dripped with heavy disdain. "I wonder what the hell he said to her."

"Yeah me too." Jeremy agreed.

"So where's Autumn now?" Aiden asked.

"I'm sure she'll be back any minute." Chance jumped in, "God, I hope she'll be ready to talk."

"Me too." Jeremy agreed again, but this time with a voice softened.

"So she knows then?" Lloyd asked. "Everything? I mean. About us?"

"Not everything." Jeremy said. "She doesn't know about Amy."

"Jesus." Aiden's voice was no longer irritated and impatient sounding. A sad underlining tone tainted his words. "How do we tell her bro?"

"I don't know." Jeremy answered his brother somberly. "There isn't really an easy way of say it. I mean keeping our sister's death a secret is big."

"Yeah," Aiden agreed. "I don't even like talking to each other about her. I can see why you didn't say anything. Especially to just a neighbor."

Autumn pinched her face and cringed at the dig.

"She's more than *just* a neighbor." Jeremy defended. "I should have at least mentioned Amy to her, especially when she told me about Maylee. They're just fucking alike, haven't you noticed that?"

A moment of silence offered Autumn the image of Aiden either nodding or shaking his head. She had no idea which, but the question gnawed itself around in circles inside her stomach. Her heart ached for Jeremy, no wonder he was so pushy with her before. The fact that he was standing up for her, and so obviously guilt stricken about his deception, even though he had no clue as to her eavesdropping meant something.

"We shouldn't have lied to her at all." Chance jumped in again.

"Do you want me to talk to her first?" Lloyd offered. "I mean, if it's too hard for you guys to tell her about Amy, I can do it, really."

"I don't know." Jeremy's voice clearly indicated that he was considering the offer. Aiden still had nothing else to say on the matter. "It's gunna' suck, but it really should probably be me who tells her. I mean, Autumn's a good person, a good friend, I've compromised her trust enough."

"We all have," Chance said.

"Yeah," agreed Lloyd, "I guess you're right. We should probably get inside and watch for her to get back. We wouldn't want her slipping past un-noticed again."

Autumn was lost, yet grateful that she'd been speeding on the way home. Being in such a hurry to get to Josie paid off. That little bit of insight on her boys at least gave her a glimpse of understanding. In a strange way she felt better, like they could actually be trusted. A light head shook back and forth in disbelief and confusion atop of Autumn's neck. *Jeremy and Aiden had a sister? Who was she?* And, *what about Lloyd and Lucas, could they really be trusted? How could there possibly be more secrets?* She forced her eyes from the kitchen linoleum and looked up at Josie.

Dampened tear streaked cheeks glistened from the brightness of the overhanging light above Josie's head. The swollen side of her face had healed some since the night before. It allowed her to open both eyes equally. Under all the bruising Josie was a beautiful girl. Autumn was curious at the cause of Josie's fresh tears, hoping that she'd be able to finally offer some useful insight.

"Amy," Josie whispered. "I knew her."

The air caught in Autumn's chest. She led Josie carefully to a seat at the table, and gently helped her to sit. Without letting go of Josie's hand, Autumn took a seat across from her and told her slowly and very clearly.

"We don't have much time. They're going to see my car and most likely be at the door very soon."

Josie only nodded, tears continued to stream down her face, but she didn't say a word. She couldn't do anything but agree with Autumn, and listen.

"We still don't know who we can trust. I need to talk to them before they come up here and find you. Okay?"

Josie's voice cracked as she forced a few words through the tears. "Let them come up. All of them."

"Are you sure?" Autumn questioned soft and cautiously.

"Yes," she whispered, "I need to do this."

Josie's tears subsided and she stared at the abundance of marks on her own arms. Amy's face followed by the still shot of Jessica from the news broadcast that morning flashed through her mind. She'd been close to Amy, very close. They spent months locked away together. Josie knew how close her friend had been to her family before she was forced from her home.

Aside from the men that killed her, Josie was the only person who knew everything that had happened to Amy. Josie owed it to her murdered friend to bring a little bit of closure to the brothers she'd heard so much about. A part of Josie felt as if she already knew both Jeremy and Aiden personally. Hearing their voices and knowing she'd have a chance to meet them felt surreal. Josie nodded slightly to herself trying to accept the whirlwind of everything Autumn's unexpected appearance had brought about. She then sucked in a lungful of oxygen, ignoring the still sharp pain in her ribs, and then let it back out slowly.

"I have to do this." She repeated.

Autumn could tell by the hesitation in Josie's eyes that there was much to talk about with Jeremy and Aiden, yet she didn't want them to push Josie any further than what she could handle. This was a very delicate situation, and Autumn knew exactly what she needed to do. She rounded the table and knelt before her tattered guest, continuing to hold hands gently.

"Josie." She spoke slowly. "Please, if you need a break then take one. They *are* police. They have to follow a certain protocol, and once you see them there's no turning back."

Josie nodded, a lone tear fell fresh.

Autumn continued quickly, "I'm going to tell them about you before I invite them up. But, I also have to do it before they invite themselves. I have to go right now. Okay?"

Josie responded with a simple, "'kay," and a sniffle.

"Take some coffee to my room and lay back down. I'll be back up in just a minute. I'll lock the door behind myself."

Autumn took the steps two at a time. She wasn't surprised to find Jeremy and Chance nearing the bottom of the stairwell. They were headed in her direction, walking shoulder to shoulder. Each of their faces wore grim somber expressions. Like a couple of teenagers ready to fess up to a parent after being busted skipping school.

Jeremy wore his jeans casually as usual, but Autumn's eyes were instantly drawn to the badge dangling around his neck by a thick silver chain. It looked good there, she noted, oddly enough it seemed to fit. Chance looked as dapper as ever. His clean cut charcoal tinted suit was tailored perfectly. Autumn's heart skipped a beat at the sight of him, just as it had the night before.

She stopped on the bottom step, feet frozen still to the concrete. *How the hell was she going to do this?* She wondered as the tears already stung at the corners of her eyes. As anxious as she felt, she could see the shame and sorrow in each of their faces. Chance had already come clean, but she was yet to break words with Jeremy.

The secret was out, he'd been lying and using her for weeks – pretending to be her friend. Yet, in light of the hideous act she was forced to display with the dirty cop Alex, partnered with the knowledge of Jeremy's sister, she just couldn't find the anger inside that she wanted so badly to have. There was only understanding and compassion in its place.

The men stopped before her, and Jeremy opened his mouth to speak. Before he had a chance to defend himself, or even voice an apology, Autumn stopped him on impulse.

She threw her arms around his neck in a deeply meaningful embrace and sobbed lightly. After an initial moment of shock and hesitation he wrapped his arms around her middle, accepting her swirl of forgiving emotions. An unspoken sigh of relief escaped his chest, and a ten pound weight was lifted. Autumn felt his chest sink from the release and held him tighter while he hung his head and buried his face into her shoulder and hair. She sniffled, then quickly and consciously forced a little composure. Then she spoke softly into his ear.

"Can we go back to your place to talk? Instead of mine?"

Jeremy pulled her out of the embrace, but continued to hold her by the shoulder with one large reassured palm. The other hand was used to wipe away a drop of embarrassing moisture from his cheek. He then took a look at the wetness on his fingertips with a disappointed smirk and shook his head in disbelief.

"Fuck, I'm glad you're not mad at me Autumn."

"I never said I wasn't mad." She corrected graciously, "I just understand. That's all." Then she sniffled again and wiped her face clean too.

"I can't believe I just cried... like some baby." He added.

Chance intervened by offering Jeremy a brute slap on the shoulder.

"Don't worry about it man, she had the same effect on me last night. Your secret's safe."

Autumn chuckled despite herself, and took a long suggestive look at Chance. There was so much to be said. Their unexpected phone relationship had grown into something. There was an unexpected connection between the two, and now that the air was cleared of any secrecy, Autumn felt the want for him all the way into her bones. He was over a foot taller than her, and those sharp unmerciful eyes of his drilled into her soul. Suddenly, she was again very acutely aware of his scent – that fresh musky smell that she'd been dreaming about. The one that made her chest thump and her knees buckle.

"We have a lot to talk about." She said before placing her fingers intimately into his.

The interlocking of their hands fit, it was nice and comforting on both ends. For the first time in weeks Chance felt at ease. Despite the situation at hand,

and being so far away from his home, he felt like he was in the right place. He was determined to help Autumn. They were finally on the same page, and would be able to work together. He wanted so badly to find Maylee, to heal every pain that Autumn had ever had to endure.

Jeremy soon opened the door to his apartment allowing his guests to shuffle past and make themselves comfortable. At first the conversation was light and awkward, but after a few moments of beating around the bush, Jeremy finally swallowed his nerves and began telling Autumn about Amy.

Autumn reached up to accept a framed photo of Amy. Aiden passed it to her without removing his gaze from the carpet. He'd avoided any sort of eye contact since she came in. Unlike Lloyd, who was the first to greet her at the door, sporting his official title proudly around his neck to match Jeremy's. Autumn noticed immediately the difference in the two.

Lloyd's decoration sported the word 'Lead' and his step had a particular bounce to it. It was as if a cloud of freedom was following him around amidst the open honesty. Once Jeremy went into the details of his sister, Lloyd jumped in to explain to Autumn how he'd been leading up a secret undercover division in Denver for nearly two years. He'd handpicked Jeremy and Aiden to join his team a few weeks after Amy went missing. She was found dead shortly after.

As far as the local department was concerned the brothers had quit their positions as ranking officers and decided to live out their day to day lives apart from law enforcement. Lloyd was completely at ease spilling the beans to Autumn about the details of the operation. He'd been observing her, and admired her love and dedication to Maylee. If it were up to him completely, then he would have clued her in at least a week sooner, but the crew found it best to work together and vote in such a decision. Lloyd even wiggled onto the couch making sure to wedge himself between Autumn and Jeremy.

Autumn found herself sandwiched between Lloyd and Chance without an ounce of breathing room. In a way it was comforting. All questions about Lloyd were quickly put to rest. She listened closely to the order of ranking in the crew and even more carefully to the details of Amy. Aiden, on the other hand seemed very off. The way he paced the floor while Jeremy explained Amy's murder to Autumn was unsettling.

"She was found by an abandoned building, next to a dumpster." Jeremy explained quietly. "She had been raped, starved, severely beaten, and there was a substantial amount of heroin in her system."

"Oh my God." Autumn whispered. "I'm so sorry."

In the photo Amy wore a yellow summer dress and her kind innocent eyes illuminated happiness. She looked gorgeous, standing in a field of tall grass with blue skies ahead. Jeremy was right, they did look a lot alike. Autumn felt like she was staring into a mirror, fifteen years earlier. Thoughts of Maylee was suddenly suffocating. The words 'raped', 'heroin', 'starved', and 'beaten' jabbed into Autumn like a knife to the chest. She held onto the hope that Maylee may have been seen alive so recently. Autumn could hardly fathom such brutality, and imagining those things happening to her own niece was overwhelming.

She swallowed the lump in her throat. It was finally time to work together. There was so much to do, and time was ticking. Autumn felt like everything was coming to a head, and if they didn't act fast then it would continue to escalate until the top blew off causing another major catastrophe.

A fresh, sickening premonition was building within Autumn. There was a reason she went into Craig's house the night before. She knew that as a fact, and felt the truth of it deep in her bones. Something big was going to happen, very soon, and uncovering Josie was only the beginning.

"I have a secret, too."

Every eye in the room suddenly snapped up in Autumn's direction. Even Aiden, for the first time since she walked in was giving her his complete and utter attention. His brows pulled up in the middle with concern and the corners of his lips pulled downward. With an unwavering glare, Aiden held his breath waiting for Autumn to finish the start of her confession.

Chance put a warm hand on her knee, the tips of his fingers melting slightly between her thighs. The comforting intention of his touch was felt in her entire body. Her core heated, and her chest pulsated. *God, it was all too much.* Autumn didn't know if him being there was helpful or distracting.

The anxiety of what lay ahead, mixed with the fear for Maylee and Josie, added to the powerful pull she felt to the man at her side. His touch was exhilarating, and there was nothing to be done about it until everything else around was handled. Autumn's mind snapped back to Josie, almost as quickly as Chance's touch had pulled it away.

"Last night. Something happened."

"What do you mean, something?" Chance urged.

"I. I." Autumn hesitated.

The attempt to say Josie's name out loud felt like a betrayal. Even if Josie did agree to this, and to go as far as the request to talk to Jeremy and Aiden. They were still cops, just like Alex. No matter how much Autumn trusted them, the future held nothing but question for Josie. The need to protect Josie was strong. Autumn felt responsible for her.

"Autumn," Lloyd spoke smoothly in a comforting tone. "It's okay. We want what you want. Now that you know who we are, just let us help you."

"A girl." Autumn finally found her voice. "I found a girl."

Jeremy jumped to his feet.

"And you're just barely telling us? Autumn, what the Hell?!" He demanded.

Autumn's heart stopped at the suddenly tense feeling that washed over the room. It felt like the air had been sucked out of the apartment with a vacuum hose.

"Where?" Aiden questioned angrily, "Who? Was she alive?"

"Please sit down." Autumn insisted.

She tried with everything she had to make her voice calm. She knew they would panic, that was the whole point on warning them all before tossing Josie at them like food for a pack of hungry wolves.

"She's okay. But before I tell you anything else, you all need to calm down and let me explain."

After a moment of contemplation, Jeremy resumed his previous place on the couch next to Lloyd. Aiden remained at a stand, but the expression on his face smoothed some. An antsy foot tapped on the floor, and he folded his large muscular arms over his chest. The red tint of his cheeks lightened some as he unloaded a lung full of anxiety.

"Well," Aiden pushed, still refusing to sit. "Spill the beans, Autumn. Hopefully it isn't too late for this one too, yeah?"

He waved a suggestive hand toward his sisters picture, and suddenly Autumn got it. She understood Aiden's root of strange behavior. He wasn't spiteful, he was grieving. Autumn knew firsthand the strange things people do, and the odd reactions they have when losing loved ones. She felt a ping of Aiden's pain, and held nothing against him for treating her like an outsider.

"Like I said. She's okay, and I know where she is now. I'll tell you everything, but you have to promise to listen to me before storming out."

Autumn straightened her back, and waited for a response from the four burly detectives surrounding her. Responsibility sat heavily on her shoulders, and she wasn't going to let Josie down. Or Maylee, for that matter.

Autumn needed to reach a hand inside herself and grab hold of that strength she knew was in there somewhere. The same strength that she was able to conjure up when she pulled Josie out of that crack house of pain. The bravery she used that morning when she'd forced herself to accept a phone number from a very man that had tortured Josie, and possibly even Maylee. The thought made her insides tighten.

"Okay?" She asked an octave louder, staring directly at Aiden.

Aiden nodded his head slightly, and raised his brows in disbelief. He waved an arm in front of his middle, allowing it to sweep through the air in defeat. Then he flopped himself into his chair and said somewhat sarcastically.

"Proceed."

And, so she did.

Meanwhile, Josie took Autumn's advice and laid back down in the bedroom to relax her sore body while she waited. Thoughts of Amy, Jessica, Mary, Maylee, and all the other tortured girls danced circles in her haunted mind. She recalled the stories Amy used to tell her about her brothers. Aiden and Jeremy, Amy's brothers who she was certain would save them all. Amy had so much faith in her family, insisting that despite the other cops and political leaders who had harmed them, that not all law enforcement was in on it. Amy assured Josie time and time again that they would come to the rescue any day, and to never lose faith.

The first time Josie had escaped the clutches of Craig and his abusive thugs, she went straight to the local department. She followed Amy's encouragement and asked specifically for either Jeremy or Aiden, only to be informed that they'd quit after Amy went missing. At the time it all finally made sense to Josie, and the harsh truth of it all bashed into her like a swinging bat connecting to a solid surface.

Amy's murder was an act of revenge. It was personal, and much harsher than the usual treatment of the girls. It wasn't until Josie was tucked into a hospital bed the day after her first escape months earlier, being guarded by an officer by the name of Alex, that the real motive behind Amy's murder came out. Josie lay in Autumn's bed and let the memory of that terrible day consume her.

Other than beeping monitors the room was quiet. Clean pastel walls surrounded her, and through the small window in the door Josie could see the backside of a policeman's uniform, as he was stationed to guard her. It was an hour after visiting hours had closed. Only her family had been notified of her location, and there was yet to be any kind of news briefing in regards to her return home after the abduction so long before. The nurse on rotation to take care of Josie for the night had just made his rounds, so Josie was expecting nothing but peace and quiet to sleep and heal. Unfortunately, what she got was the exact opposite.

The door to Josie's hospital room creaked open and the officer slipped inside, locking the door behind himself. His face was familiar, but she couldn't quite place where she'd seen him before. *Was it before the abduction, during, or even in the previous twenty hours of chaos upon her return?* Josie wasn't sure, but she did know she'd seen his face, and the question of it made her instantly freeze in the bed. A white hot chill moved from her toes to her fingertips.

His eyes smiled from his cheeks. It was an eerie excited look. There was nothing caring or protective about him. Even the way his sure steps moved across the floor, slow and precise rang predatory. Suddenly, she remembered. Josie knew exactly why his face was familiar. He'd been there when Amy died. He played a part in her murder – a big part.

Alex eased himself to a sit on Josie's hospital bed. With his body brushing up against hers he leaned over her, pinning her down with one arm. His other arm was used to slowly pull the warm comforting blanket away from her body, and open the side of her gown. Josie closed her eyes tightly with her entire face pinched. A nervous heart pounded in her chest and the air pulling into her lungs struggled to flow, with short choppy breaths.

She couldn't try to run, or even scream out. Josie knew exactly what would happen to her should she defy him. If not right then, it would be later. She would pay dearly for the escape as it was, but a second attempt to get out of the clutches of the very man who offered the final blow that ultimately took Amy's life, could easily mean the same fate for herself.

As Alex slid his hands from her breasts, to belly, then below her panties, he breathed hot air against her neck. Forceful fingers pushed inside Josie violently, then he closed them into a tight fist. It pinched her painfully, and as she gasped he squeezed harder. With a clenched fist the uniformed officer grabbed ahold of Josie by the core. Then he smiled a full toothed grin, only inches from her face.

"You remember me, don't you?"

Josie remained stiffened, her entire body clenched in pain, and every inch of her face was strained. Violently, she nodded with neck and shoulders tense.

"Good," he whispered.

Then he broke way for the washing sink with a disgusted look on his face before moving to the window. The glass was lifted allowing a breeze to flow through the air. It caused a chill to spread the surface of Josie's now exposed skin.

"Craig will be here any minute. It's cool enough out for his trench coat. So you'll be a good girl and hide inside. Unless you want to go out like your friend. It's your choice."

Chapter Nine

The way Josie was able to steady her voice, and get through the details of Amy's, helped Autumn to see her in a new light. Since the risky move in taking her home the night before, Autumn had seen Josie as merely a victim. With every word flowing from Josie's swollen lips, and with every pained tensing around her bruised eye. Autumn's perception of Josie grew to something wholesome and real. Strength and perseverance suddenly shined through.

Respect and admiration filled the emptied, questionable cracks of Autumn's perspective. Josie had withstood more than any woman should be forced through. She had every reason in the world to crawl in a hole and die, never to be seen or spoken to again. Yet, here she was… Josie was bearing witness to the heinous murder of her dear friend, and to the dead girl's family nonetheless.

After all the disgusting, painful, and even humiliating acts Josie had undergone, she was still willing to take a risk in a room full of men she'd never met, and had no reason to believe or trust aside from the hope of delivering justice. *And, at what cost?*

Autumn watched Jeremy and Aiden slump lower and lower at the shoulders, listening in defeat. Autumn prayed silently that Maylee had the same inner strength as Josie. Given Maylee's upbringing there was hope. After telling the details of Amy's death, Josie moved onto the details of her second abduction, the time she was slipped out of a hospital window. Autumn froze stiff the second Alex's name floated into the air.

Autumn tightened her grip on Chance's hand and their eyes met as a result. Chance recognized the name from his conversation with the boys earlier. He was well aware that Autumn had been approached by Alex, but they were yet to discuss the conversation. The shade of Jeremy's face lightened and even his lips suddenly looked to have a lifeless dulling to the tint. They all remained quiet and let Josie talk.

"After I was finished with my punishment from Big Braun, my owner, I was sent to stay in that basement. Alex was put in charge of me until my next trip to the healing house to be sold again. Big Braun said that I didn't deserve to stay in his house after my escape. He said that he was finished with me and that whoever bought me next wouldn't take it as easy on me as he had."

"What was your punishment?" Aiden finally croaked through the tears.

Josie hung her head forward in shame, and spoke in a mere whisper.

"I was hung by my wrists and ankles for days. Every man in the operation took their turn beating me with a cane, and they made all of the other girls watch. I was made into an example."

The bowels in Autumn's stomach knotted and the sickness she had the night before threatened to return full force.

"Who is Big Braun?" Lloyd asked softly.

"I don't know his real name," Josie explained. "That's all I've ever heard him called. Us girls weren't allowed to address him at all, or even make eye contact. We were usually drugged around him, and forced to keep our mouths shut, no matter what."

"Can you explain what he looks like?" Jeremy asked somberly with a straight face and eyes glued on the carpet a few feet in front of him.

"He's short and stout, maybe in his late forties or early fifties. He has red hair with a bald spot on top."

"I've seen him!" Autumn jumped in.

All eyes snapped up to look at her.

"This morning. He was at Craig's house."

"Lucas did mention a new face at the house today. He must've been there because of your escape." Lloyd said as he turned his attention back to Josie.

Lloyd reached a comforting hand over to touch Josie's but she jumped and pulled away. Her shoulders tensed with the fear of his touch. He understood her jumpiness and set his hand back into his own lap discreetly. Then he nodded to himself and drew in a deep breath before speaking.

"Guys, I think this young lady needs to rest. She has talked enough for right now and should lay down and get comfortable. Aiden and Jeremy, I think you two deserve a breather too after hearing about Amy."

"No." Aiden jumped in. "I'm not taking a break until that mother fucker Alex is behind bars or dead."

"Me either," Jeremy insisted. "He was my partner, how didn't I see it? I'm not stepping away now. Not today!"

"I'm sorry," Josie whispered with a new round of tears beginning to well. "I loved Amy. Her memory and faith in you guys has kept me going all this time. Alex told me her death was revenge, because you stiffed him with a new guy. Her life meant nothing to him, to any of them. I'm so sorry."

Jeremy thanked her and then excused himself to the bathroom. He had to blow some steam alone, and no one could blame him. They all sat in silence and listened as he beat an angry fist against the bathroom countertop a room over. Autumn thought of everything else they had to go over.

The pictures, her conversation with Alex, she hadn't even told them the license plate number. The picture she had taken of Alex's arm was probably pointless, yet she still needed to share all the information possible. If nothing else they could use it I court, God willing they got that far. Autumn didn't want to push it as Josie had just spilled so much information about her only friend's sister.

There was so much to do, and so much to talk about, Autumn didn't even know where to start. Rather than jumping right into the day's tasks ahead, Autumn offered to help Josie back to her bedroom to get some rest. Rightly so, Josie's hands were shaking even more violently from the start of a withdrawal. Her vision was beginning to blur, and her breath was starting to hyperventilate. Josie accepted Autumn's help gratefully, and leaned into the support of her body.

After Josie was settled in Autumn's room with a tall glass of ice water and some minor pain killers, the team set to work. They weren't all in agreement on what to do with Josie, but after her last experience at a hospital, they opted to let her stay there where she was comfortable, and let the withdrawing pass in waves under the team's own supervision. Jeremy took it upon himself to volunteer to stay within arm's reach of her at all times.

No matter the tasks ahead, or what members of their undercover team was in and out, he'd help Josie and protect her. Jeremy felt like he owed her much more. This is where he was needed the most, and if nothing else he would protect her in Amy's name. Bringing Josie water and holding her hair when she inevitably puked and ceased from withdrawal was the least he could do.

Lloyd and Chance worked shoulder to shoulder setting a plan into motion, they made a great team. Autumn admired their dedication, and was shocked to sit in and listen to all of the details Chance had memorized about the missing girls involved, as well as Craig and the other 'muscle', or so he called them. He was even able to identify the names of the girls in the photos Autumn had stolen, just from a glance at their faces. He knew everything about these girls. From the dates and locations they were abducted, to the color of clothing they had on the last time they were seen.

The team set up a research station in Autumn's apartment. Lucas showed up with all of the equipment they could possibly need and more. His muscular arms were on full display as he packed in tables, chairs, a couple of boxes filled with paperwork, laptops, and a printer.

There was a lot to do and little time to do it in. The team needed Jeremy to work his magic with the database, and he refused to leave Josie's side. This alone was enough to dub Autumn's apartment as the new main location for the case work. Autumn's map was soon pulled down and replaced with a cork board just as large.

Along the bottom of the board, each photographed girl was pinned up next to the missing person photos turned in by their families upon their abductions. They were lined up in order by the dates they went missing cross referenced with geographical location. Above the girls where photos of Craig and the other two 'muscles'. Autumn's strings came in handy as they were used to tie which girls were taken by what men.

Autumn fetched the men drinks and snacks and for the most part she tried to stay quiet and out of their way. She observed them, mostly Chance. The way the men addressed each other was an admirable mix of casual, yet professional. Previous to this day Autumn had only seen the joking side of her boys. Jeremy, Aiden, Lloyd, and Lucas laughed and teased one another to no end. They were at ease and knew every quirk the others had. Lucas would mimic Lloyd's laugh and once in a while he'd even replicate the exact snort that sounds from the back of his nose.

This day was different. Much different. Autumn watched closely and admired the professionalism in them while they worked. Although, they were still just as utterly comfortable with each other, they seemed to speak a whole different language. Each detective filling the space of her apartment complimented another. They searched database after database, cross referencing and searching for any kind of link between addresses, names, families, political ties, professions, and even the license plate number Autumn had memorized.

Unfortunately, all they could come up with was one dead end after another. The human trafficking ring they were dealing with was smart. They covered their tracks. There was only one card trick left in the deck and it was one that no one seemed to agree on. Autumn knew what she had to do, and it was all a matter of convincing the men to allow it. Chance and Lloyd refused to let her do it, but Autumn was determined. After a couple hours of persistence and failures in linking numbers or clues to Big Braun's face, Autumn had no choice but to put her foot down.

"I'm calling him." She announced.

Lloyd shook his head at her, knowing exactly what she was talking about, but turned his attention back to his laptop just as quickly. They were blowing off her attempts to help in the only way that would actually make a difference. Their lack of faith after everything she had brought them so far was starting to get to her. Autumn understood if it wasn't for her, Craig would still be flying under the radar, and Josie would still be tied up in that nasty basement. Enough was enough.

"Would you ass holes just listen to me!?"

Autumn shouted over the sound of typing fingers, and brainstorming conversations. The room stilled, and for the first time since Autumn revealed Josie's existence, she had the detectives complete and utter attention.

"We all know that the only way to get anything accomplished is going to have to be through this Alex creep! Would you all just give me some fucking credit and let me do this? For Maylee!"

Chance jumped in first with a hesitant stutter, "Autumn I, I, I don't think…"

"Don't even start," She interrupted. "As far as I've came and as much danger as you dipshits have let me throw myself into without even knowing who the hell you all were, there is no way you are going to hold me back now!"

"He saw you running when Josie escaped them, Autumn." Jeremy said, "you don't know what this guy is capable of. I know him better than anyone here, and he's dangerous. If he suspects you then the whole thing could be a trap."

Autumn sighed in defeat. What Jeremy was saying rang true on every level, but in the big picture made no difference. Her meeting Alex may be their only choice, so she had to try. If Maylee was really seen with Craig, then Autumn had to take the risk. No more time could be wasted.

"I'm the only person here that has a chance of getting to this guy, now please let me try." She pleaded.

"He's a cop Autumn!" Jeremy was getting angrier and angrier by the minute. "He notices things. That's what he's trained to do. He approached you for a reason, and it wasn't just because he wanted to take you on a damn date!"

The sound of a timid clearing of a voice squeezed its way into the kitchen. Autumn and Jeremy stopped their argument before it had a chance to escalate at the sight of her. Josie leaned against the wall with a hand on the back of a chair to steady her balance. The swelling of her eye had gone down immensely, but the bold color of its bruising stood prominent against the shade of her increasingly pale skin. Shaking knees struggled to hold her weight, and her voice was all but gone. Clearly the withdrawals from whatever drugs Alex kept her pumped full of was taking over every part of her.

Autumn and Jeremy both rushed to her, with one on each side, they gently helped her to sit on the loveseat. This was the first time Josie had emerged from Autumn's room in over an hour, and with each appearance she looked worse.

"You have to let her." Josie whispered, hardly able to speak through the shaking of her voice.

"No," Jeremy shook his head, yet his face had melted from anger to worry. "I can't let him around anyone else. I can't."

"Neither can we." Chance agreed, backing him completely.

Autumn rolled her eyes. She was just as frightened as everyone else at the circumstance, or worse. Yet, she saw it as an opportunity – one that they couldn't afford to pass up.

"Don't you think they would have found me by now?" Josie questioned with pleading eyes. "I mean, if he suspected her, he would have followed her here. He wouldn't have let her go so easy. If Alex actually believed that Autumn had anything to do with me, I'd be dead already."

"She's right." Aiden agreed. "Alex is smart, but one thing he isn't is patient. You know that, Jeremy. He's never been one to sit and wait."

Lloyd dragged a fold up chair across the floor. Directly across from Jeremy on the loveseat, he straddled the back of his seat. His arms folded in front of himself as he leaned on the chair's frame for support. He and Jeremy stared deeply into one another's eyes yet neither of them spoke.

The moment was intense. Aiden watched the stare down from a foot away, waiting with his arms folded across his chest. Chance could do nothing but bow his head to the floor, and kneed his temples with his thumbs. Chance knew what was coming, and he knew there was nothing to be done in protest. Autumn was right, and so was Josie.

"Fuck, alright." Jeremy finally cracked. "But I swear to God, if anything happens to her, Lloyd it's on you!"

Lloyd nodded in agreement. "You're right about that."

* * *

Autumn stood in front of her closet in a towel, rummaging through her clothes. *What the hell do you wear to a black tie date with a crooked cop?* She'd just taken the fastest shower of her life, shaving her legs at a record speed, and had twisted and pinned her hair to the crown of her head in waves of tight ringlets. The phone call to Alex had been nerve testing. He'd sounded excited to hear from her and wanted to prove that he had better taste than take-away tacos. He'd told her that he had the night off, and would love to take her to a country club if she was available on such short notice. After playing it cool and trying her best at quick witted flirting over the phone she agreed.

Josie was encouraging, and she informed them that Alex would never take her to such a high-end, public-figure type of place if he'd expected her to have any kind of involvement, and especially not if he was setting her up. Jeremy and Aiden agreed to the logic and were able to relax some once the evening's events were put into play.

Autumn found a dress that would reveal just enough, yet still be able to hide the wire they'd be concealing underneath. She'd also be wearing a necklace embedded with a small camera. The plan was in place, and Lloyd contacted a few more detectives that Autumn was yet to meet. It was a risk that she was completely uncomfortable with, but they had no choice. Jeremy assured her that he'd been working with them for a very long time, and he trusted them completely.

Jeremy and Aiden explained to Autumn that these men stay separated from the crew for a reason, and that they'd also never been a part of the local department. They were a separate division of undercovers, investigating drug trafficking and they only collaborate with Lloyd when needed, as both organizations are often intertwined. In order to maintain complete discretion, all uniformed officers are kept in the dark as to their identity. These men had also been watching Alex for some time in the drug business, and he was yet to figure them out. The men would be able to go unnoticed inside the club with ease. The news was only somewhat reassuring.

Two of the new men were to stay parked down the street from the club and listen in. They'd be close enough and prepared at all times to enter the club if needed. Two more would stay inside the building and sip drinks in the bar to keep a closer eye out for familiar faces and anything out of the ordinary. Lloyd and Chance played their lead roles well, as they plotted, strategically placed men, and prepared plans to execute in all possible scenarios. Autumn was impressed and although she was scared out of her mind, she was as ready as she'd ever be.

Three years of doing nothing was too long, and it was finally time for Autumn to fight back and do her part in finding Maylee. This opportunity was a sharp edged knife, digging into Autumn and forcing her to put herself in a place she never dreamed of being brave enough to enter. All caution was thrown out the window, and she was beside herself. Trudging ahead in the skin of a woman she no longer recognized.

The dress she chose was shoved in the back of her closet amongst a bunch of items that she hadn't worn in years. She recalled packing her things for the move and debating on whether or not to throw it out. Thankfully she'd decided against it. For this date, it was a perfect fit, as it was made of stretchy enough material that it would still fit after losing so much weight. Autumn considered herself to be a bit of a hoarder when it came to clothing, and she liked to dress for 'the mood' as she called it. For the first time in her life the attachment she had for attire collecting came in handy.

Josie was fast asleep on Autumn's bed, so she moved around her room as quietly as possible. As she pulled the little black shrink-to-fit dress out of its plastic dry clean bag, she recalled buying it. A large grin formed across her face at the thought, and she shook her head in disbelief of the innocence of her memory. Autumn lay the dress out on the bottom corner of her bed, a few inches from Josie's toes, and allowed herself to drift off in thought to a previously carefree time.

When Autumn bought this dress, she'd been out for an afternoon friend date at a small coffee shop, just a few blocks down the road from work. On the walk back they'd been laughing and joking about how every girl needed that perfect little black dress, even if she never actually wore it. Randomly enough, as they were joking about the matter, they passed the window of a dress shop with the absolute perfect 'numbers' hanging on mannequins for display. They'd squealed and ran into the store to try the dresses on at the mere sight of them. Autumn chuckled at the memory.

Autumn let her towel drop to the floor, she slipped on her possible, as she called them, and a robe. After sliding the dress from is bag and folding it carefully over an arm, she quietly exited the bedroom. Thankfully, Josie was finally in a deep enough sleep to let her body heal rather than convulse in withdrawal. Autumn hoped that she'd sleep through the evening, at least until she got back from her date. *If she got back from her date.* The air caught in her throat at the question, and she forced herself to choke back the rising fear along with all the *ifs* that seemed to be taking over her thought process.

Autumn poked her head around the living room corner to inform the men she was ready for them to help with the wire before she put on her dress. She'd never seen so many men blush at once as they looked around at each other in embarrassment. Autumn smiled and rolled her eyes assuming they'd all done it a dozen times, yet because it was her things were different.

"Chance, do you mind?"

The pink hue of his cheeks was adorable. The shade faded and he flashed Lloyd a triumphant grin before looking back at her. As Chance followed Autumn into the bathroom he noticed a small birthmark on the back of her neck, at the base of her hair line. It was tiny and in the shape of a heart. The way her hair was swept up showcasing the mark, caused a lump to form in his throat and his heart to drum harder in his chest. He closed the door behind them and stared at her, mesmerized.

The room was small, allowing him to take in the lingering scent of her previous shower. Lavender shampoo floated around the still humid air, and her vanilla bean body butter made him weak at the knees. She stood a mere foot in front of him with a full length body mirror behind her. He could see the birthmark in the mirror, peaking out at him from the neckline of her soon to be removed robe. He swallowed hard, and fiddled nervously with the wire in his hands, amazed that a woman could actually make him so nervous.

"Well this isn't exactly how I imagined taking my clothes off for you the first time, but I guess it will do."

She chuckled nervously, and he twitched between the legs in response.

Autumn stood before Chance and fiddled with the opening of her rob, exposing the base of her cleavage. Her attempt to make a joke of the situation didn't work. Nervousness still consumed every part of her, coursing through her veins like an electrical current, and his failure to laugh at the humor didn't help. Chance stood wide-eyed and stiff as he stared at her.

After a few awkward quiet moments that seemed like a lifetime, he finally forced his feet to take the small step necessary to close the short distance between them. Body heat radiated, their chests brushed against one another, and he could feel the rise and fall of her breath.

"Everything about you is perfect."

He whispered into her lips just before planting a soft kiss on them. His warm hands slid the robe off of her shoulders and it landed on the floor in a heap. One hand gently touched the base of her neck, and the other glided slowly down her silky skin and stopped to rest on the smallest curve of her back. He pressed his forehead against hers and closed his eyes softly. Breathing her in, wanting to claim her as his own.

Autumn finally relaxed, like softened putty in his arms, she melted in the chest. He reluctantly pulled away, and took a deep look into her eyes. Then he pulled her back close, took a satisfying look at her entire body from behind in the mirror and whispered in her ear.

"I can't wait for tonight, when I can have you to myself."

Soft kisses were planted all along her neckline. Autumn could feel the heat from his body against her exposed flesh. She was drawn to him now more than ever, and he couldn't bear the thought of leaving him to meet up with another man. Such a dangerous man at that.

Chance strategically placed the wire to Autumn's inner thigh and hip, up her abdomen, and underneath the base of her bra line. With each stick of a tape strip he continued to kiss his way down her collarbone and tickle his fingers across the surface of her skin. Autumn's legs nearly buckled beneath her at the feel of his soft mouth and curious hands.

As soon as the equipment was in place on her body, their lips again met. This kiss was much more passionate. Their tongues moved in a natural rhythm of its own, a fitting tune, utterly in sync. Chance reached his hands down behind Autumn to pick her up at the thighs. With an equal mix of grace and power he lifted her to the counter allowing her to wrap her legs around his waist.

Autumn moaned quietly into his mouth, she wanted to feel him inside of her – every inch of him. Yet, she was acutely aware of the abundance of people in her apartment, along with the lack of time. Chance was also painfully in tune to the situation. He wanted their first time together to be perfect. He wanted to take his time, and to please her the way a woman deserves to be pleased.

No sooner than their bodies pressed together with her legs squeezing him around the middle, he pulled away from the kiss. With foreheads touching they caught their breath. Her chest touching his with each rise and fall.

"If we kiss again now, I don't think I can stop." He whispered.

"Me either." She admitted while tightening her grip on his belt.

"I guess we better hurry, we don't have much time."

Chance helped her down from the countertop and straightened his baby blue button up, that was rolled at the elbows. Then he tousled his hair and watched her slip on her dress. After pulling the back zipper together for her and double checking that the wire was completely concealed, Chance brushed the birthmark on the back of her neck with one last kiss and left the room.

Autumn looked herself over in the mirror. Before her stood what appeared to be a confident beautiful woman, yet on the inside her nerves were doing somersaults in the pit of her stomach. They stomped on her guts violently, and pounded on her chest. She noticed her own fiddling fingers and made a mental note to stay conscious of them. *Don't fidget and pick at your nails, Autumn,* she thought. Whatever that was that just happened with Chance she wanted more of, and inserting herself into the unknown on a date with a violent killer had her in a state.

Autumn closed her eyes and let out a long sigh before sliding on her favorite pair of toeless black stilettos. She stood tall once more to admire the woman staring back at her. A strong frame, dark hair, and thick makeup made it hard for Autumn to see herself through the disguise of this beauty. It was a good thing, and it gave her a confidence boost. A sensual slit up the side of her dress reached mid-thigh. It exposed her long, firm, and very tan right leg.

"This is your chance, Autumn. You can do it." She told the stranger in the mirror before walking out to meet her fate.

Lloyd was the first to break the awkward silence and drop-jawed faces.

"You look great Autumn. Are you ready?" he asked.

Autumn held her head high and looked over to Chance and then Jeremy before nodding her head in agreement. She grabbed a small black handbag embedded with jewels that she had sitting by the door. It contained only a small amount of cash, her phone, and minimal makeup incase the need for touch up should occur. Any form of identification was left behind, just in case.

Chapter Ten

A private drive twisted and swirled up a hillside on the northern outskirts of the city. One side of the road overlooked the twinkling lights of Denver in the dark. The view was stunning, but it wasn't until the actual building came to view that it took Autumn's breath away.

It was a three story building, and made almost entirely of giant open windows. The men and women inside on the second floor were visible from the Valette drop. It was an elaborate dance floor, and the dressy couples inside spun and moved in rhythm. Autumn stepped out of her car and glanced around at the abundance of Valet men who were climbing in and out of Ferraris, Porsches, and Audis. It made Autumn miss her old car. She looked at her sedan as she closed the door and sighed.

This was certainly a classy place, and it made her wish she could experience it with Chance. She slipped her keys to a young man with a silver bow tie and a friendly smile. In return he handed her a ticket, then gave her a small wink and held his hand out, leading her toward the building. He walked her up to the first step, kissed her hand, and then turned back to her car. Autumn didn't wait by the large glass door long.

A small herd of very young attractive women made their way past her. They giggled with excitement and anticipation for the night ahead. Although their perky pushed up breasts, and youthful glowing faces reminded Autumn of her age, she refused to compare herself to the young tarts. Autumn felt more at home dressed up and ready to sip wine at a five star club than she ever did running the streets of Denver's not so finest. She straightened her back and reminded herself of the shape she was in. The beautiful and confident image of herself in the mirror before she left her apartment swirled in her mind.

The dress Autumn had on was far sexier and a much better fit than any of the dresses the naive young women around her was wearing, which was also a giant confidence booster. Her age only added season to her perfection. She stood tall awaiting her date, and she looked around until she spotted him stepping out of a brand-new Cadillac.

It was freshly waxed and the wheels were shined. Autumn let her held breath out slowly and turned the position of her body so that her necklace was pointed directly at him. With the intent of giving the men behind a screen down the road a good view of him.

Alex looked up at her and grinned. He handed his keys to the Valet and all but skipped over to her.

"Wow Erin, you look delicious."

"Thank you." She winced on the inside.

Autumn made a conscious effort to smile from her eyes as he slid an arm around the small of her back to guide her inside. Thought of that same hand violating Josie at the hospital screamed at her from the back of her mind. She let her eyes wander to the dressy loafers laced on his feet, the same feet used to stomp the life out of Amy. Autumn could feel his eyes looking down the length of her body as they walked. It made her feel violated and uncomfortable, like a slab of meat cut to perfection. But, she hid it well and leaned into him with smile.

"I'm glad you decided to call me," he announced.

They moved slowly past a tall lady in black dress slacks, welcoming guests. The woman had checked the couple before them for a membership, but with Alex she only smiled, letting him pass as a well-known and welcomed guest.

"So, what do you think of the place?" he asked. "I told you I had class."

He bragged as he swept a hand around them to advertise. The room was enough to bring any poor girl to her knees. Even Autumn had only seen a few places that compared in beauty. The ceilings were tall and covered in paintings. The floors were marble and there were giant beams randomly placed throughout the mostly open space with carvings of dancing couples to decorate the length of them. They were holding up the ceiling, and strategically placed between dozens of sparkling chandeliers. The entire scene was absolutely gorgeous, and nearly took the breath from Autumn. The music playing was classical and soft.

"It's really nice." She smiled trying her hardest to hide the growing anxiety that seemed to be spreading through every inch of her body.

"Shall we start with a drink?" he asked.

"That sounds perfect. It's been awhile since I've dressed up like this for a date, excuse me if I'm a little nervous."

Autumn hoped that if she made up an excuse for her nerves right off the bat, then he may overlook them later. She didn't want to worry about stumbling on her words or getting jumpy. He smiled a big toothy grin as if he was proud of himself. The lie seemed to have fooled him, unless he was really just *that* good an actor, she thought. He was after all a crooked cop, and made himself a career of fooling people. She couldn't believe or trust him in any way. Alex led her to the bar.

"I reserved us a table on the second floor. It overlooks the garden out the back, you'll love it."

"Don't you have to get reservations to a place like this... like say, I don't know... *weeks* in advance?"

Autumn emphasized the 'weeks' as if she were calling him out on a bluff. Alex chuckled charismatically, and his eyes sparkled with pride.

"*Most* people do, yes," he agreed, matching her emphasis. "I'm on a special guest list."

"Awwww," Autumn allowed her face to lighten, appearing intrigued, "And how does one get on such a list? This place is to die for."

The second Autumn's statement escaped her she wanted to bash her head off a wall. *To die for, really Autumn?* Of all the things she could have said, it had to be '*to die for*'. Her stomach twisted and she prayed that her nerves didn't show in her face at the mistake of word choice. Alex only giggled again, he seemed to be enjoying the start of conversation.

"Well, Erin, you're right about that, it is definitely to die for."

The sound of her fake name being spewed into the air was a reminder of how well she'd acted that morning. It reassured Autumn that she was better at this than she ever thought she'd be. She pictured Maylee's face as she listened to Alex and weeded through his words. The entire conversation was spent praying for him slip up and spill the beans on anything that might lead Chance, Lloyd, and the rest of her boys to something useful. His handsome smile widened and he continued.

"Let's just say the owner is a close friend. We've been *golfing* together for years."

The way he accentuated 'golfing' made Autumn wonder what he was actually insinuating. She decided not to push the subject, as she tried not to give herself away. Every word out of Alex's mouth was spoken with the same confidence and handsome smile that he had earlier that morning. He was easy to be around and after the first few sips of wine at the bar, Autumn could feel her nerves beginning to melt away. *This might not be so bad*, she thought, *he's charming and we're in a very public place, there's nothing he can do here.*

"We can take our time here at the bar, I have the table for the whole night."

Autumn took another sip, as his eye contact remained intact.

"So, I have to ask."

With excellent posture Autumn swiveled on her plush bar stool to face him directly. She leaned an arm on the bar to her side, and crossed her ankles. Alex mirrored the body language, leaning even closer to give her his complete attention.

"How is it, that a guy from my neighborhood plays golf and is personal friends with a person who owns a place like this?"

The lie came easier than she thought it would, as she fooled him into thinking she was from the same part of town as Craig. His smile seemed innocent, and the spark of his eyes intrigued. After leaning in even closer, so their faces were a mere three inches apart, he spoke smoothly.

"I could ask you the same type of question, Erin. How is it a woman from that part of town carries herself with the confidence you do, and just so happens to have a dress like that lying around for short notice dates at a place like this?"

A nervous heart thumped in her chest, but she held the unwavering eye contact, and smirked confidently at his question. Pretending to have no idea who he truly was came naturally, and it surprised the hell out of her. Autumn imagined herself to be on a first date with a stranger that she'd actually met for the first time in the parking lot. Keeping her quick witted responses simple yet satisfying was key.

"This is my sister's dress, she's much richer than me." She smiled proudly, "your turn."

"What's your sisters name?"

"Jackie. You still didn't answer my question."

Finally Alex broke eye contact. He leaned back in his chair and chuckled, completely satisfied with her returned quizzical banter. He nodded to himself and took a swallow of his wine.

"That neighborhood isn't where I'm from. I just go there to play poker with a couple of old buddies once in a while."

Alex then turned back to face her, and smiled his devilish grin. He placed his hand on her exposed knee and continued.

"I like you, Erin. You're fearless, beautiful, and confident. I don't usually bring dates here, but there's something about you." His handsome smile returned full swing. "Now, you didn't answer my question. How is it a girl like you lives in a hood like that?"

The question came out light, playful, and sent a chill straight through her. *Think fast Autumn, think fast, he's a cop, you suck at lies, he'll know if you're lying.* Autumn's mind spun until it was dizzy and confused. She opted to sprinkle in a little honesty to go with the lies.

"I just moved here, actually. I wanted to be closer to my family, but was limited on cash flow. I had to find the cheapest place I could until I got on my feet. Your turn."

"I'm an open book."

"Hmmm, what to ask?" she played while drumming her fingertips to her chin. "Your poker friends, they don't exactly seem like gentlemen. Have you ever heard the saying that 'you can always tell who a man truly is by his friends, and by the way he treats his mother'?"

She reached down as she spoke grabbing Alex's hand that was now rubbing circles around on the inside of her knee. She peeled it off of her while attempting to hold a flirtatious smile. She set his hand back onto his own lap.

"You'll have to prove yourself to be the gentlemen you're claiming to be before you can help yourself to my legs."

She winked at him and grinned as she finished her sentence. Autumn then sat up a little taller and took another sip of wine, wholly proud of the way she was carrying herself. It was all coming easier than she'd expected. Weird enough, she was starting to get a bit of a rush from the deception. Especially when he got a twinkle in his eye as she flirted. Chance was sure to be watching the whole display, and Autumn could only imagine just how jealous he'd be. Although, she did assume he'd have to be proud of her reaction to Alex's touch and the way she held her ground.

"Well if you must know, I treat my mother like a queen. And I wouldn't really call those men my buddies so much as occasional business partners. Besides, they're not all that bad if you get to know 'um."

He stared at Autumn with adoration as he watched her down the rest of her glass of wine in one gulp. Then he waived the bartender back to them by holding up a hundred dollar bill. Alex placed the paper on the counter and told the attractive man behind the counter to, "Keep Erin's glass full of their finest wine all night".

"You know, I don't usually go for girls from your side of town but there is something different about you. I honestly struggled to see you living there until I just watched the way you chugged that wine."

He giggled a little before he finished the comment.

"Now it all makes sense."

"What do you mean, it makes sense?"

"You're not from where you run, you take way too good a care of yourself. But, judging by the way you drink, you're not used to this type of country club environment either."

"Oh, and you can tell all of that just from the last five minutes of being around me?"

"Yep." Alex chuckled. "Well, from that and from the way you were able to ignore and blow of Jack when he threw his body at you last night. It takes a secure woman to react the way you did. It didn't seem to bother you at all, and I admire that about you. Your reaction to him is what interested me about you. You're stronger than most women, I can tell. Then when I saw you this morning, I couldn't help but ask you out. I don't know what came over me really."

Alex blushed and briefly looked at the floor. He seemed shockingly vulnerable. Autumn wondered if he meant what he was saying, or if it was all a part of his act. *He must be pretty damn good at his job*, she thought. Or just the opposite, he must be great at playing the good cop as he was recognized and decorated, yet here they were.

Autumn watched the bartender refill her glass. She picked it up taking another sip, and carefully thought about the direction she needed the conversation to go. *You're in charge here*, she told herself.

"Well, you're right about one thing and that is I'm not from here. But you're wrong about the blowing off your friend part. It was all I could do to keep running and not say anything to that pig."

She took another sip of her wine and then smiled back at him. "Why don't we go and get that table you bragged about. I don't want to sit here and talk about myself all night. I want to get to know more about this strange man who spends his time in the hood playing poker, and then turns around and takes women out to the classiest place in the city."

She leaned back in toward him and stared into his eyes. Again, her attempt to flirt seemed to get the best of Alex. His cheeks pinkened a shade darker, and he looked down at his feet with a sly grin. After the short second of adorable shyness, he suddenly seemed to develop a different kind of nervous tension in his neck. He glanced around the bar as if looking for someone and then fidgeted in his seat while drumming his fingernails on the glass of his drink.

"Excuse me for a minute, Erin. I just spotted another partner, and we have some important business to address."

His eyes found their way back to hers, and he straightened his tie before putting the most confident smile yet on display.

"Don't move a pretty muscle, enjoy this wine, and I'll be right back to escort you to our table."

Autumn nodded in return and picked up her glass as he smirked and explored the length of her entire body with wanting eyes. She displayed it confidently, immune to whatever sick thoughts he concealed. He then swallowed his wine just as fast as she'd drank her first. Alex set the glass down carefully, glanced up and down her body once again and grinned before leaving her alone at the bar.

Autumn's heart lowered a notch, continuing down its ever sinking path. The bar was busy, full of men in fine tailored suits and women with expensive jewelry, veneer smiles, and too much makeup – a perfect match to her own masked pores. Autumn wondered which men were supposed to be watching them. She turned slowly on her stool to face forward. The bar was rounded and it covered a giant portion of the corner of the room. Autumn could see all the way around it.

While sipping the expensive fine wine, she watched Alex out of the corner of her eye. He stopped in front of a man who had his back inverted from the bar, making it impossible to see his face. Alex's expression however, was in perfect view and it was unreadable.

He shook the man's hand and then glanced over to give her a grin and a wink. She smiled back with half of her lips and then turned her attention back to the bartender until she could no longer feel his eyes on her. She looked back over out of the corner of her eye as the man Alex was speaking to rotated his body to face the bar. Autumn gasped instantly and put her hand up to her hair, trying to block her face from sight.

Standing right there next to her date was none other than Craig himself. Autumn turned in her seat to slightly to conceal herself from Craig's view. With shaking hands and a racing heart she grabbed ahold of the necklace around her neck. She held the chain out and spun the diamonds in the center of her fingers. *Lots of women fiddle with their jewelry*, she thought, *just make it look casual.*

The camera was small and attached between two fake diamonds that hung elegantly from the chain. Autumn made her best effort to point the camera toward Alex and Craig, if only for a moment before she let it drop back down onto her chest.

Autumn sat at the bar nervously twirling her wine glass, waiting for Alex to return. All she could do was pray that Craig didn't accompany him back to her, and that he didn't happen to recognize her from across the room. Autumn drummed her nails on the top of the bar and closed her eyes to say a prayer in her head. Just as her eyes opened back up she could feel the heat of a body standing directly behind her, and the breathing of a man on her neck.

A hand ran softly down her arm and stopped at her drumming fingers. The large hand intertwined its fingers into hers, stopping their movement. Autumn's breath caught at the lump in her throat. Her heart stopped abruptly in her chest. *Please don't let this be Craig*, she repeated in her head. Alex's voice broke out in a whisper at the nape of her neck.

"What do you say we go get that table?"

Autumn let the air out of her lungs allowing her hand to accept his. Slowly, she spun to face him and stepped off the stool. Craig was nowhere in sight and she couldn't wait to get out of this room and further away from him.

"That sounds great," Autumn answered. "I'm famished."

Alex slid his arm around her waist and led her to a beautiful winding staircase. Autumn was already starting to feel the effects of the wine as she walked up the marble steps in her stilettos. She hadn't realized how much she'd already drank, or how fast. She needed to keep her wits about her and she'd be unable to do so if she was drunk.

This must really be good wine, she noted, glad that they'd be eating. That'd surely help her regain sobriety, but until then she'd need to back off the booze. The table was just as gorgeous as Alex told her it'd be. The garden was directly beneath them, and it was lit from every angle with small golden lights. There were flowers of every color and the most beautiful waterfall she'd ever seen.

Autumn imagined it being Chance sitting across the table from her in this magical place. What she would give for that. Autumn stared out the window in aww and silence until the waiter approached the table. Alex ordered for himself and for her. She watched him with a playful grin as he took her menu, folded it up, and handed it to the waiter.

"Do you always order for your dates?"

"I don't usually have dates, but when I do… no. I really just wanted to look cool." He giggled playfully. "That and I wanted you to taste the duck."

Autumn giggled back. It was much easier than she'd imagined it to be to relax around Alex. He seemed like an easy-going man, and had she not known better then he'd probably be able to make her feel genuinely comfortable with ease. She wondered how such a seemingly nice guy could possibly have done all the things Josie explained.

Every time Autumn started to enjoy herself, thought of all the photos of naked and beaten women hanging on her kitchen wall practically slapped her across the face.

The conversation had a smooth flow as they spoke. She told him the very same story that she'd rehearsed over and over with Jeremy the week she told him about Maylee. They talked about her love for running and how badly she wished she could afford a gym pass so that she wouldn't have to subject herself to the dangers of the city's back streets. Talking about this gave her the perfect opportunity to ask about Craig and the gang of men he played poker with.

"I'm not really fond of your friend, Jack was that his name? Tell me, what kind of business is a classy man like you in that would possibly make men like that your business partners?"

She asked the question casually as the waiter returned with their food. She assumed that the distraction of the food would take the pressure off and possibly bring out some unintentional honesty from Alex. He laughed a little at her question and took a long admiring look at their overflowing platter of roast duck before he spoke.

"Well," he paused, "I guess you could say I'm in the import export business. Those men are sort of the muscle of the company. They do all the lifting and shipping."

He smiled a full and seemingly innocent grin as he offered her a fork full across the table. Autumn could feel his eyes on her mouth as she accepted the bite. She played her part well and let a small groan of pleasure at the taste rumble from the back of her throat.

"Anyway," he continued after adjusting himself in his seat. "I don't think you really want to be bored by business now, not with this delicious meal in front of us."

He stared into her face, pleased with himself. Yet, the word choices he used in explaining his so called business, along with the attempt to change the subject didn't go unnoticed. It also didn't go un-recorded. Autumn could tell that he was going to play hardball with any more details about himself. She'd have to wait just a little farther into the date before she could pry any further.

Alex was right about the duck, it was positively sinful. Autumn ate very slowly and savored each bite. They talked about how beautiful the scenery was. She told him about how much she loved to garden and about the flower bed she had before her move. She made up the name of a small town on the complete opposite coast before laughing at his jokes. The night would be coming to an end soon and she knew that she had to get more information out of him.

"So who was that man you were talking to at the bar?" She asked casually.

"Oh that was Craig. I'm sorry to have left you like that. We actually have a business meeting tomorrow at a boss's house. I was just asking him a few questions about the details. It saved me the call later, anyway."

Alex smiled, leaned across the table and grabbed Autumn's hands up in his.

"Any more questions before I whisk you away on the dance floor?" He asked in a tease.

Before she had a chance to answer, or say anything for that matter, he stood up, rounding the table to her side. Autumn forced her lips to raise at the ends, and reached up to take his hand. Alex led her to the dance floor.

Autumn was embarrassingly impressed at the man's moves as he spun her around in his arms. She'd never been a very good dancer herself, so it was nice to have a man who could twist and sway her from one side of the dance floor to the other with such ease. The music was tasteful. The fact that he hadn't taken her to some new hip place where she might actually have to move her hips made her sigh with relief while they spun smoothly around the floor, joined together as one.

The second song in was a slow one. They moved sensually to the tune. Alex had one arm draped around the small of her back and was holding her hand to his chest with the other. Their bodies were pressed tightly together and she was surprisingly comfortable in his arms. She rested her head against his shoulder and forced the images of the nasty things he'd done out of her head. With ease, she replaced them with thoughts of Chance.

The scent of Chance's cologne filled her nostrils, and the tingle left by his fingertips seared across her skin. As the song came to an end, she pulled in a deep breath and reminded herself that it was in fact Alex whose arms she was snuggled into and not the man she'd imagined.

"It's getting late Alex, I think I should get going before this dance leads to another drink."

Autumn pulled away from him casually, displayed a grin of content, and then asked him to walk her out to her car. He agreed and waited by the gorgeous staircase while she went to fetch her purse from the table and quickly use the restroom before they left.

As she stood next to Alex waiting for her car in silence, she could feel that he was just as nervous as her. It seemed a bit comical, and she could tell by the way he kicked his shoe into the ground and fiddled with his suit jacket that he was legitimately anxious. Autumn was proud of the way she handled the entire date, and was even more proud of the way she was getting out early, completely unscathed.

"Thank you for tonight," she told him. "It was perfect."

"Will you let me take you out again sometime?" He asked. "There's something about you Erin, and I just can't quite get a handle on it."

He grabbed her hand and smiled his devilishly handsome grin at her before kissing the outer edge of her fingertips.

"Maybe you'll let me pick you up next time, like a real date?" He teased. Autumn nudged him playfully with her shoulder.

"Well, I don't know if I'm ready for that, just yet."

She chuckled lightly to herself and looked at the ground for a few seconds before making eye contact.

"I'd love to go out with you again sometime. You said you have business tomorrow? What if I meet you after you're done? Maybe something a little more practical." She returned the banter.

"Yes," he beamed, sounding a little too excited. It reminded Autumn of a kid in a candy store. "He actually lives just up the hill a few miles from here, and that is where we will be. It might take us a few hours to make the exchange and plan out the details."

Alex stopped himself and stumbled on his words. Autumn could see the realization in his eyes of what he just said. She kept her calm, and her face unreadable. She lifted her eyebrows slightly and leaned her face toward him, indicating for him to finish speaking and waited, as if she had no idea what he'd just done. Inside, she was reeling. He straightened his back, adjusted his tie, and forcefully spoke in a more professional tone.

"I mean, I have the meeting at 7:00 tomorrow night and I'm not sure how long it will last. Do you mind if I just call you when I'm finished?"

Alex now looked concerned like he knew that he'd said too much. Autumn kept the conversation and the mood casual.

"Sure, since I called you earlier, you should have my number right?"

"Um, yes, I think so."

Alex pulled a phone out of his pocket. He chuckled to himself without looking up, then put it back in his pocket and pulled out a different one.

"Sorry 'bout that. I like to keep business and my personal life separate." He pressed a few buttons, pulled up the recent call history, and confirmed her number. His face was again friendly, handsome and unreadable. He was calm and confident as they said their goodbyes. He kissed her hand just the same as he had a few minutes before, and he even opened the door to her car like a gentleman.

Autumn watched as he tipped the Valet. Rather than waiting for his own car, he went back into the club. Autumn wondered if Craig was still there as she started her car and tried not to completely speed away. As soon as she was out of the circular drive and on the road her phone rang. She pulled it out of her purse and answered it to hear the sweet sounding pitch of Chance's voice.

He instructed her to stop at a gas station down the street. Apparently, Jeremy and Aiden insisted on keeping her apartment secured with Josie, and he invited her kindly back to his hotel rather than the apartment. Autumn was reluctant. She wanted to check on Josie herself, but at the same time she needed the alone time with Chance. She whispered an agreement before hanging up the phone, nerves growing by the second.

The road from the club twisted and winded back down the hillside. Autumn sighed and slumped her shoulders over. After taking a few short breaths alone in her car, it all sank in. With a tight shaking fist she grabbed a hold of the necklace, tearing it off of her neck, and threw it onto the seat next to her. She felt dirty and used, wondering how anyone could work undercover and actually like it. The fact that she had somewhat enjoyed Alex's company now made her skin crawl. She pictured him abusing women the way Josie had described. Over and over, she imagined a scene of him holding a whip with Maylee in chains.

"Why can't I get this shit out of my head?" She screamed at the top of her lungs.

With one hand on the wheel she reached the other up the bottom of her dress and grabbed ahold of the base of her wire. It took a few strong tugs to rip the entire thing off of her body. The tape stung as it detached from her stomach and rib cage then pulled away from her between the knees.

Autumn finally pulled into the gas station with tears streaming down her face. She stepped out of the car, stormed around it, and threw herself into the passenger side, knowing that Chance would climb in and take over the second he saw the state she was in. The door slammed at her side and she bashed her fist against the dashboard.

"Damnitt!" she shouted.

Only a little bit of a childish embarrassment pooled in her chest, as Chance climbed in the driver's seat. He looked over just as she wiped a tear from her cheek.

"You have every right to feel upset and out of place right now, but you did an amazing job. And...," he hesitated before his face turned up in amusement, "I just have to say it."

His grin was growing as she glared over at him, curious as to what the hell could be so damn funny at a time like this.

"Jeremy was right, you do look really cute when you're pissed."

A well-manicured middle finger shot up from Autumn's closed fist. Chance chuckled a little to himself as he put the car into reverse and pulled back out of the parking lot. Autumn assumed that he must have seen her stamping around the car followed by a punch to the dash. As upset as she was, she realized how ridiculous she must look throwing such a fit. Especially in such an over the top sexy dress. Autumn reluctantly joined in his amusement and let out a small huff before she unraveled with a frustrated growl.

"Three years, Chance! It's been three Goddamn years, and where am I?"

She shook her open palms in front of her as if holding a box and trying to figure out its contents.

"I'm drinking wine and dancing with a murderer! I flirted with him, like some bimbo, and all I want to do is get out of this disgusting dress. I probably even smell like him!"

Chance reached over the top of her to grab a stack of napkins he spotted in the pocket of her door. With one steady hand on the driver's wheel, he used the other to wipe the tears from the visible side of Autumn's face. The notion stopped her rant and forced her to sob quieter. She grabbed the stack and held them against her entire face to cry into. Chance placed a comforting hand on her exposed knee, and spoke very solemnly.

"Autumn, don't beat yourself up. I'm so proud of you… We all are."

She sniffled, uncovered her face, and blew her nose, refusing to look in his direction. Nonetheless, she listened to him very intently. Hanging onto his touch and encouragement as if his were the only decent voice left in a world of destruction.

"You've single handedly made more progress in one month than a ten state span of an undercover team of officers and detectives alike. If it wasn't for you, Josie would still be locked away, getting beaten and raped, Craig would have never been found, and more importantly we wouldn't know about whatever big exchange is going down tomorrow. Autumn, this is huge. It could be the biggest break we've ever have."

"I saw him Chance, I saw Craig."

She whispered in shock as the impact of the entire situation continued to sink in deeper.

"You handled it perfectly," he encouraged.

"He could have seen me. He could have recognized me. What if…"

Autumn's voice trailed off into some incoherent mumble. She knew that the police only really cared about making arrests. Aside from Chance and Jeremy, Autumn felt like no one even gave a damn if Maylee was there when they busted this Braun guy or not. This is what truly had her on edge, and saying the words out loud made it feel that much more real to her. She collapsed her face into her hands and again screamed at the top of her lungs in frustration.

"Not only all that, but you know the car Alex was driving?"

"Yeah," she managed.

"You gave us a perfect view of him and the license plate together. While you were in there dancing, and keeping him stalled, Jeremy worked his magic and gathered information. He pulled the name it was registered under, and it happened to be of a man who's been dead for five years."

"What's that supposed to mean?"

"A lot of criminals take the identification of deceased people. They use their name and social security numbers to purchase credit cards and issue fake ID's. Jeremy and Aiden traced three different credit cards issued to this same name."

"Oh my god." Autumn whispered under her breath.

The more she heard, the less she wanted to know. It was like the entire night was a tornado. One that kept gathering momentum and ripping apart more and more, feeding off of the destruction of everything in its path. Chance tightened the grip on her knee and rubbed circles on her skin with his thumb while he continued.

"One of the fake credit cards was used to purchase a hotel suite for the last two weeks. Your video feed offered real hard evidence that Alex is a fraudulent officer. It gave us the kind of evidence that can be used in court, Autumn. He's definitely a dirty cop, and now Lloyd will finally be able to legally follow him. They now have two men planted at that hotel for the night, and depending on how things go tomorrow they'll be able to get a warrant for the room, as well as permission to investigate this meeting."

"Why don't they search the room tonight? What if there are girls are there? What if Maylee is there?"

This new information sent Autumn into a panic, she needed to know. Patience wasn't a luxury, with the sickening premonition that something very bad was about to happen. Something even worse than what already had. She'd come too far to let Maylee slip through her fingers, for the mere notion of patience.

"We can't do anything that might screw up tomorrow night. Whatever Alex and Craig have planned, it must be big."

"But Maylee…"

"Autumn, I'm sorry." Chance cut her off. "There's too much at risk. Try and think of it this way. If Maylee is there tomorrow, we will be too. But if he leaves her behind, then by standing back and watching them all tonight, then at least we'll know where to look."

Autumn nodded and the tears continued to flow. She understood what needed to be done, and she had faith in Chance, but that didn't make any of this waiting any easier.

"Craig has been off the map until now, thanks to you. If he's kept Maylee with him, then at least we'll know where he's been staying."

Autumn's tears slowed, and she stared at Chance wide-eyed while he spoke. This was amazing news and it gave her a fraction of hope. Finally she felt a little less used, and a bit more productive. Her hopeful fingers gripped his hand tightly, pulling it from her knee in order to intertwine it with her own. The back of her seat cushioned her head for the rest of the drive. She closed her eyes and pictured Maylee's happy smiling face until they pulled into the small parking space to the side of Chance's hotel.

Chivalry was at its finest as Chance moved around the car to open the door for Autumn. As she stepped out he stood his ground. He shut the door and then leaned up against her, pressing her body against the car softly.

"I wish it could have been me dancing with you tonight."

Autumn took in the words and inhaled his scent. She ran her right hand up his stomach, across his chest, and stopped at the base of his shoulder. She closed her eyes and confessed to picturing him the whole time she was with Alex. He wrapped her face into his hands and forced his lips onto hers. The kiss was rough and passionate. Autumn's entire body tingled as she felt the warmth of his hands moving down to cup the base of her breasts, around her hips, and then to her back.

Chance was unable to stop himself as he felt the curves of her body. It didn't matter that they were in a parking lot, hidden only by the increasing darkness of night. It was only a preview of what was to come, and stopping now wasn't as necessary as it had been earlier that night in her bathroom. They were drawn to one another on a new level. Every inch of Autumn ached for him, and she could feel the need of his touch crawl beneath her wanting flesh.

Chance couldn't wait to get her out of the parking lot and into his room where he could ravish her. Autumn shoved him away from her to catch her breath, otherwise she would've ended up stripping him down right there on the spot. Taking the initiative was bold, but she couldn't handle the wait any longer. Autumn grabbed him by the hand and quickly led him through the cars and into the building.

"Room one ten," He managed through a shortened breath.

"First floor, perfect."

Autumn picked up the pace, leading the way as she marched in her heels to his room. He followed in tow, watching the swing of her hips. Before Chance dug through his wallet to find the room key, he swung her around to face him. He picked her up effortlessly by the thighs wrapping her legs around himself in a deserted hall of his dimly lit hotel. He pushed her against the freshly painted wall, and let his tongue go to work one last time before entering the room. They kissed in waves of long awaited passion.

She held herself in place by squeezing her legs tightly around his waist. He dug out his key card and opened the lock. The door slammed shut behind them as they threw themselves in the room. With clothes flying in all directions, they didn't hesitate. Chance needed to feel her body against his, every part of her. The exposed flesh, sweat and moans linked the two together in a hot mess of pleasure.

Autumn allowed herself to crash around him over and over. He now held a piece of her that no one else had. For the first time since her marriage Autumn had broken the promise she'd made. She'd given her heart and her body to another man, and it felt amazing. Chance offered everything she'd been missing and more. With the stress of the night and the anticipation of what the next day was to bring, Autumn's emotions were heightened, and her weak spots sensitive. Her legs shook around him, and he reacted to her touch in such a way that there was no turning back from.

Chance was a changed man, belonging to her. With every moan that escaped her he pushed deeper. Relishing the night, every second of it. He was no longer obsessed with this woman after a nightly phone call, she was finally his. He was in love, in every sense of the word. He loved her body, her touch. He loved the way his fluttering stomach reacted to the humming sound that came from the back of her throat. He loved the way she exploded around him.

Even more than loving every physical detail the night had to offer, he loved what had developed over time. Their late night conversations that had led up to the night. Chance loved Autumn's determination. He loved the way she had no idea how strong she actually was. There was no denying it, Chance was utterly in love with this woman, inside and out. Finally she was his.

Chapter Eleven

Lloyd paced back and forth in his office on the North East side of the city. The sun had just broke way over the rooftops of the city's tallest buildings. He'd needed a break from that stuffy apartment of Autumn's, and this was the closest place of his own to Chance's hotel. It was right down the road, so they'd be meeting him there soon, before making way to the rest of the crew.

He was wearing down the freshly laid carpet. The smell of the once welcomed cinnamon burning candle was now starting to make him nauseated. He stomped directly to the source of the smell and blew much harder on it than needed. A small line of smoke rose into the air from the corner of his messy desk. Papers were strewn across the oak finished top of nearly every one of his office furnishings.

Lloyd didn't spend much time there, as his entire cover depended on his 'job' as a mechanic. He'd 'called in' the night before, claiming to have a stomach bug. He'd told ol' slick top to find himself another guy for the job for at least a week until he 'felt better'.

This office looked like it was plucked directly out of a Good Housekeeping magazine. He was on the thirteenth floor of an unexpected office building with oversized windows overlooking the city, and the golden name plate on his door read Dr. French D.M. The multiple identity charade was sometimes confusing and irritating, but absolutely necessary. Lloyd had three locations or "jobs" as he called them. The whole doctor status was merely for a sign on the door. One that would leave him untouched, unquestioned, and unbothered long enough to take an evening or two every month to make quiet untapped phone calls, and to catch up on paperwork.

The walls, floors, and chairs were white, and the large corner desk with surrounding cabinetry were solid oak. The drapes were a tasteful orange with a hint of blue around the edges which tied in nicely with the abstract paintings on the walls.

Lloyd had the entire morning mapped out. He'd given Chance the address of his office the night before while they were spying on Autumn and Alex. Jeremy and Aiden had been up in intervals throughout the night. They'd kept an eye on Josie while they compiled as much evidence as possible. They spent the majority of their night cross referencing names, fingerprints, license plate numbers, addresses, and acquiring everything necessary for search warrants. Josie had been sleeping deeply for nearly twenty four hours coming down, only waking for a few minutes at a time to use the bathroom and ask Jeremy to fetch her water.

The team opted to stick together and work this way through the night and on until they followed Alex and Craig to the exchange that coming evening. They'd planned on having a break only in the afternoon to rest. Apparently Alex had gone straight home from the club the night before with some random woman, and they were yet to surface. Craig on the other hand, had left the club much earlier than Alex. He made his way back to the hotel they'd traced via the credit card about thirty minutes after the undercover in the club had witnessed him speaking with Alex.

Lloyd poured himself yet another cup of coffee. He scooped in one heaped spoonful of sugar and took a sip before continuing his pacing in the center of the office. He had another half an hour of time to kill before Chance and Autumn were said to arrive. He had nothing to do but wait. His mind wasn't in the right state to catch up on his piling paperwork, and he was in no mood to clean.

Finally, he opted for a couple of quick phone calls to each team of men tailing both Alex and Craig. Discovering that the woman Alex took home from the club was just leaving, and Alex was having coffee on his porch, he appeared to be in no hurry to leave. Craig was still locked inside his hotel room with a *do not disturb* sign on the door. So far the morning was quiet.

Soon Autumn followed Chance into the office sporting a proud smile. A styrofoam container was placed ever so carefully on Lloyd's desk. The breakfast food inside the container smelled heavenly. Lloyd hadn't realized how hungry he truly was until the scent rising up filled his nostrils.

"Wow!" He declared as he opened the container.

Inside the styrofoam was the beautiful sight of banana pancakes smothered in rich syrup, strawberries, and a heavily whipped cream topping. Lloyd dug into the heaven sent meal the second Autumn set the fork beside him. He couldn't help it.

Chance and Autumn took a seat next to each other on a small over cushioned couch across from Lloyd's desk. Autumn sat with her back straightened and her legs crossed. Chance leaned back a little more relaxed and slipped his hand over her thigh. Lloyd noticed the way they seemed to complement each other, and actually felt a little bit sheepish for the way he'd been hitting on Autumn for weeks.

Neither of them were surprised to hear about Alex taking home another woman. Autumn recalled his confident mannerisms and how at ease he seemed to be with himself. She thought about his welcoming smile and his warm eyes. Even the feel of his arm draped around the small of her back while they'd danced had been strangely comfortable. Thinking back made her pray that she'd never have to see him again. It also confirmed her decision to skip her run that morning.

Lloyd explained that he was able to speak with the hotel Craig was staying in about their security cameras. Apparently they used a web based program. They'd given Jeremy access codes for a direct stream to the hotel security, which he in turn linked it into Lloyd's office computer for the morning's research. Lloyd typed out a few passwords and then turned the screen to show Chance and Autumn a view of the hallway to Craig's room, as well as the front counter and the entryway. Autumn admired the immaculate lobby.

"Oh my God," she gasped. "He really must be making a lot of money doing what he does. How long did you say he has been staying there?"

She stared at the computer screen with her mouth slightly open and listened closely to Lloyd. He informed her that the hotel records show the name of his fake identity checking in and out for weeks at a time over the course of the last two years.

"Are they able to pull the recordings of the last few times he stayed? Was there anyone with him?" Chance asked.

Autumn's heart raced waiting for Lloyd's answer. The center of her palms were getting clammy and she flicked her nails together to keep herself from chewing them.

"That was one of the first questions we asked. Apparently, the recordings only save for two weeks. After that the system will automatically delete, unless saved manually."

Lloyd took a close look at Autumn's face. She didn't seem satisfied with his answer. Wrinkles of concern bunched between her brows and at the corners of her lips as she pursed them into a tight line. He continued on the insight, hoping to offer her a little bit of encouragement. The fear and concern for her long missing niece was written in every detail of her face.

"I focused in on the hallway to his room. I've been here for over an hour already this morning reviewing every last second of video feed available. I've fast forwarded until he was there and watched every time he came in and out of the room. It seems like he carries in enough groceries to last a few days at a time and then he doesn't leave. He's never accompanied in or out by anyone and he doesn't allow a maid to clean his room. That *do not disturb* sign is on the door at all times. He even fetches his own towels and blankets from the staff to avoid their assistance."

Lloyd paused the screen, zoomed in and pointed to the small plastic sign hanging from Craig's door. Autumn stared at the *do not disturb* words as they hung there in real time from that handle. She took in a deep breath as she realized that she was staring at the exact place Craig was located at that very minute.

"So that is it?"

She whispered the simple question, more to herself than to the men on either side of her. The impact settled and quickly turned to the beginning of a built up rage.

"That's where he is right now? Maylee could be in there with him and all we're doing is looking at the outside of his door on a fucking computer!?"

Her words were getting louder and her voice was starting to shake. Autumn fought back the tears and looked back and forth between Chance and Lloyd. Voicing her unspoken plea with her eyes. Her head was growing foggy, and she turned her attention back to the *do not disturb* sign.

"There's got to be something we can do."

She wiped her face and spoke the words through her rapidly forming tears of shock and despair.

"Maybe we can distract him and search the room when he leaves? Something! Anything!"

Chance could do nothing but whisper an apology and promise her they were doing everything they could. He reminded her again, by speaking ever so lightly into her ear about the risks. Lloyd stood to hand her a tissue and again top off his cup of coffee.

Autumn accepted the tissue and tried to settle and compose herself. Falling apart now wasn't an option, not today. The tears were swallowed with a gulp before she pulled a small make-up compact out of her purse and touched up the mascara smudges on her face. Autumn then stood, pulled down the bottom of the form fitting floral print top that she'd bought that morning from the hotel gift shop, and helped herself to Lloyd's coffee center.

As Autumn let the richly brewed coffee run past her tongue and down her throat she focused on the shaking of her hands. She wondered how she'd possibly get through the day without having a nervous breakdown. The known exchange was not meant to take place until later that night. Autumn wondered if she'd be able to make it that long without having a heart attack or strangling some passerby on the street.

Autumn stood by the coffee machine for several minutes just sipping and thinking. She looked around and admired the beauty of Lloyd's office and then slowly returned to her place next to Chance. He wrapped his arm around her waist, welcoming her in. The warmth of his body was comforting. While leaning into him and listening to their conversation, she continued to swallow the much needed caffeine.

Chance and Autumn remained in Lloyd's office for nearly an hour as they discussed every detail. The ins and outs of the case for the last few years were laid out in the open. Processing the details was nearly impossible for Autumn. It all seemed to blur together, weaving in and out of her thought processes like a shark in shallow water. Sometimes, certain information would bite down giving her imagination a nasty nibble. Other information would swim off in a blur, leaving her lost and unable to see what lay ahead.

The three of them brain stormed on suspects in and out of the bureau, name dropping political figures, and the known wealthy class men. Even the club owner of the restaurant Autumn had wined and dined at was researched. He had a mountainside estate, miles out of town with a ranch, and it seemed nothing tied him to the group. Every angle they approached offered nothing but dead ends. Left and right, they covered every piece of information they had, trying to find a missing piece. A piece that might tell them exactly where they might be led that night, so they could prepare properly.

Just as all the weeding through and brainstorming began to bring about a very stressful headache for Autumn, the sound of Lloyd's phone crashed through the room. Chance resumed his place on the couch next to Autumn and they waited in silence, listening in on Lloyd's call.

Autumn watched the peak of Lloyd's brows raise with shocked excitement, followed by the concern of his lips tightening into a straight flat line. He rubbed a hand down his face pawing at the skin, not saying much more than the occasional, "uh-huh", "oh my God", and he finished it off with an, "okay, make a list of anything you can think of that'll be useful. Chance and Autumn are here, and I've gathered all the paperwork I needed, so we're on our way back to the apartment now."

The two sat tall on the edge of their seat, waiting for an explanation.

"That was Jeremy. They finally pinpointed the balding redhead that you saw on the porch of Craig's house."

"Thank Christ," Chance said. "Who is this douchebag?"

"His name is Braunson Vinchelli."

"Vinchelli, as in Craig Vinchelli?" Autumn jumped in.

"Big Braun," Chance mumbled, making the connection.

"Exactly, he's a very distant cousin of Craig's. He's also the widower of an adopted sister to the clubhouse owner that we've spent hours trying to tie in. Fuck, how did we miss this?" Lloyd cussed himself.

He slapped a flat palm on the surface of his desk. Pens rattled, and Autumn flinched.

"This guy's wife passed away six years ago, and he still lives in a mansion she'd inherited, it's just up the road from the clubhouse. Apparently the place is enormous, and it sits on a ten acre secluded lot. The parcel is still listed under her maiden name, which is different from the club owners."

Lloyd shuffled through stacks of papers and files, shoving them into briefcases as he spoke.

"Josie's waking up too. She's finally hungry again, and she's asking for you Autumn, we'd better get moving. We've got a lot of work to do before the damn night rolls around."

On the drive, they made a quick stop at a grocery store for enough food to tide everyone over the entire day. Autumn sat in the car waiting while Chance ran in to shop. She pawed and reeled at her wrists, trying to stop the shaking of her hands. She'd thought that being alone in the car for a minute would give her a little peace and quiet to clear her head, but it seemed to be doing just the opposite. Anxiety was setting in. Maylee stared up at her from the photo she'd dug from her purse, as she held back the tears that were forming in her eyes.

"Today's the day, Maylee. I'm here for you." She whispered.

Autumn couldn't help but to think about the hotel Craig was staying in. She couldn't get the image of the door to his room with the big fat *do not disturb* sign hanging so casually out of her head. Autumn was so deep in her thoughts that she didn't even notice Chance making his way through the parking lot. As the car door opened she jumped in her seat and gasped for air. She looked up at Chance with clouded eyes and shock etched on her face.

Chance didn't need to speak. He eased into the car in silence, granting her the respect of continued silence, and started the engine. A strong hand slid itself to the spot on her leg that was quickly becoming its usual resting place. It fit, it belonged there. Stop light after stop light Autumn slowly regained her composure. Her body trembled less and less and her breathing started to come a little smoother.

The photo remained on Autumn's lap. She was unable to tuck Maylee away again, at least not until they arrived at the apartment and she was rendered no other choice. As they pulled into the parking space she stared down at the photograph and let out a sigh, before forcing it back into her purse. They walked to the building and up the steps hand in hand. Each with a paper bag full of food in the other arm, ready to feed the crew, along with Josie, and prepare for whatever daunting future the day held for them.

Chapter Twelve

Autumn secured her holster around her waist before slipping on a loose black tee. Then she wiggled her feet into a pair of boots that laced tightly up her leg. An extra clip for her pistol sat on her nightstand, bullets loaded. With a steady hand Autumn shoved it into the already tight pocket of her jeans, and then slid the gun securely into its holster.

She took a long heart throbbing look into Josie's healing face. Her bruised chest rose and fell with steady healing breath. Josie had been kept comfortable with very strong painkillers since Jeremy took over her caretaking. He was like a mother bear, constantly checking up on her. He'd even went so far as to help her wash up, as well as rummaging through Autumn's clothes to keep her dry and comfortable after each round of feverish sweat.

He did his best to live up to the man his sister had bragged him up to be. Of course, Jeremy wouldn't allow Josie to be any less comfortable than she absolutely had to be. He catered to her every need plus some, and vowed to keep it up no matter what lay ahead. The team would move forward to Big Braun's estate without him, as he refused to leave her side. Josie's comfort and trust was his number one priority. She'd been abused and betrayed before after seeking help in escape. On his honor it'd never happen again.

Autumn watched Josie sleep, feeling guilty that she'd wished it was Maylee in her bed. The swelling of Josie's face had eased up immensely, and the color of each bruise on her face and arms had changed in the mere two days' time. A heavy sigh forced Autumn's lips to protrude from her face, and her shoulders sagged some with the weight of Josie's baggage. Before leaving her yet again with the fear of no return, Autumn planted a soft motherly peck on Josie's sleeping head.

"I'm so sorry for what they've done to you." She whispered.

The sight of her apartment full of armed and busy men was much to take in. New faces blended in with the familiar. Jeremy was particularly anxious, even after claiming to trust each and every one of this undercover drug task force division, he seemed to be watching Autumn's bedroom door like a hawk.

They'd been there for hours, preparing. One man in particular took a certain liking to Autumn. Dawson was his name and he was quite possibly the most courteous man she'd ever met. He insisted on calling her ma'am and offering up his seat every time she entered the same room.

There was also a woman, Special Agent Stailey. Autumn was equally surprised as she was relieved to meet this woman. Stailey was an FBI agent assigned to oversee the operation. Lloyd had failed to mention that he'd been reporting directly to a woman the entire time. Stailey only made herself present on special occasions leaving the details entirely to Lloyd.

Today was deemed at the top of such occasions. She and Autumn hit it off well. Stailey was close in age to Autumn and put up with half as much shit. She was tough. The kind of tough that Autumn always admired and wished she could replicate. A sharp blonde bob framed Stailey's face and her features were well defined, including her squared shoulders and hips.

Autumn leaned against the wall, shoulder to shoulder to Jeremy. By mirroring his exact body language, she folded her arms over her lower chest, and crossed one foot over the other. He looked down at her with an approving smirk.

He was ready for this, they'd been working toward this night for years and he finally had a chance to bring justice to the operation that killed his sister. As badly as Jeremy wished he could be going with them all to Big Braun's estate, he was content to stay at Josie's side. There would be no prying him away from this girl any time soon.

"You're pretty great with her." She told him.

"Yeah," The smirk faded away, and his eyes pulled to his feet. "I owe it to Amy. I have to make sure her friend stays safe this time."

"I'm still mad at you for lying to me."

"I know." The smirk slowly returned to one half of his face.

"Thank you," she mumbled, then peeled herself from the wall.

Autumn took a step to join Chance and Stailey as they stood over an elongated fold up table. It was covered from one end to the other with a property map, as well as ATV and motorcycle trail maps of Big Braun's estate. Before she could completely move away from Jeremy, he grabbed her lightly by the arm, causing her to spin back to face him gracefully.

"Be careful tonight, okay? Remember everything we went over at the range."

Autumn recalled every word that Jeremy and the boys ever told her at the shooting range.

"I promise I'll be careful. I remember everything."

"Breathe, don't panic, use your head Autumn."

"I will."

"Keep your finger off the trigger unless you're absolutely sure you're ready to pull it. You got that?"

Autumn offered him a solemn nod. His eyes widened and his nostrils flared slightly with concern as he pulled his face in closer to hers. He lowered his voice so that no one could hear this coaching except for Autumn. There was a void in his eyes, something she'd never seen before. Something about his look rang regret with a twinge of loneliness.

"Once you've taken a life, Autumn, there's no turning back from it."

The pain in his words was thick, and a hint of moisture formed at the outer edge of his eyes. Autumn threw her arms around his neck. With all the new found honesty between them, Autumn wished she had the time to really talk to him. To get to know her friend for who he really was. Perhaps if prayer and luck is on their side, along with all of this planning and preparation they could all make it back in one piece. Then she could get to know Jeremy for who he really was, rather than just a punk kid who happened to be the most friendly apartment manager in history.

He hugged her back tightly, then pulled her away to take a stern look in her face. The unspoken conversation resonated deep inside Autumn's chest. It was serious, he cared immensely about their friendship, Autumn could feel it crawl in her bones. Once the moment was accomplished and he was sure that the seriousness of all his advice was pounded deep enough in her stubborn head, he let her go.

"Hurry guys, look," Aiden hollered through the room of busy worker bees, grabbing their attention. "Craig's finally gunna' leave his room."

Autumn pushed her way through the small crowd, and stood next to her new friend, Dawson. He draped an arm casually around her shoulder and leaned in close to her ear to ask quietly, with a low respectful twang.

"How ya' holdin' up, ma'am?"

Autumn's eyes were glued to the monitor, "I'm not sure," she told him honestly under her breath.

They all watched as a member of the hotel staff delivered a baggage cart to Craig's room. The bell hop knocked on the door and then walked away without offering to help, or even waiting for a tip. It seemed routine, and completely normal. Autumn's stomach knotted and flipped as she watched Craig grab the cart and wheel it into the room. She reached up and squeezed Dawson's hand for support as it hung casually by her arm.

Lloyd looked down at the silver watched on his wrist. It was five forty five. Craig's moving around only confirmed it as the time to get going. He watched the monitor just as closely as the rest of the crew. All but Jeremy, who remained in his watch guard position by Josie's door.

They had a lot to do on the estate to prepare. They'd go in as close as the ATV trails would allow, and the rest of the way would be closed in on by foot. They'd need to surround the house, as well as place at least one sniper on a hill or in a treetop close by. They'd need to be in place at least a half an hour before seven, yet they couldn't move any earlier than now so as not to be spotted. Alex's little slip up on his date with Autumn was everything.

Lloyd looked over at Autumn with pride. He'd worked hard on this case for years, and was yet to get this close. He'd needed her to show up the way she did. When he first heard from Chance and learned of her coming, he was excited for such a break in the case, but he'd never expected it to get this far. Autumn was the sole reason for the month's progress, and Lloyd knew it. To be honest, he was even a little bit jealous of Chance. If he didn't respect and enjoy working with the guy so much, then he'd probably hate him.

It only took a couple moments of anxiously staring at the screen before Craig made his way out of the room. He was pushing a giant baggage cart in front of him. The cart was stacked with five oversized square luggage bags. They were all black with large wheels on the bottom. Three of the bags had a green band wrapped around the metal pull handle at the top. The other two were color coded the same way except they were white and pink.

Stacked on the smaller top shelve of the cart was another bag. This bag was made of entirely different material and was a solid blue color rather than black. It was bulky, very bulky, with a big round lump in the middle. Josie had told them about how they moved the girls around in luggage. They'd be drugged and then shoved into large bags in the fetal position so they'd fit.

Lucas confirmed to have seen the two other 'muscle men', like Craig, travel with very large awkward luggage. They traveled in and out of the city often, so there was never much question about the luggage. No one would have imagined them to actually be that bold and coy with moving the girls around. Josie had quoted them while explaining. She said they'd brag about how easy it all was.

"No one expects what they're looking for to be right under their fucking noses," Craig had said once while shoving Amy into some luggage right before Josie.

Autumn stared wide eyed at the luggage cart as Craig pushed it through the hallway of their hotel. Aiden pressed a few letters on the keyboard and then the screen split into two showing the lobby and the front door. Craig pushed the bulky bags past the front desk as well as a handful of guests. Not one person even glanced at him. Josie's quote of Craig's own words stung like salt on an open wound.

"No one expects what they're looking for to be right under their noses."

Moisture welled in her eyes, and she thought, *it's her, it's Maylee, she's with him, it has to be my Maylee.* Before the lump in her throat had a chance to grow into something bigger than just a lump, Chance was at her side with an arm around her waist. Dawson pulled his own arm away. Autumn buried her face into Chance's shirt. She breathed in his scent with a couple of long therapeutic pulls to compose herself before looking over at Lloyd. His eyes were locked on her face, waiting.

Lloyd didn't know exactly what to expect from Autumn at this point. So far she'd done nothing but surprise and impress, so he hoped tonight would be the same. They were all thinking the same thing, knowing that it was likely Maylee in that bag, but no one said it out loud. Maylee had been seen with him more than once, and not so long ago. Craig was attached to her and kept her separate from the other girls.

Lloyd had interviewed dozens of escorts over the years that had mingled with the ring of traffickers. Some of them had been introduced to a few of the kidnapped girls held captive including the one Craig called 'M'. He hadn't told Autumn about these women, or about 'M'. He didn't have the heart for it and neither did Jeremy or Aiden and Lucas. Sadly, up until now they were always a step behind Craig and could never pin him down.

A couple of the prostitutes that had met 'M', claimed that she never did more than sit in a corner and stare at her feet. Craig kept her close and called her his girlfriend. She was scrawny, sickly, and always drugged. She was never allowed to mingle with any of the other men involved, or the girls held captive. She was sad and lonely, barely a match to the old photograph that Autumn clung to, but alive nonetheless.

Lloyd let out a sigh, feeling like he'd betrayed Autumn even more than she already knew. But there was hope. As soon as Autumn shared his unspoken look of confirmation, she gave him a nod. Telling him she was ready.

"Alright men, let's move." Lloyd said.

Autumn knew that she had to remain calm or else they would make her stay behind. She steadied her breath and listened to every detail of Lloyd and Stailey instructions on the way. They handed her a full camouflage outfit to throw on over the top of her clothes.

Chance hadn't been happy about her tagging along, but he knew there'd be no fighting her. If they didn't allow her to join, she'd find her own way. Hell, she'd even use Alex if she needed to, and he wasn't having it. Jeremy was on her side that morning, insisting that she was an excellent shooter and could hold her own. Even Aiden had surprised them all by insisting that she be there. She'd proven herself, and deserved to see firsthand how the night played out. She was strong and smart, she could be of help.

Lloyd informed her to dress fast while they drove because there would be no time once they arrived. Autumn slipped the clothes on quickly and pulled her hair back out of her face. She promised the men and Stailey that she'd be able to keep up and stay quiet.

In no time at all they were at the base of an ATV trail that headed up into a line of trees just outside of town. It only took the men a few minutes to unload all the bikes. Chance and Autumn were on the last bike out of the four, with Lucas riding backwards behind her, gripping tightly to the rack. Autumn clenched onto Chance around the waist as they bounded down the trail and into the trees. The road was rough and it took Autumn a few minutes to get the hang of it. She'd never ridden a four wheeler, and it was a thrill she hadn't expected.

She held on tight and peaked around his shoulder. The dust was thickening as they closed in close behind Lloyd's bike. Stailey's short hair whipped in the wind behind Lloyd, and two other policemen clung onto their ATV's the same way Lucas was. Lucas was the size of both the men combine, and needed the rear end of an entire ATV to hold him.

The two other rides were just as packed with body mass. They made the ride quick. Every bump on the trail and every downshift of a gear for speed caused the adrenaline to all but consume Autumn. Dawson had done a quick ride over the trails a few hours before, to familiarize himself with the surroundings and to be able to lead the way. He had picked out a perfect place to stash the bikes. They made it in record time. It was far enough away from Big Braun's place that they wouldn't be seen or heard. The rest of the way would be spent on foot.

When the bike came to a screeching halt, Chance had to peel Autumn's fingers apart from around his waist. He helped her off the bike, ran his hand down her cheek softly and planted a warm soft kiss on her unsuspecting lips before pulling her by the hand into the trees behind him.

They moved quickly, quietly, and shuffled through the brush in the exact order planned. Autumn was just as nervous as she was impressed. She stuck with Chance, hand in hand they jogged into place. Autumn watched the ground in front of her intently, avoiding any large sticks or shrubs that would make too much noise. She took her steps as quickly as the rest of the men with ease. The adrenaline and anticipation of it all kept her feet moving quickly, and her lungs breathing steady, despite the workout that was clearly getting to a few of the men who weren't in quite as good of shape as herself.

Dawson was the first to become winded. Because he'd been the one who scouted the place earlier and was leading the way, Stailey gave him a nudge to the shoulder and an icy stare when he slowed to catch his breath. Autumn held her head high and reminded herself of her strength. Dawson forced an apology through struggled breath, before picking the pace back up. The heat from the day was starting to wear off and it was now a comfortable temperature as they made their way through the shade of the trees.

Autumn was grateful for the concealment. She was a little shocked that there could be such a place in the middle of the desert, and understood how it was possible for this Braun guy to run such an operation there. The place was perfect, convenient, secluded, and well hidden. Dawson stopped and waved the entire team over to duck down behind a large boulder. They all huddled in close.

"The house is just over that hill." Dawson said.

With a large flat palm Dawson used his entire hand to point in each direction. The hill he indicated was fairly tall, but didn't contain much vegetation. Only a few shrubs sat on top.

"It isn't much, but it's the place we talked about being the best for a sniper to see the private drive to the house."

Lloyd nodded in understanding, "Lucas and James, you know what to do."

Autumn continued to pay close attention, absorbing every word and studying every face. After spending time with Lucas at a shooting range she was comforted to know he'd be the one watching their backs. She was yet to see him handle a gun the size of the one that was now strapped to his back, but she had faith in him. James was another new face. A handsome one with a confident smile. He wasn't quite as large as Lucas, but with his abundance of tattoo's and matching neck muscles, the two seemed to complement each other.

Dawson continued, "this tree line here drops below that hill and surrounds the place." He pointed his whole hand again to the East. "There are a couple of weak spots that might be tough to get through unseen, we'll have to really watch our backs there. But for the most part there's plenty of vegetation to keep us all concealed for as close as a hundred yards all the way around the house."

"Good work, Dawson," Stailey complemented. "Lloyd, lead the way."

"Alright team, we've been over this plenty of times, you should all know what to do. Stay in order and keep your distance from one another. I'll lead the way, and we set up position. Find your spot and hold steady."

Lloyd glanced down at his watch before finishing up his orders, looking mostly at Autumn as he spoke. He had to make sure to get the point across.

"We only have twenty minutes, it's not much time, but it will seem like forever. We have to be patient. Once the perimeter is secured, no one is to move a muscle. Hold steady until told otherwise, is that clear?"

"Yes sir."

"Loud and clear."

"You got it."

They all complied in their own words, and those who didn't whispered their agreements nodded in silence. Autumn admired the unite. Together they were a well-trained machine. They'd each been tested before and placed in situations forcing their skills and agility. Autumn noted Stailey more than the rest.

Special Agent Stailey was alert at all times, forcing herself to be in tune with the nerves of the men around her. She placed a hand around Lucas's wrist and squeezed. No words were needed. She'd stick by his side, and in turn she became his number one priority. He understood her stern look completely.

"Autumn," Stailey's hushed voice was firm and demanded her attention. "I'd advise you stay put right here out of harm's way."

Autumn shook her head suddenly in a panic, but before she could speak Stailey kept going.

"But, since I have the feeling you won't sit still," she tilted her head and lowered her brows accusingly, "I just want to tell you, be careful. Stay with Chance no matter what you see."

"I will," Autumn promised.

"I'm not messin' around. Even if you do see your niece, or if anything awful happens, you have to trust us, do you hear me?"

"I do."

Autumn nodded her head in stubborn agreement. She wasn't a child and she didn't appreciate being treated like one. The urge to shout at them all about how she was the only reason they were here now was swallowed. Ultimately, Autumn let out a hard sigh of defeat and kept her mouth shut.

"Okay then." Stailey turned back to Lloyd, "let's not waste any more time."

"Let's move," he instructed them all in return.

Autumn surprised Lloyd again with her collected compliance to the warning from Stailey. He grinned to himself with pride as he carefully navigated the team through the scattered vegetation. Once settled in place Autumn leaned into Chance. Silently they waited. Their position offered a clear view of the driveway along with a straight shot to a large beautiful bay window. Autumn pulled up the binoculars that hung from a harness around her neck and shoulders to peer inside.

Chapter Thirteen

Alex was the first to arrive. He showed up empty handed in the same black Cadillac he'd driven the night before on his date with Autumn. She focused her binoculars on him as he parked the car and climbed out. Three men in suits accompanied him. They stepped out of each passenger door of the Cadillac, adjusting ties, and straightening hair. Chance leaned toward her and whispered in her ear.

"The one in front's a senator. We've expected him to be tied in for some time, but until tonight haven't been able to prove anything. The other two are new, I've never seen them before."

The man he was talking about was in his late sixties and looked it. His hair was white and thin. It was combed over to the side and he wore a very loose fitting suit. He couldn't have weighed more than 150 lbs, Autumn thought.

Autumn stared closely at Alex as he waited in front of the car with the Senator. The other two stood tall on either side of them, one with a tight grip on a large black briefcase. Autumn held her breath as she watched the redhead man she'd seen before walk out of the house and into the driveway to greet them. *Big fucking Braun*, she thought to herself.

The next car to pull in was a midsized SUV, and Autumn's body seized as she watched Craig step out of the driver's side. Close in tow, three of the men she'd seen playing poker at his house exited the vehicle. Including the jackass who hollered and humped the air at her. The sound of Alex's voice while he described his friend at the clubhouse rang through, "*Jack isn't so bad.*" Autumn lowered her eyes in a glare at him. The fear in Josie's face as they hid on the side of Craig's house the second she heard Jack's voice told Autumn otherwise.

"Pig," she mumbled, the word dripping with disgust.

Chance tensed at her side, shoulder to shoulder, yet he remained perfectly still. Alex and the suited men he brought stood to the side and supervised as Craig and his guys pulled three suitcases out of the trunk of the car. They were identical to the bags they'd witnessed Craig wheeling out of the hotel less than an hour before. With eyes glued on the bags, Autumn waited and watched closely. The bulky bag made of different material was nowhere in sight. The handles of the bags still had the colored tags intact. Autumn fought the urge to speak to Chance about her observations, managing to keep silent and watch. She knew her place, as the night began to unfold before her very eyes.

Autumn observed as Alex made eye contact with Jack and the other two poker pigs after they'd wheeled the bags into the house and then came right back out. He pointed back toward the cars. The men hung their heads in defeat and climbed into their places in the back seat of his Cadillac, rather than the car they'd came in. They looked like whipped dogs obeying their masters.

Autumn shook her head slightly, wondering how the world could be so cruel. She thought about Josie and what had happened to her by the hand of the men in front of her. *Where's the other bag*, she wondered? Autumn was determined to keep her eyes on the car Craig arrived in, no matter what else happened around them. She had a gut feeling that if Maylee was with Craig he would keep her separate from the rest, and he wouldn't let her leave his side.

Once the raunchy card players were settled in the back seat of Alex's ride, and the rest of the men had disappeared into the house, Craig came waltzing back out, and to his car. He appeared to be pulling at something, moving it to the edge of the seat. Autumn couldn't quite tell what it was. She strained her eyes through the lenses of her binoculars trying to see past him and into the car.

There was a small window of clarity allowing Autumn to peer into the seat. Sitting right there on the leathered bucket seat of Craig's car was *the* suitcase. The one with the different material and suspicious bulge. Autumn sucked in a breath and held it. Her and Chance both kept their eyes glued on Craig. He leaned in over the top of the bag and then back out. He was opening the zipper of the bag and pulling the top material down.

Craig shifted his body, blocking their view. Autumn let out her breath and sucked in a new much bigger lungful, on the verge of passing out. After a few more shifts and adjustments Craig backed away slowly pulling whatever was in the bag out of the car. He stood and straightened his back. Autumn gasped as she watched Craig pull a seemingly lifeless body out of the suitcase in the back seat of his car.

His back was still turned to her but she could see the girl's legs dangling to one side of him and long blond hair on the other. Autumn's heart pounded in her chest and her eyes clouded. She blinked rapidly trying to focus clearly. Just as Craig turned to walk toward the cabin there was a loud overbearing noise closing in from above them all. Both cars were parked just a few yards from the small landing pad.

Chance draped his arms around Autumn and held her close as the noise grew louder and louder. She wiggled and squirmed trying to escape his grip. She had to get close, she had to see the girl. *Maylee,* she thought, *I'm coming, I'm here.* Autumn couldn't take her eyes off Craig and the limp girl he now held in his arms. Craig ran with the girl into the house, before the helicopter dropping down could land. Autumn wasn't able to get a clear view of the young girl's face as he jogged to the porch and out of site.

Autumn dropped her binoculars and turned to Chance to shout at him over the sound of the landing helicopter.

"That was Maylee, it had to be her!"

It continued to drop down, the noise was too overpowering, he couldn't hear her words. He didn't need to, her lips were clear to read, and it took everything he had to restrain her. He yelled back trying to be heard over the constant thump of propellers.

"You have to hold still!" He yelled. "Wait! We have to wait!"

Neither could hear their own words as the sound of the helicopter closed in. Chance looked over the top of Autumn giving Lloyd a nod through the struggle. Autumn looked through the trees at Lloyd who was crouched down with a radio close to his lips, ready to give the orders as soon as the bird was shut down and un-manned. The helicopter would need to be secured quickly as well as the house. There'd be little time.

Meetings like this, with political leaders, the kind important enough to bring in an actual plane never take long. They're very risky, so the criminals involved never lingered. Lloyd and Chance were both well aware of this fact, knowing that there was no time to call in any more help than what they already had. It was time to move in and put a stop to the entire operation. This was their opportunity to shine, possibly the best they'd ever get. Time to bring justice and take the risk of going all the way.

Autumn's body shook and the adrenaline shot through every part of her. It felt like her nerves were jumping out of her chest and running circles around her. Her mind was unclear. Autumn didn't care about the helicopter, all she could think about was the limp girl being carried into the house by Craig. She continued to shout over the noise.

"I have to get down there! I have to get to Maylee now, before they hurt her!" For a brief moment, Autumn broke free of Chance's strong hold, she lifted her body to her hands and knees. Just before taking off in a sprint Chance was able to fumble then rise to his feet and grab her around the waist. Back to the ground she was pulled, legs kicking violently causing dust to stir up from the dry dirt.

Chance tucked Autumn's arms between his chest and hers, and wrapped himself around her, engulfing her completely. She flung her body from side to side and kicked her feet trying to break free. He yelled into her ear at the top of his lungs in an attempt to be heard over the engine of the helicopter's swinging propellers.

"If you go down there they'll kill you and they'll kill her to!" He yelled. "You'll both be safer if you wait!"

Autumn heard his words as the sound of the propellers died down to a whisper and then vanished. She pressed her face into his chest and sobbed. The woods were once again silent. The tears streaming from Autumn's face burned against the dust and dirt in her eyes.

"You have to pull yourself together Autumn, and we need to watch what is going on down there. If he has kept her alive all this time, then he's not going to hurt her now." Autumn nodded her understanding into his chest and wiped the moisture from her face with her sleeve.

As soon as she calmed, Chance resumed his position with his rifle in hand. He looked so sure of himself and steady as he set his sights through the scope of the gun. Doing everything in his power to save Maylee was a priority to Chance, second only to keeping Autumn close and out of harm's way if at all possible.

Autumn looked down the hill at Lloyd who was slowly and silently making his way close to the tree line. The entire team was moving in, like bugs they crept and weaved, ready to make their move. Autumn forced her shaking hands to pick up the binoculars and bring them back to her eyes. She watched carefully as the helicopter pilot left his bird behind, empty and unmanned to join the crew in the house.

Chance placed his finger in his ear and strained to hear Lloyd's cautious instructions as they ran into a small speaker inside of it.

"Copy." He whispered quietly into the radio secured to his shoulder.

Chance whispered so quietly to Autumn, she had to strain to hear him. He was inches from her, yet the words seemed to blur together. The lightness of her head grew and black spots were showing up to block chunks of her vision. *Shake it off Autumn,* she told herself. *Be strong, you can't pass out now.*

"We have ten minutes to secure the plane and the house. Stailey called for backup. Plenty of cruisers will be here within ten minutes along with plenty of medical help. The team has to move now that all the men are inside."

"Good," she whispered back, "I have to get to her."

"No." His hushed voice was stern. "I have to keep you safe. We stay here while they move in."

Insult salted the wound, she snapped back.

"I don't need a babysitter!"

She whispered angrily with a stomp of her foot.

"Autumn…"

"Stop! If I don't get to her, I'll never forgive myself, and if you hold me back, I'll never forgive you."

A stressed hand pulled on the skin of Chance's face as he tried to rub the anxiety away.

"I know," he finally replied. "God, you're stubborn!"

"Let me go." She pleaded, "Please Chance, it's her. I know it's her."

Flush and dirty were Autumn's cheeks. Chance grabbed them in his hands and planted a firm kiss on her pleading mouth. The shards of grey in his eyes pierced into hers trying to find a way to bring her comfort.

The rest of the men made their way from tree to tree down the hills on each side of the house. They blended in well with the surroundings and would be hard to spot from the untrained eye. Chance picked up his rifle and started moving down the hill quietly hiding behind each tree and shrub. Autumn followed in tow, mirroring his moves exactly. They stopped and crouched down behind a small patch of brush and cedar. It was as close as they could possibly get to the house and still stay behind the rest of the closing in crew.

Aiden crouched down next to the porch with the barrel of his pistol pointed at the door. He was ready to pull the trigger on anyone who may come barging out with a weapon. There was a sliding door out of site on the other side, and a basement exit in the back, each with a man mirroring Aiden's stance. Lloyd and one other was hunched down behind the Cadillac containing the men who had lifted and moved the suitcases, yet were uninvited to the house. Autumn watched the last remaining detective in the field with them hustle across an uncovered opening and up the steps into the helicopter.

Autumn and Chance listened quietly, seconds seemed like an eternity. Everything was still completely silent, the calm before the storm. No gun shots were a good sign, as three men snuck inside the house through a large window.

Soon the shouting began outside at the Cadillac, followed by the *pop pop* of gunshots. Autumn didn't know where to look or who to watch. Dawson and Lloyd tackled down Jack and the other pigs who were trying to get out and away from the Cadillac.

More gunshots soon sounded from inside, along with incoherent shouting. Aiden, who'd been crouched down by the door, held a gun to the first man's head as he tried to run out. Finally, with the front door now open Autumn could see past them into the house. In a split second she could see Craig picking up the same limp girl off of a lounge next to the door.

"Maylee!" Autumn shouted.

Autumn could recognize that face from a mile away no matter how sickly, or how long it'd been. Autumn's entire chest sunk to her toes. Chance grabbed her arm.

"No Autumn! You have to stay here!" He yelled again.

Autumn fought herself, willing her legs to stay put. Alex was the next to try and escape from the house. He shot the man by the back door in the temple. The man dropped to the ground in an instant pool of blood, soaking the bullet proof vest that was strapped to his lifeless body. Chance let go of Autumn's arm, took a quick aim, and shot. His bullet hit Alex in the back of his neck and he fell lifeless. Alex's body lay next to the man to die to at his own hand.

It all happened so fast, the image danced circles and pulsed in Autumn's eyes. Clutter and confusion filled her head. As the gunshots died down and the shouting ceased Autumn rose to her feet. Chance jumped up next to her and again grabbed her by the elbow.

"Wait until we get the okay from Lloyd." he demanded, this time much more dominant. "They have to search everything and make sure the premises are absolutely secure."

"Let me go."

'I'm not going to lose you because you're so fucking stubborn."

The angry tense of his face melted at a very look into Autumn's eyes. He stared at her with sympathy. The pain and confusion in her eyes was spewing out at him, he ached for her. From the pit of his belly to the tips of his fingers, he felt her grief. They were as one, he'd likely never again have a moment of solace without feeling firsthand the emotions that surged through her. Her pain was his to bear.

Alex's hadn't been the first life Chance had taken in the line of duty, and he knew it most likely wouldn't be the last. Death he could deal with for now, but the look of betrayal in Autumn's face as he held her back wasn't so easily tucked away.

Autumn tossed her arm in the air throwing his hand aside. Like a caged lion she paced, hands shaking rapidly at her sides. Occasionally, she'd grab her hair at the base of her scalp and let out a low muffled scream of frustration through her teeth.

A whistle soon sounded from the porch. Autumn glanced over to Lloyd, the culprit of the noise, and he waived them to the door with caution. She took off in a sprint forcing a shrill screech of panic the entire way.

"Maylee!... Maylee, I'm coming for you!"

The tears streamed down her face as she ran, hurdling Alex's dead body, as it blocked the entry. The pale cold skin of his face was blank, lifeless. Torn, bloody pieces of flesh were all that was left of his neck.

"Maylee?"

She wailed into the entry room past them all. The congressman along with the Big Braun and one of the other men in suits were on their knees against the wall, arms cuffed behind their backs. Autumn frantically looked through the wandering task force men, the same ones that had spent the afternoon in her apartment. Only this time none of their eyes met hers. She forced her way past Lloyd who was trying desperately to calm her.

"Autumn, they're not here." Lloyd told her, his quiet shameful voice snaked into her ear, muffled as if he were under water. "We've looked everywhere, I don't know how they got out."

"What do you mean they're not here? Who is they?" She shouted back, trying her damndest to look around him.

"Craig, or the girl he carried in. We've searched everywhere. We don't understand where they could've went."

"Maylee! It was Maylee, I saw her!..." Furiously she screeched, "How could they have left?"

Autumn was fuming, heart trying to escape the confines of her ribcage. From room to room she ran, shouting Maylee's name through her tears. She'd seen Maylee and knew they had to be there somewhere. *They had to be.* After pushing her way past and through the men surrounding her, shoulders bumping, the walls started closing in around her. Failing lungs refused to pull in breath and her knees were increasingly weak.

Finally she made her way back outside. The sliding glass doors in the rear end of the cabin offered her passage, and gasped in a pull of fresh air. A patch of soft grass cushioned her knees as she collapsed on the ground, burying her face into the dusty palms of her hands. Autumn threw her head back and looked into the sky.

"Why?" she screamed.

How could this happen? How could they have gotten away after all of that? Autumn didn't understand, nothing processed. She was lost, confused, completely heartbroken. As she knelt down on the ground she felt a warm arm slip around her. Autumn couldn't look up out of her hands or even see through her tears if she were to try. With a giant sniffle of snot, she could smell Chance's scent. She threw herself into his arms allowing him to hold and comfort her.

Blue and red lights began pulsing around them and the stillness was torn apart by sirens. The men shuffling through the house became mute. Before long, new voices joined the familiar, questions were demanded and rights were read. Everything seemed to be lost and the most precious item in the case was missing. Unless they found some kind of clue as to where Craig could have possibly disappeared to, to Autumn the entire thing was pointless. Handling Maylee's loss a second time around was unbearable.

After sitting on the ground and sobbing into the comfort of Chance's arms for several minutes, he was finally able to talk Autumn into moving to her feet. With his warm hand gently cupping her cheek bones, she glanced through her clouded eyes and took in the sorrow of his gaze. He wrapped his arms around her waist and whispered.

"I'm so sorry, my love."

His sympathy fell on deaf ears, and the knot in her throat was nearly impossible to get past.

"I'm not leaving until they find something," was all she could manage to say through the cracking in her voice.

Chance didn't need to respond, he understood and would stay by her side as long as she insisted on being there. The sun was going down and Autumn feared if they didn't find something soon then the darkness would close in and Maylee would be lost forever.

Autumn replayed the scene over and over in her head. She closed her eyes tight and remembered the small window of sight she had through the crack of the front door. The sickly and unconscious Maylee seared in her memory. The image was perfect. It hit her like a semi-truck to a brick wall.

"They have to still be inside!" She insisted.

"Autumn the men have looked everywhere. They can't be inside. Craig had to have gotten out somehow."

"I saw them Chance! I saw them inside after the house was already surrounded. They have to be in there still, they didn't have time to get out! I saw Maylee, I know it was her!"

Autumn shoved herself out of his arms, determined feet carried her back into the house. All that remained inside were the two cuffed men in suits that arrived with Alex and the Senator, along with Lloyd and Aiden. The rest were shuffling the other suspects single file to the waiting police cruisers, and tagging the dead bodies out back. Forensics were pulling in, ready to do their job.

This left the rest of the place somewhat empty and seemingly quiet. As Autumn stomped across the kitchen floor in her boots she noticed a change in the tone coming from her noisy shoes. The short square heels created a hollow sound from beneath the freshly laid hardwood. It'd been far too noisy with the dozens of men for her to notice the first time walking through. Now it was unmistakable.

Autumn stomped her foot on the kitchen floor. She walked a couple of feet to her right and then stomped just as hard on a different panel of wood.

"Chance, Lloyd, hurry! I think I found something!"

The two were at her side in seconds, along with Aiden and Dawson. Her four soldiers, ready to storm the gates at any possibility of finding her niece.

"Stop right there!"

With a flat opened hand, she indicated for them all to stand in the doorway, and off of the switch in flooring. She didn't want anything to interrupt the vibrations of the boards as she stomped around, making sure the noise from her boots was all they could hear. After watching Autumn jump around across the length of the kitchen, and listening to the different sounds coming from the floor beneath her, all four men understood her sudden excitement.

"Hurry," Lloyd said. "There has to be some kind of a door somewhere."

They rushed in and started moving around the kitchen furniture. There was an area rug underneath the table and chairs along with a floating island that moved with ease. They couldn't find anything under them. Autumn paced back and forth in frustration before looking over at Aiden as he crouched down to his hands and knees. Next to the far wall by the sliding glass door, he ran his hands across the edging and pushed down every couple of inches.

The others must have noticed as well because they too dropped to their knees, following Aiden's lead. As they met up to each other in a corner of the room there was a soft *click*. The small sound rang through followed by a *creek*, and the floor lifted.

A three foot square door popped up granting access to a short flight of stairs. The crease of the door fell perfectly into the seams of the hardwood concealing it completely. Each man instantly stepped back and drew their guns. Lloyd hollered outside for help. Of course, Autumn insisted on following them down into the hidden basement cellar, she'd have it no other way.

Chance tucked her behind his own body, sure to put himself before her as they made their way down the steps and into the dimly lit space below. The smell rising up was rancid. It filled their nostrils causing one of the uniformed officers to gag and pull his shirt up over his mouth and nose. Autumn followed his lead, taking the same step to muffle the scent. It smelled like rust, mold and urine. Autumn peaked her head out around Chance. Nothing could prepare the crew for the God awful scene ahead.

Aiden stood shoulder to shoulder next to the uniformed officer who was first down the steps. A long tunnel of barred cellar doors had been right beneath their feet all along. There were ten cells in total, five on each side. It was dank, with the wreaking of rotten flesh. Aiden and the officer each pulled a flashlight from their belts, shining a light down the tunnel.

At first the beams of light revealed nothing but a clearer view of the cinder blocks and bars. But after a few steps in, the tortured girls inside the cells became visible. One at a time, fingers gripped the bars, and muffled cries sounded, accompanied by a few coughs and hardly coherent pleads.

The far end of the tunnel was a dead end wall. Leaning against that wall were the missing suitcases that had been wheeled in by Craig's men. Autumn walked behind Chance and the others through the tunnel. Each of the girls were either handcuffed to the walls of their cells or passed out on the damp concrete floor. The ones who were awake sobbed at the sight of their rescuers.

The team stopped just before reaching the last two cells, parallel to each other. Aiden turned back to Autumn with a dreaded look on his face. Her chest fell to the floor, as the feeling in her legs began to disappear. In a split second she was pushing herself past them and yanking on the bars trying to open the block.

"Maylee!" She cried at the top of her lungs, "Somebody please help me open this fucking door!"

There was something more, Chance could feel it in his bones. The girls, half alive, naked, starving and beaten wasn't the only thing wrong with the pit of a secret basement. He strained to look around in the dark as Aiden tried to help Autumn pry Maylee's cell door open. Only Aiden and the few uniformed officers had flashlights. Dawson, Lloyd and himself were at their mercy in the dark.

One of the men with a light searched the floor and walls for a key, while the other few pulled at doors and locks trying to get the cages open to free the missing girls. He placed a hand on Lloyd's arm.

"Did you see that?" Chance asked Lloyd. "I think something moved behind those bags."

Dawson took a step forward. With his pistol drawn he led the way. There was only a few feet between the bags and the cage door of Maylee's cell. There wasn't much space, and the darkness was consuming.

Just as one of the officers turned to join them with the light, there was a rustle causing the top duffle bag to crash to the floor. The clatter of the wheels on the bag echoed in the space and for a split second Chance caught a glimmer of a reflection as the light bounced off of a metal blade.

"Autumn!"

Chance screamed her name as he dove for her. Sharp and jagged was the edge of Craig's blade. It cut through the flesh at the base of Chance's neck, sinking in at a downward angle as they crashed together to the floor.

Dawson's reaction was instant, jumping on top of Craig just as Chance took the entire blow to protect Autumn from the blade. The explosion of Dawson's pistol was deafening as he popped off three rounds. With a repetitive twitch of Dawson's trigger finger, blood and brain fragments plastered the cinderblock wall. Craig's now headless body twitched with nerves before going completely limp.

It was too late, Chance was breathing his last breath. The long black rubber of the blade's handle was still protruding from his collarbone, as warm scarlet fluid emptied from the wound. He coughed, causing a few chunks to flow from his mouth.

Autumn scrambled to his dying body, and hunched over him not knowing where Craig's blood stopped or Chance's began.

"Please," she pleaded. "Please Chance, breathe."

With his hand in hers the last lungful of air slowly released, and his chest sunk in death. He was gone. The one man she let herself love after so many years of loneliness, dead. In a split second he'd given his life for hers.

The air became thinner and thinner with every breath Autumn inhaled, until she collapsed. In the pool of Chance's blood her body limped and everything around her changed from a high pitched buzz to darkness.

Lloyd bent down amongst the mess and pulled a large ring of keys from the belt of Craig's headless body and handed them to one of the officers. Roughly he wiped the splatters of blood from his face along with the quickly forming tears of his own. He turned to the officer now holding the keys to each and every girl in that basements freedom.

"Get her out first," He pointed to Maylee, her head bobbing around slowly from the wearing off effect of her drugs. "Make it snappy, we need to get them all out of here and up to the paramedics fast."

The uniformed men went to work as a team. They stepped carefully over Chance and Craig's lifeless bodies, and began unlocking cage doors.

"Aiden."

"Yes sir."

"Help me with Autumn. I want Maylee within arm's reach when she wakes up, and neither of them are to leave your side, from here on out. Do you hear me?"

Aiden did as he was told with no response. He scooped Autumn into his arms and turned for the stairs with the officer holding Maylee two steps behind him. Her breath was warm and her limp body heavy in his arms. Aiden carried her with honor. He pictured Amy in a cage. The thought of it made him sick and caused a salty tear to mix in with the sweat and dirt on his face. He thought of

Jeremy and Josie back at the apartment as his eyes adjusted to the light outside the basement.

Once outside, Aiden and the officer walked shoulder to shoulder carrying Autumn and Maylee in their arms to the first ambulance in site. Aiden climbed in alongside the paramedics.

"Thank you," Aiden whispered the words into Autumn's ear vowing to follow through with his orders. No one would ever harm Maylee again, he and Jeremy would see to that. He lightly held her soft bony fingers, lowered his forehead to her hand and sobbed.

* * *

Autumn stirred, squinting through the blinding lights around her. All she could see was the blank icy stare of Chance's gaze. It was burned in her mind, the first conscious thought a memory. She was stuck between sleep and awake, unable to move her limbs or pinpoint anything except the beeping of monitors. Her toes tingled and fingertips twitched.

Just as she gasped for air there was a faint moan. It was no more than a couple of inches from her ear, and it was familiar. The most familiar sound in the world.

"Maylee!"

Autumn shot up to a sitting position. Everything that had happened flooded back into her mind, front and center as if she were still trapped in the basement curled up next to Chance as he exhaled his last breath. Autumn's panic was settled by a touch. *Her* touch.

Autumn closed her eyes gently and felt the hand in hers, skinny and warm. A long relaxing breath was inhaled as she closed her fingers around the boney ones laced in with her own. She looked down to see Maylee's beautiful blue eyes staring up at her, curled up on the same hospital bed with a beating heart in her chest. Autumn's mind raced as she ran her free hand gently through Maylee's hair and whispered the simple words she'd been waiting three years to say out loud.

"I missed you, Maylee."

About the Author

A SIMPLE LIFE: THROUGH THE EYES OF AN UNEXPECTED AUTHOR.

Growing up in a small town had more than several advantages and disadvantages. Saying that my childhood was sheltered is nothing short of an understatement. Unlocked doors, cleared streets, and the quiet of a trustworthy neighborhood were all welcomed features of my hometown. As a small child I baked cookies with the old lady down the road. I sat next to my kindergarten crush in sun day school, and literally rode my bike in the middle of the road without a care in the world. We didn't have what kids have today. We actually had to use our imaginations to have a good time. There were no smart phones, tablets, or 64s to keep us occupied. We were perfectly content to play with our stick guns and a water hose for hours on end... And I loved it! Along with my scrapes and bruises I also maintained a simple, happy for the little things attitude, and of course a great tan.

Now that I have made my childhood out to be nothing but cherries and smiles, I have to point out the disadvantages that came with the small town upbringing-- before the world of electronics took over the young mind. One word distinctively comes to mind... Boredom! As I grew into adolescence I no longer cared much for silly toys, dancing, baking, or crafts. I rebelled like many young adults do.With a sever chip on my shoulder and a lack of coordination in the sports department, I spent the majority of my time partying. Nothing too outrageous, mostly close friends,fires, and beer.

As much as I would love to say that living in a small town gave me an overactive imagination and love for books, that is unfortunately not the case. I cared more about having a good time than I did about school. I was voted wild child twice in high school. I cheated my way to passing grades.

It wasn't until I was settled and married with a child on the way that I found my love for the literary world. Rearing out of my mid twenties left me a bit more mature, having to find more important things to do with my time than re-occurring nights at the bar. This is when it started - I read one book after another for a few short years, then decided to give writing a bash. I'm completely amazed at the love I developed! Once I started putting the world of imagination that has long been trapped in my overactive mind into a keyboard, the transformation of self began. A new aspiration in life has formed. I want nothing more than to be known as the unexpected novelist who took the literary world by storm!

Lightning Source UK Ltd.
Milton Keynes UK
UKHW012334050221
378341UK00009B/454/J

9 781034 348672